The Josan
and
The Jee

The Josan and The Jee

a novel by
William Karl Thomas

MEDIA MAESTRO - BOOK DIVISION

Cover photo and design by William Karl Thomas
Copyright © 2013 by William Karl Thomas

ISBN 978-1-62768-001-1

Printed in the United States of America

This book is a work of historical fiction within which many real persons and/or events have been described. However, all of the dialogue, all of the non-historical persons, and many of the events, are a product of the author's imagination, making any resemblance of such characters to real people purely coincidental.

Published September 2013

MEDIA MAESTRO - BOOK DIVISION
P.O. Box 50672, Tucson AZ 85703
(520) 303-7806
info@mediamaestro.net
www.mediamaestro.net/books.htm

FOREWORD

This novel is loosely based on the author's experiences in Korea during 1953. The first two chapters of this book are based on tales told the author by these three women over the course of that year, tales he believes to be absolutely true. The balance of the novel is a work of fiction with no intended relation to anyone living or dead. This foreword is to impress upon the reader the reality of the horrors of war, and the heroism of these women who survived that war.

TABLE OF CONTENTS

Chapter One
SURVIVAL

The bayonet blade made a crunching sound as it pierced her father's body and narrowly missed the twelve year old girl as she lay petrified in the sack he had carried over his shoulder. Her father's body arched upward, creating a small window of light which revealed his bright red blood running in riverlets down the shiny blade of the bayonet, then narrowed to a thin line of grey light as the blade withdrew and his body relaxed, pressing her down into the muddy rice field.

Sook Cha continued to hear the 'pop pop' of gunfire that had heralded the arrival of the North Korean soldiers who had overrun this small band of sixteen children being led South by her father, a Seoul Policeman who had remained at his post until the very last minute. After he despaired of stopping the looters, he gathered together this collection of abandoned children and, carrying his small sleeping daughter in a cloth bag over his shoulder, he herded them through the rural areas to avoid the North Korean invaders who marched together with clanking mechanized armament down the main thoroughfares.

The 'pop' of gunfire diminished as the screams and pleas of the children increased. The most distinguishable sounds to Sook Cha were those of her closest friend, Ling, who lay only a few feet from her and, from the painful entreaties Sook Cha could hear, was being raped. Only a few months earlier, Ling had celebrated her thirteenth birthday and privately and proudly revealed to Sook Cha the budding of her

1

womanly breasts. At that time they had discussed the future possibility of marriage and the mystery and anticipation of offering their virginity to their future husbands. Now Ling screamed in agony as the soldier savagely entered her virginal opening, laughing and verbally deriding her in the process.

In what seemed like an eternity, but was actually less than an hour, the cries for mercy and sounds of agony reached a crescendo and then diminished. The multiple rapes progressed to multiple murders, and, one by one, 'pop' by 'pop,' crunching bayonet by crunching bayonet, the voices and lives of the youngest to the oldest children were extinguished.

Sook Cha lay in trembling fear stricken silence, afraid that the sound or movement of her breathing would reveal her presence beneath the dead body of her father. She was also paralyzed with guilt, feeling obligated to rise up and defend her father and Ling and all the children she had come to know in their three day journey South of Seoul. But she knew that gesture would be futile and fatal, and she tried to estimate the time since the last scream and whimper subsided, since the last soldiers boot made a sucking sound as it pulled out of the mud and they retreated from this field of horror. And still, Sook Cha waited; waited until the last light from the cloudy overcast sky began to fade.

With apologies to her father and a sustained sense of guilt that she had not come to their rescue, Sook Cha pushed her father's body to the side and crawled out of the slit in the blood filled bag made by the bayonet. She cautiously peered around the horizon for any lingering North Korean soldiers, then respectfully rolled her father's body onto his back. The blue of his usually scrupulously clean uniform was almost entirely obliterated by mud and blood. The chest

2

pocket where his silver Policeman's badge had been was ripped open, probably by the soldier who murdered her unarmed father and wanted a trophy to go along with a bogus story about defeating him in a fair fight. She tried in vain to count the number of bullet holes in his body, and marveled that none had penetrated his body to reach her. She hoped he was aware that his body had shielded her and that, because of him, she had survived.

A light snow began to fall as she stood up and surveyed the carnage around her. A few feet away Lings nude spread eagled body was turning blue white, exaggerating the contrast of the bright red blood that still oozed from her crotch and the bayonet wound in her small chest. Three other girls and two boys, all between the ages of ten to thirteen, were displayed in nude postures of rape and bearing bayonet wounds. One kneeling boys head was completely buried in the mud, his upended posterior feeding a trail of blood down his legs and back. Sook Cha pushed his body sideways to destroy the obscenity of the tableau. He had been shot in the back of the head and part of his face destroyed by the exit wound, but she recognized him as Kim, the boy who had always tried to help her and of whom her father had said with a smile, "He likes you."

Finally, tears welled in Sook Cha's eyes. She ran to Ling's body and threw herself across her chest, clinging to her and sobbing into her frozen hair as Ling's open eyes stared at the darkening sky. After a long time, Sook Cha's sobs softened into labored breathing. She rose on her elbows, stared at Ling's face, and vainly tried to close Ling's frozen eyes. Sook Cha moved closer, gently kissed Ling's lips, then breathed warm air on her eyelids and closed them.

Sook Cha rose, noting that Ling's blood now stained Sook Cha's clothing at her crotch and her chest.

3

A laugh began to form in her chest, but, somehow, could not arrive at her mouth. Instead she looked to the night sky and then to the horizon, and said aloud, "Not today. Not today." She criticized herself for not observing where the sun had set so she could determine South, but decided that, since the children had all walked behind her father, a line drawn through their collection of bodies towards him would point South. She cautiously crested the first ridge, surreptitiously surveyed the terrain around her, and headed toward whatever remained of her native South Korea and civilization and sanity.

****

Sook Cha had been a city girl and knew little of farming, but she had been an educated girl and knew how to learn and adapt to new situations. Traveling through the war damaged and often neglected fields of rice, cabbage, garlic, onions, parsnips, carrots, turnips, and other local crops, she was able to forage sustenance and even learn a little about agricultural technology. She knew that human waste was used as fertilizer in some crops, so she learned to distinguish safe drinking water from potentially dangerous drinking water, how to clean and whenever possible boil water and foods, and that eggs from any source, fowl or reptile, are the easiest source of protein.

Most dead bodies had been robbed of their valuables, but she managed to acquire a metal cup from a dead soldier, better hiking boots from a dead woman, and a broken half of a machete from a dead farmer, probably left by others because it was broken. She found a flat surface on a granite boulder and, with much effort, ground a crude point on the broken machete

4

turning it into a sort of 'Bowie' knife. Now she had a weapon at least adequate to fend off snakes, vultures, and rats. Snakes she didn't mind eating, vultures she didn't like the taste of, and rats she couldn't bring herself to eat.

Her progress South was painfully slow, largely because she was wisely and meticulously careful. She figured out the strategy of avoiding open areas where she would be visible in daytime, populated areas which would attract North Korean soldiers bent on rape and pillage, and restricting herself largely to terrain that was tough to navigate and therefore avoided by others. She had a smarter schoolgirl's knowledge of what a compass and maps were all about, and, though she mostly zigged Southeast and zagged Southwest, she managed to stay in a generally Southerly direction.

At one point she was caught stealing vegetables from a farmer. Later she realized how stupid she had been to be so docile and let him march her to what passed for his barn. Instead of appealing to his wife as she had planned, they were after all South Koreans, he tied her up and told her that if she didn't cooperate he would hand her over to the North Koreans. Apparently his survival strategy was to be a collaborationist. Over the next two days he attempted to sell her to neighboring collaborators, at one point describing her as a bargaining chip to curry favor and protection from the North Korean Army. In order to make herself less saleable, she frowned, snarled, spit, and attempted to bite anyone who approached her. The third day, unable to sell her, the farmer decided to sample the goods before handing her over to the North Koreans. He tied her hands and feet to four posts and started to undress when his wife appeared, fending him off with a wooden pitchfork. She released Sook Cha, scolding her for not cooperating with the sale, but affirming she would not condone murder, handing her over to the North Koreans, or letting her husband debauch her.

Now she was even more cautious. When she found what appeared to be a safe place, she was inclined to stay there even longer. She had lost her machete come Bowie knife, and life was a little more complicated without it. When she observed a fully clothed North Korean soldier lying inert for several hours in a remote location, she considered the possibility that he might be dead and a source of valuable needed equipment, including a knife or other possible weapons. She approached cautiously and, when within striking distance, she picked up a huge rock, so large she could barely lift it over her head, intending to smash his skull and insure her safety.

Suddenly her feet were pulled out from under her as the soldier rolled over and grabbed her ankles, the rock barely missing her head as it fell from her hands. Her back and buttocks were scraped along the rocky ground as he pulled her over to the low hanging branch of a tree. Describing her as a 'nice little toy' he had found, he bound her hands behind her and her feet together and elevated to the tree branch.

He pulled out a beer and offered her some, lifting her head and pouring some in her mouth, which she promptly spit back into his face. He angrily dropped the beer, reached behind his back, and brought forth a 45 caliber automatic pistol which he cocked and pointed at her forehead, saying, "Maybe you'd be a better toy dead than alive."

Sook Cha pictured the massacre of her father and the other fifteen children, and she wondered if any of the rapists had persisted after the children expired. She considered whether living would be worth what followed, feeling certain that, whether she cooperated or not, he would eventually kill her. Two reasons to survive came to mind; one, to be able to tell others what she had experienced, and, two, to reserve the possibility of escape or, sweet justice, to kill him.

The soldier stood up, straddling her head and saying, "Okay, let's see if you're willing to drink what I offer you or if you'd rather be a dead toy." He opened his fly and proceeded to urinate a stream up and down her body, ending for a long time on her face. He then lowered his face to hers and, pointing the gun at her temple, added, "Wanna' spit that back in my face?"

Sook Cha remained silent, rationalizing to herself that, since she didn't open her mouth, she couldn't spit it back anyhow. In the ensuing hour, the soldier proceeded from raping her mouth to her vagina to her anus, a traumatic introduction for a barely thirteen year old virgin to what should have been one of life's most rewarding experiences. As Sook Cha assessed the bleeding and pain in her vagina and anus, she reasoned that he had refrained from his threats, each time she showed a glimmer of resistance, to beat and defecate on her. He even allowed her to walk a few feet away to retrieve a hot beer from his tote bag. She carefully inventoried its contents, noting nothing she could use as a weapon. The only apparent weapons were the forty-five automatic pistol in a right side holster and designated 'Property of the U.S. Government,' probably salvaged from a dead American soldier, and a small hunting knife strapped to the calf of his left leg, both of which he re-belted to his nude body after disrobing.

When he placed her atop his body, she could not reach the knife on his calf. But when he placed himself atop her, she could reach the forty-five pistol. She carefully removed it from its holster, pointed it at his

7

head at an angle that would not possibly cause the bullet to exit in her direction, and attempted to pull the trigger, but unsuccessfully. When he finished his last orgasm, she was in a panic and unable to return the pistol to its holster. For the first time, she feigned sexual excitement and succeeded in getting him to resume sex. She did not know about the dual safety devices on a forty-five automatic pistol, the little side lever that locks the barrel slide, and the rear grip lever that requires simultaneous compression of both the lever and the trigger in order to fire. She did not consciously reason how it operated, but kept trying every combination of its different devices until, by happenstance, it fired into his right temple and blew a silver dollar size chunk out of the left side of his skull. At the age of thirteen, Sook Cha experienced having a dead man's corpse atop her tiny body for the second time.

When she felt his autonomous system began to urinate into her vagina, she quickly pulled her knees to her chest, placed her feet on his chest, and flung his body six feet away where it continued to empty the contents of his bladder and bowels.

She could hear male voices some distance below the hill react excitedly to the gunshot. Despite the pain in her vagina and anus, she quickly put the gun and knife into his tote bag, sadly decided his boots were much too large for her, but grabbed the clothes he had placed nearby which, thanks to his disrobing for sex, were not bloodstained. She moved uphill in the opposite direction of the men's voices, painful step by painful step trying to find a path around the hill that would not scrape her nude body too badly, but a path that was not so easy the soldiers would follow it and overtake her. By the time she heard them discover the body, their voices were very faint and she knew she had achieved a safe distance, even though she dare not stop until she had used her last ounce of strength.

****

Sook Cha's new modis operandi was to disguise herself as a boy in the soldiers modified uniform. She cut her hair very short with the hunting knife, cut the military buttons and emblems off the uniform, and cut the pant legs and shirt sleeves to her approximate size. The bulkiness of the oversize clothes helped to hide her budding breasts and any feminine curves to her tiny body that might attract males. She practiced using what she thought sounded like a guttural male voice, in case she ever had to actually act the part.

As she sharpened the knife on a granite boulder, she regretted that she had not thought of cutting off the soldier's penis, but the urgency of the moment had precluded that. She laughed at the thought, wondering what she would have done with it, and reasoning that it would have been a little too late to have served any vengeful purpose.

She pondered over the pistol's operation, trying to figure out what had made it fire, the knowledge of which would make it a powerful defensive weapon. She deduced how to reload the clips from the ammunition in the tote bag, how to extract and insert the clip expertly, and how to pull the slide back and let it spring forward carrying the initial round into the firing chamber. But fear that the sound of its firing would draw attention to her kept her from experimenting with the possible combinations that might make it fire. Still, she practiced drawing and cocking it rapidly should the need arise, remembering the sound it made as the soldier cocked it and held it to her head, and how intimidating even just that sound could be.

Sook Cha knew enough about biology to fear that she might be at risk of being pregnant. The wounds in her vagina and anus had stopped bleeding and the pain had long since gone away, but when she felt anything in her abdomen, she tried to guess if it was hunger or the beginning of life. She usually chose a remote high ground on which to sleep at night, affording her a strategic overview of her locale when she awoke, usually a hilltop with no visible paths leading to its crest. There she would build herself a nest with a camouflaged overlay so no one would see her unless they actually walked right over her. A little more than a month after her rape, she woke in her nest to discover the commencement of her menses, a bloody discharge so thick with matter that she didn't know whether she should celebrate her introduction to womanhood, or cry for her stillborn child. She decided to abandon her current befouled nest.

****

One morning she awoke on her newly chosen hilltop to view an idyllic scene below, a narrow curving road leading across the rice paddies with a moon bridge reaching across the principal waterway that curved beneath it and reflected its semi-circular shape. The road was too small for most modern vehicles, it had been bombed into disuse on both sides of the bridge, and yet the bridge was intact with its perfect circular symmetry when reflected in the still waters. Sook Cha remembered a wall print in her parents home which depicted such a bridge.

10

Sook Cha was drawn to the bridge which was inaccessible without wading through knee deep water or, as Sook Cha decided to do, building a small wood and straw raft to navigate the stream and rice paddies. Reaching the bridge, she discovered it had a small embankment beneath one side, the shadow side when the sun was at high noon. This, she decided, was the safest place she could be during the day when she had to forage for food, and the surrounding water offered reptiles and fish, as well as abandoned rice seedlings and other edible wild crops. Sook Cha cleared a space for herself on the embankment and decided to make it her day camp for a few days, returning to the hilltop for safety at night..

On her third day at the moon bridge, Sook Cha was paddling her raft back to the bridge when she saw a small military vehicle stopped at the bomb crater on one side. Two North Korean soldiers dismounted the open vehicle, one with a holstered pistol hesitated by the vehicle, the other with a rifle with bayonet who traversed the bomb crater and headed toward the bridge. At first Sook Cha assumed someone had seen her there and these men were sent to check it out, fearing at worst she would lose her small stash of rice seedlings and dried plums, and that she would have to vacate the area. Then she thought she saw movement under the bridge. She reached in her tote bag for the small plastic coated map salvaged from the soldier, rolled it into a tube, and used the tube as a sighting telescope to view under the bridge. By excluding extraneous light, it made the shadow areas more visible.

There she saw a young woman clutching a baby, desperately trying to keep the baby from crying out, and an older woman gesturing for her to stay hidden as the older woman exited the other side of the bridge and tried

11

to create some distance from it before she waved her hands and yelled at the soldiers to distract them, acting like a crazy woman. "Hey Soldier! You seen my dog? I look under bridge, but he not there. He big brown dog, with froth on his mouth. You help me find him this way, okay?" The old woman kept moving away from the bridge, trying to lure the soldiers away. The soldier with the rifle walked to the other side of the road nearest the old woman, then took aim at her.

Suddenly the baby let out a brief cry before the young woman covered the infant's mouth. The soldier at the vehicle cautioned the rifleman to stop, and, without having drawn his pistol, started to move toward the near side of the bridge.

Sook Cha's raft had come perilously close to the bridge, a point at which she would lose her cover, a point of no return. Sook Cha wondered if there had been silent witnesses to the murder of her father and rape of the children, witnesses who made no effort to stop it. She wondered if there had been a witnesses to her own rape, and all the possible reasons why they made no effort to defend her. Sook Cha knew, beyond a shadow of a doubt, that if no one intervened, in the next few hours these two women and the baby would be dead. She also knew she had not learned how to fire the 45 caliber pistol.

Sook Cha pushed the raft aside and stood up as tall as she could within firing distance of the soldier nearest the bridge. She pointed her pistol at him, cocking it noisily and holding it in both hands, with her feet planted firmly apart. She spoke with her best imitation of a boy's voice. "That's my mother, she's crazy. The dog bit her. You leave now, and I help her find the dog. When I find it, I kill it so it wont bite you, too."

12

The soldier's looked at each other and laughed uncomfortably. They knew Sook Cha had the 'drop' on the nearest soldier. The rifleman started to aim at Sook Cha. Holding her ground without flinching, she yelled at him, "You point at me, he dies." The nearest soldier smiled painfully, gestured to the rifleman to lower his weapon, and slowly moved his hand toward his pistol. Sook yelled back, "No gun, or you die." The nearest soldier raised his hand away from his holster. After an awkward five seconds, she added, "You go bye bye now. I kill mad dog for you."

The nearest soldier grunted assent and retreated to the vehicle, gesturing for the rifleman to join him. The two drove off swiftly, looking over their shoulders as Sook Cha continued to keep her pistol pointed in their direction. As soon as they were over the horizon, Sook Cha pulled her raft to the bridge and, as the two women tried to thank her, she said, "No time. They come back quick with more soldier. Put baby on raft. I show you safe place." And the party of women waded down the stream in the direction of Sook Cha's hilltop night time hideaway.

****

Sook Cha could tell that Young Mamasan's clothing, though torn and muddied, was expensive and her manners were upperclass. Old Mamasan had been Young Mamasan's housekeeper and was originally a farmer's wife. They both expressed their gratitude to Sook Cha excessively, until she told them, "Stop. No more 'thank you.' I did for you because no one did for me. Hereafter, we do for each other. But I am boss. You don't listen, I leave you. Understand?" The two women looked at each other, then nodded assent.

13

At fourteen, Sook Cha's height began to shoot up, and pulling off her role as a boy or young man became easier, even though the pistol remained a prop more than an operable weapon for her. The greater need to feed three and a half people was offset by Old Mamasan's knowledge and expertise as a farmer. She knew more edible plants, animals, and means of storage than Sook Cha had learned, and she taught these to her tactfully without challenging Sook Cha's authority. Old Mamasan made the food tastier than Sook Cha ever could, and saw to it that Sook Cha had clean clothes and a comfortable bed wherever they camped. Both Young Mamasan and Old Mamasan deferred to Sook Cha as if she were the man of their household, even though Young Mamasan was a decade older and Old Mamasan four decades older. They recognized that she was an adolescent girl who had been greatly traumatized, that she had survived through initiative and by taking control, and they wisely did not challenge her need to maintain that control.

Sook Cha had mixed feelings for these women and this baby. Her mother had died when she was young and she had little contact with her grandparents, so the nurturing behavior of Old Mamasan was a strange experience for her which she enjoyed, but which she could not respond to emotionally. It was Old Mamasan that helped Sook Cha learn how to deal with the mystery of her menses, a mystery that was compounded and conflicted by the association of rape and traumatic vaginal bleeding.

Sook Cha had been taught democratic principles by her father and saw Young Mamasan as a potentially spoiled elitist, but slowly began to recognize that Young Mamasan had not been given a choice when her teen age beauty had attracted a wealthy older husband and her father had thrust her into a life of luxury. At heart Young Mamasan was a fair and honest person, willing to wash Sook Cha's clothes and even rub her feet at the end of a long days trek. At times, Sook Cha identified Young Mamasan with Ling, her childhood friend whose cold white corpse she had last seen in that field of horror, and she wanted to hold her and protect her and believe that Ling was alive again.

Even the baby gave Sook Cha conflicted emotions. There were spontaneous moments when its smile would evoke happy feelings and the desire to cuddle the child. But there were times when the baby reminded her of the tiny corpses on that field of horror, and she would have to turn away from the child to help erase the grisly details of that scene.

The trio of women continued South, their progress sometimes impeded and sometimes aided by their numbers and increased body of knowledge. After many days trapped on their latest safe hilltop while they heard bombardment all around them, they woke one morning to see American and Australian forces marching north on the roads below. South Korean civilians began to dot the sides of the road, waving and cheering the Allied forces who occasionally responded by tossing out cans of K-rations and candy bars.

Young Mamasan was delighted by the sight of the Allied forces and prepared to go down and cheer them on. Sook Cha looked through her curled up map tube at the distant soldiers in their vehicles and their multi-colored hair and skin tones, a frown beginning to form on her brow. Young Mamasan donned her one remaining formerly fancy but now tattered dress and began to head downhill, but Sook Cha grabbed her arm in restraint. In her sternest male voice, Sook Cha asked a needless question, "Where are you going?"

15

Now Young Mamasan began to have a slight frown and answered in an apologetic tone, "To greet the Allied soldiers. They are on the side of South Korea. They have come to free us."

Sook Cha maintained her grip on the young woman's arm. "You're a pretty girl. They are men. You'll get in trouble."

Young Mamasan smiled imploringly. "But they're on our side. And they say the Americans are rich and generous. Don't you understand, they're on our side."

Still holding the young woman's arm, Sook Cha's brow knitted almost angrily. "They are men. If they get you alone, they'll have only one side," and, with her other hand, Sook Cha gripped her own crotch like a man.

Young Mamasan shook Sook Cha's grip free of her arm and turned to face her with a condescending smile. "Okay, then you come and protect me." With that she turned quickly and headed down the hill. After a moments hesitation and without changing her frown, Sook Cha caught up with the young woman and stayed closely behind her. When they reached the roadside, Young Mamasan turned around and said, "We forgot the baby." She looked around her and, among the thin collection of civilians, she spotted an unattended five year old boy, picked the child up, and displayed him to the passing soldiers. The first Hershey bar that arrived she gave to the child. The following occasional khaki colored small cans of jelly and crackers and candy bars she kept handing to the frowning Sook Cha, saying, "Hold this."

After the first contingent of soldiers passed and Young Mamasan returned the boy to his searching parents, along with a small portion of the collected

16

foodstuffs, the two women headed back up the hill. Sook Cha still frowned her disapproval and, to emphasize it, she started emptying her pockets of all the collected foodstuffs and making the young woman take them, forcing Young Mamasan to lift her skirt to carry them all. In a slightly defensive voice, Young Mamasan said, "Don't worry, Sook Cha. I am not a naive young girl, but we each have to play to our strengths. I know how to take care of myself."

Sook Cha increased her pace, passing the young woman by as she said angrily, "No you don't. Without someone's help, you'd be a rotting corpse under the Moon Bridge by now."

Young Mamasan's jaw dropped as she stopped abruptly in her tracks. Now it was her turn for her brow to knit angrily before resuming her climb to catch up with Sook Cha.

Chapter Two
HOME AGAIN

Young Mamasan had been married to a much older politician, a Minister in President Singman Rhee's cabinet. She had lived a brief life of luxury in a palatial home in the center of Seoul. Her wealthy husband had died and her beautiful home destroyed in the initial bombing of the North Korean invasion. The value of the paper currency of her fortune, the banks in which it was deposited, the paper deeds to her property, and the government and halls of record in which they were recorded, all these had vanished overnight with the invasion. The very ground on which she had lived was now being bulldozed to make way for new government buildings to house a new Allied supported government.

Old Mamasan had once tilled the soil on the outskirts of Seoul with her husband, a tenant farmer who had been killed by the retreating Japanese towards the end of World War II. The Japanese had practiced the traditional but inhumane tactic of burning all food crops and killing all male population as they retreated, thereby leaving no resources to their advancing enemy. An additional tactic was to have their soldiers with venereal diseases rape all remaining attractive women in the hopes of infecting and thereby further debilitating their enemy. The diseased Japanese soldier who thought Old Mamasan was still attractive enough to attempt to rape, died with a wooden pitchfork through his chest, wielded by Old Mamasan.

With no land to farm, she migrated to nearby Yeong Deungpo, one of the poorest suburbs of Seoul.

There she became a housekeeper to Young Mamasan's widowed father, helping him raise his teen aged daughter in the modest 50' x 50' structure on an alley beside the railroad tracks. The large double wooden doored gate to the alley was once a bright red, very rugged, and the only entrance in or out of the modest mud brick house. The mud brick was once covered with a brilliant white stucco.

The doors opened on a small three sided cobblestoned courtyard, each side with a shallow four foot deep hardwood veranda raised one foot off the courtyard floor. The three rear bedrooms were marked by their sliding paper and latticed doors. The wood door just inside the left gate hid a primitive toilet that required periodic removal of the 'honeybucket' beneath the toilet seat. The area just inside the right door showed the upper lips of six giant earthen jars protruding above the wood floor and submerged 5' into the ground, each capped with a heavy earthen lid.

In these jars, Old Mamasan had created the classic Korean dish known as kimchi, a pickled concoction of cabbage, carrots, turnips, onions, garlic, horseradish, hot peppers, and other ingredients which, when aged six to twelve months, was too spicy and odiferous for most foreigners. By rotating the six jars to insure a properly aged product, Old Mamasan had provided food for the household and enough extra to supply small nearby eateries with the classic dish, thereby providing some modest additional income for the household.

It was to this house in Yeong Deungpo, that the quartet of Sook Cha, Old Mamasan, Young Mamasan, and Babysan now returned. The pot holed once brick paved now muddied streets were lined with badly damaged houses and sections of bombed out rubble where men, women, and children in rags looked like an army of ants as they pilfered building materials to repair their own dwellings. Street vendors, looking more like beggars in rags, offered a variety of used items, displayed in straw bags and cardboard boxes, varying from a mismatched collection of plastic combs and cigarette lighters and cigarettes, acquired legally or illegally from Allied soldiers, to a variety of homemade candy and finger food that smelled and looked delicious, but ran the risk of contamination. Every so often a shopkeeper and his family stood guard at the doorway of their repaired and re-established business. And every so often a cluster of yelling children surrounded an Allied soldier, most often American, the soldier in search of a little R&R (rest and recuperation), the children in search of whatever generosity he may bestow or whatever was in his pockets.

When the quartet first arrived at Young Mamasan's parental home, it was in shambles, the little remaining stucco creating a jig saw pattern, and the red gates retaining only faded traces of their original red paint. Upon entering, the quartet was confronted with a collection of squatters, three males and two females all dressed in rags and, like themselves, obviously undernourished. For a moment, Sook Cha despaired as she saw the look of compassion on the faces of Old Mamasan and Young Mamasan. But fate stepped in as Old Mamasan attempted to assess the damage to her earthen jars, and one of the men, thinking she was going to take the tiny residue of food in them, attacked her with a broken rake handle.

Sook Cha swiftly drew and pointed her pistol at the man before he could strike, and the entire group was galvanized with silent tension. Sensing her strategic advantage, Sook Cha moved to the rear center of the

21

house and, gesturing with the pistol, she herded them all, one by one, out the gates and into the alley, ordering them "never to return" and locked the gates from the inside with its huge wooden bolt.

Young Mamasan and Old Mamasan looked at her as if she had done something wrong, their eyes brimming with tears of compassion for the evicted refugees, their mouths forming entreaties for the needs of the refugees. Sook Cha frowned at them as she returned the pistol to its holster hidden beneath her shirt. She yelled at them, "No! No! How dare you criticize my decision. I did not save you to die of their diseases. I do not gather food for them to eat. You are my family. I protect only you. I feed only you. Do you understand?"

First Old Mamasan dried her eyes and soberly nodded assent, then Young Mamasan followed in suit, and Babysan broke the tension by gurgling an unintelligible but smiling positive agreement. Then the three women set about cleaning and restoring their sadly neglected reclaimed home.

Aside from the dwindling supply of salvaged building materials from the bombed out rubble on some remaining streets, there were no newly manufactured goods of any kind, other than what could be bartered for or stolen from the Allied forces. When she could get the raw materials, Old Mamasan knew how to make soap from Borax and animal fat, glue from oxen hooves, and various cosmetics from petroleum jelly, mineral oil, baking soda, salt, sugar, and various food flavorings derived from the juice and skin oil of various fruits and vegetables. Old Mamasan's resourcefulness helped the women return to the civilized lifestyle of clean and sweet smelling bodies, clothes, and living environment.

In the densely populated suburb of their new home, food was not as easily scavanged as in the thinly populated war torn farms they had previously traveled. Old Mamasan's revival of her kimchi production required time and capital, of which they had little. Hired labor, skilled or unskilled, was a buyer's market. Even posing as a boy laborer, Sook Cha was a small and scrawny looking boy, rarely and last hired, and first fired. A noticeable blow to her vision of herself as the 'man of the house.'

Several elements had changed the dynamic of the trio of women. The war was over and Sook Cha's role as savior and protector was, if not completely gone, at least reduced to a make believe male bouncer to discourage thieves and horny men from preying on them. Young Mamasan was not only the owner of their residence, but now the head of their household. Even Old Mamasan had gained status among their ranking because of her kimchi production skill which was potentially their most likely source of income.

It was an age when few women were educated or worked outside the home. Old Mamasan fared best as a semi-skilled occasional worker for some of the re-established shopkeepers. Young Mamasan found even less occasional work as a scribe or accountant. There were infrequent offers from the a growing number of bordellos for Young Mamasan to work as a prostitute, an offer everyone in the household considered preposterous and insulting, at least until things became extremely desperate.

When one of the bordello Madames came to purchase the small supply of underaged Kimchi from Old Mamasan's first available batch, Young Mamasan invited the woman into her private bedroom to talk. After the Madame detailed the requirements of the

23

various jobs available for an attractive young woman in her establishment, Young Mamasan asked her to repeat the duties of a 'sakahachi girl,' These duties required performing fellatio, but restricted any need to disrobe, and could be minimized by the skilled addition of assisted masturbation. Young Mamasan was not a virgin and, as the widow of a quite elderly man, was acquainted with the skills of fellatio and assisted masturbation.

Sook Cha arrived home in time to see the Madame exiting Young Mamasan's bedroom, and frowned her disapproval as the woman passed her at the gate, the Madame addressing her farewell to Sook Cha as if Sook Cha were a young boy. Sook Cha questioned Young Mamasan about the Madame's presence in the tone of a jealous husband interrogating his wife. Young Mamasan's denial of any business discussion was as evasive as her eye contact with Sook Cha. Old Mamasan had been watching them, but, when Sook Cha looked at her, she too averted her eyes. Glaring back at Young Mamasan and speaking in a disdainful gutteral angry tone, Sook Cha accused her of seeking work as a prostitute.

Young Mamasan's evasive demeanor changed into a concerned frown as she stared at Sook Cha for a long time before saying, "None of us have eaten as much as one full meal a day for over a month. My baby has not had milk for over a week." She looked down briefly before staring back into Sook Cha's eyes and asking, "How much did you earn today?"

Sook Cha's eyes began to stare at the pattern on Young Mamasan's blouse as she quoted a figure that would barely have purchased a small serving of Old Mamasan's kimchi, then added, "That's not the point.

Our fortune's will improve, but our honor cannot once it has been stained."

Young Mamasan tried to take Sook Cha's hand, but it was pulled away. Young Mamasan's frown melted as she spoke more softly saying, "Sook Cha, there is nothing honorable about dying of starvation or of some disease that may take advantage of our undernourished bodies. You have to understand, I am an adult," then she continued after a brief pause, "and I am not a virgin, and I am not your wife. What I am is a refugee who is watching the two women I love and my baby starve to death. We are all thin as rails, and I am prepared to sacrifice my honor if that is all I have left to fill our needs."

Sook Cha continued to stare at the pattern on Young Mamasan's blouse as tears welled in her eyes and ran down her cheeks. Holding back a sob, she said, "Please don't do anything until tomorrow." Then she raised her eyes to Young Mamasan's, seeing tears form in the young woman's eyes, and added, "Promise me, you'll wait until tomorrow."

Young Mamasan put her arms around Sook Cha and, hugging the girl's rigid body, assured her, "Of course, I have made no commitments and we will all survive until tomorrow. Don't worry, Sook Cha, everything will be all right."

In a small voice, Sook Cha said, "Thank you," then broke free of Young Mamasan's arms, went to her room, and emerged minutes later with a small brown paper bundle that she tucked under her shirt as she exited the gate into the alley of Yeong Deungpo.

Shortly after midnight, Sook Cha returned through the gate to find both women waiting up for her, both seated in front of their respective bedroom sliding doors. Inside the gate, Sook Cha hesitated, then took

25

several steps toward the younger woman before stopping and changing direction toward the older woman. She stopped again, then finally walked over to the porch floor equidistant between the two women, placing a small brown paper bundle on the hardwood surface.

The two seated women looked at each other, then back to Sook Cha, whose eyes avoided both of them. Then the older woman approached the package and opened it, placing the contents of stacks of rumpled American currency in neat piles beside Young Mamasan, who looked at Sook Cha and asked, "Where did you get this?"

Old Mamasan had been counting the stacks of money and interjected, "There's more here than a strong man could earn in a month." Then she looked at Sook Cha with concern and a hint of suspicion.

Young Mamasan repeated her question more firmly, "Where did you get this?"

Sook Cha stared continually at the money. "I sold the gun."

The old woman made a long wailing sound, then said excitedly to Young Mamasan, "Even if she couldn't fire it, the fear of it is the only thing that has kept robbers and horny men from our door, the door of three unprotected women!"

Sook Cha glared at Old Mamasan, "Two women and a man, as far as they know!"

Young Mamasan said resignedly, "Two women and a boy, and, besides, a lot of them already know. Sook Cha, you didn't have to do this. I know how much that meant to you. And Mamasan is right, there is some concern about our protection."

Sook Cha looked at Young Mamasan with a hint of defiance. "Don't worry, I bought this to protect us," and she withdrew from her baggy pants leg a twenty four inch machete in a khaki colored sheath marked 'U.S. Property,' pulling the blade out of the sheath with a flourish.

Old Mamasan looked at the shiny blade and grunted disdainfully.

Young Mamasan looked at Sook Cha and spoke a little more compassionately, "Well, we appreciate your sacrifice, Sook Cha, and I'm sure that ... thing ... will act as some kind of a deterrent." Then she tapped the stack of bills, saying, "With this we will not starve for another month."

Sook Cha pointed to the money with the machete saying, with a raised eyebrow, "With this, you can retain your honor."

Young Mamasan nodded assent and smiled as she said, "Yes ... for another month."

****

A considerable part of the money from the sale of the gun was wisely invested in the ingredients of Old Mamasan's kimchi production. As a day laborer, Sook Cha was most often given the least desirable jobs, such as carrying the earthen jars of human waste from the individual houses to an ox-drawn collection cart which would transport it out of town to the rural areas. When Sook Cha arrived home filthy and exhausted, Old Mamasan would scrub her from head to toe before she'd allow her to cut and grate the horseradish for the Kimchi, a particularly loathsome job that made Sook Cha's eyes tear for hours despite the cloth mask she wore over her nose and mouth.

Sook Cha did not complain because, as one of the most difficult parts of the Kimchi production, it helped her maintain her diminishing leadership status after the loss of the gun and becoming the lowest paid of the three women. Secretly, she worried that if Young Mamasan became a well paid prostitute, the other two women would no longer need her. She knew they would include her as part of their household, and that they would always appreciate and acknowledge that she had saved their lives, but, with the shift in the balance of money, the resulting shift in the balance of power would probably lead the household in a direction Sook Cha did not feel she could tolerate.

The next time the Madame arrived to purchase kimchi, Sook Cha kept a wary eye on her to insure there were no private talks with Young Mamasan behind closed doors. As the Madame passed Young Mamasan on the way to the gate, Sook Cha heard her ask Young Mamasan, "Did you consider my offer?"

Young Mamasan's eyes noted Sook Cha's distant stare and replied in a muted voice, "Thank you, but not at this time."

Then the Madame looked toward Sook Cha and asked, "And what about him?"

Young Mamasan smiled painfully and replied, "No, I'm quite sure he is not interested."

Sook Cha knew she was no longer in a position to react angrily to the situation, but, as soon as the Madame left, could not resist approaching Young Mamasan and asking, "She propositioned you again, didn't she?"

Without looking up from her sewing, young Mamasan replied, "Yes, and, as before, I declined."

Sook Cha watched the young woman's hands deftly sewing the salvaged remnants of old clothes to make a new garment. She thought how beautiful Young Mamasan's hands were, like pale ivory, compared to her own laborer's hands calloused and with broken ragged nails. She asked, "And why did she ask about me? What is it that I am not interested in?"

Young Mamasan stopped sewing, took a deep sigh, looked over to Old Mamasan a distance away who averted her eyes, and then said to Sook Cha, "Come, let's go into my room." After she closed her paper latticed door and the two young women were facing each other seated on their heels, Young Mamasan said, "The last time the Madame was here, she didn't just offer me a position as a prostitute. She offered you one, too."

Sook Cha looked perplexed. "But she thinks I am a boy."

Young Mamasan's lips pursed and she looked down at the rice tatami kneeling rug she was on. "Yes, she does, and she thinks you are an unusually pretty boy, and she has male customers who like pretty boys."

Sook Cha stared down at the tatami she was kneeling on and her perplexed frown deepened. "So, I am a 'pretty boy.'"

Young Mamasan spoke in a flattering tone, "Yes, a very pretty boy. Some people think you are such a pretty boy, that you are really a girl posing as a boy."

Sook Cha's eyes met Young Mamasan's. "Soooooo! That's what you meant when you said, 'Two women and a boy, and, besides, a lot of them already know.'"

Young Mamasan looked at Sook Cha with concern, "Yes, Sook Cha. Does that disturb you?"

Sook Cha looked to one side where she saw her own reflection in Young Mamasan's broken piece of mirror, it's ragged edges hidden beneath a border of paper flowers. "Soooo, I am a very pretty boy."

Young Mamasan's concerned frown deepened. "Yes, but I told her you were not interested. Right?"

Sook Cha raised her widened eyes to the other woman. "Of course you were right." Then she smiled at her and said, "I guess, better to be a very pretty boy than a very ugly boy." And the two young women broke into giggling laughter.

It was decided that, for security reasons, Sook Cha would continue to pose as a boy. Even the suspicion that a male was on the premises, young or old, with or without a gun or a machete, would act as a deterrent to potential robbers and rapists.

Later that evening, Old Mamasan revealed to Sook Cha that neighbors had inquired of her whether Sook Cha was related to Young Mamasan as a brother, a lover, a pimp, or a lesbian lover who chose to dress in male clothing. Sook Cha felt a secret thrill in most of these images, though she would never confess that to the other two women. All she said was, "Those neighbors must be stupid to think I am a pimp when they see me go to work hauling 'honey buckets' of human waste most of the days."

****

But there came a day when even work carrying honey buckets was no longer offered Sook Cha, nor any other part time work offered Old Mamasan and Young Mamasan. The partial underaged first batch of Kimchi had mostly been sold off, and they had become desperate enough to eat the remainder.

Old Mamasan had cooked and served the meager portions of the last of their rice which the three women ate in silence. Young Mamasan set her empty bowel and chopsticks down, rose, and went into her bedroom and shut the door. Sook Cha and Old Mamasan looked at each other questioningly, then Old Mamasan collected the dishes and took them to the washing bowl, glancing at Sook Cha sideways when she thought Sook Cha was not looking.

Sook Cha approached Young Mamasan's bedroom door and knocked softly. At first their was no reply, then, after a third knock, Young Mamasan responded, "Enter." Sook Cha entered and closed the door behind her, kneeling as she watched Young Mamasan tying the sash on her best robe and begin applying Old Mamasan's homemade cosmetics; ground charcoal in petroleum jelly for mascara, and red clay rogue over a cornstarch powder base.

In a hoarse whisper, Sook Cha asked, "Where are you going?"

Young Mamasan continued applying her eye makeup, concentrating on her transformation into a traditional classic Korean beauty in the broken remnant of mirror, before dispassionately replying, "You know."

Sook Cha looked down at the tatami and cleared her throat before speaking in a hoarse voice. "The Madame, you spoke to her today?"

Young Mamasan deftly applied a pencil shaped piece of charcoal to extend and dramatize her eyebrows. "No, but I'm sure she'll welcome me, even if I'm unannounced."

Sook Cha cleared her throat again. "You know....you know that what you're considering is dangerous." Sook Cha's brow knitted in concern as she looked up at the young woman. "Those soldier's, they are taught to kill. Life is nothing to them, particularly a woman's."

Young Mamasan used a fingertip to mix the red clay with petroleum jelly and apply it to her lips, then

31

dusted her lips with the last remnant of cornstarch, then applied a fresh layer of clear jelly for gloss. "These are Allied soldiers, not North Koreans. They are here to defend us, not wreak vengeance on us for rejecting Communism."

Sook Cha looked back down at the tatami and made a hissing sound as she spoke. "They are still men, foul smelling, dirty, and diseased."

Young Mamasan closed her eyes and a trace of a smile raised the corners of her shiny red lips as she removed the cloth protecting her hair from the makeup and face powder. "Well, they eat well and are a damn sight healthier than we are. Let's hope we don't give them a disease."

Sook Cha looked up again with a pained expression. "No, really, you will be in danger if you do this. They come from strange parts of the world and they do strange things, particularly to women."

Young Mamasan turned her kneeling position to face Sook Cha. She folded her hands in front of her and looked at the girl compassionately. "Don't worry, Sook Cha. Madame has a security man, and I am no stranger myself to the strange things than men do. Besides, my contact with them will be very limited."

Sook Cha looked puzzled. "What do you mean? You will just be a hostess? You will have no physical contact with them?"

Young Mamasan looked down at her fingernails, then back up at Sook Cha. "Not exactly. Madame offers a variety of services. My service will be limited to oral sex."

Sook Cha felt her throat clutch, flashing back to how her rapist had made her gag repeatedly while he forced her head down onto his erection violently with both hands. Sook Cha tried to control the expression of disgust that moved over her face. "You mean, you're going to become a sakahachi girl?"

Young Mamasan looked at Sook Cha defiantly. "Even though it pays less, it entails less risk. And that's your concern for me, right? To minimize any risk?"

Sook Cha could not look into the young woman's face, her gaze began to wander all around the room as if she were searching for something, something she could not find.

Young Mamasan's head cocked to one side as she looked at Sook Cha questioningly. "Sook Cha, are you all right?"

Sook Cha hobbled on her knees past the young woman so she could look at herself in th broken mirror. "No, I'm not all right. I need to do something, and I need your help." She turned to face the young woman. "Help me, please, help me."

In the courtyard, Old Mamasan was drawn to the rising voices in Young Mamasan's bedroom. She opened the latticed paper covered door just as Young Mamasan turned to her saying, "She's crazy. Sook Cha's gone mad."

Sook Cha hobbled over to the two women with Young Mamasan's little makeup jars in her hands, saying, "No. I can do this. All I need is your help. It's the perfect solution." Then Sook Cha turned to Old Mamasan, saying, "Make her help me. Better me than her."

****

The Madame answered the knock at the alley back door, surprised to see Old Mamasan with an attractive young woman who looked familiar, but whom she couldn't place.

Old Mamasan managed a half hearted and obviously fake smile as she gestured toward the young girl, "This Yon Cha, the young boy's sister. She just arrive from country and wants to work as Sakahachi Josan. You put her to work, please?"

Madame's face lit up in recognition, "Ah so, I see the resemblance. As pretty as her name, Lotus Blossom. Come in, come in. Looks like she's wearing your Mistress's robe, yes? Very pretty, very pretty. Yon, if you want to work tonight, we just have enough time before business picks up in a couple hours. You do good tonight, and tomorrow I'll take you for your Prostitutes VD Card. You speak any Englilsh? No. Okay, let me teach you the house rules and a little bit of English to get you started."

Sook Cha walked self consciously in Young Mamasan's tight fitting robe and raised gata sandles. She hoped the hair extensions would not fall off and that she would not touch her face makeup which felt so strange on her skin. She tried to remember Young Mamasan's coaching in how to be feminine and how to behave initially toward male clients. Beyond that, she would not let Young Mamasan utter one word of coaching in how to perform any sexual act. But she could not reject the Madames instructions.

Madame's rules governed payment; the house takes 75% and the girl gets 25%, the girl does not handle any money other than additional tips, the men chose the girls and the girls cannot reject any paying client, and any girl caught stealing from a client will not just be fired, she will also be beaten by the security man, Madame's husband.

Madames crash course in Hooker English included; "You likee good time? You likee Sakahachi Josan? Me Sakahachi Josan! Ohhhh, you big! Ohhhh,

34

you hard! Ohhhh, you strong! No touchee there, please! Me catchee other girl, she do that for you!"

Madame's nitty gritty instructions were the hardest for Sook Cha to listen to and went like this: "The hand is quicker than the mouth and doesn't wear out as fast. The three principal and most sensitive male erotic targets are the rim just below the flange at the bottom of the glans, the testes, and the prostate gland, the search for which is an acquired skill. 'Act' is the keyword in any sexual act, and the actress who can groan convincingly and talk dirty aggressively wins the Academy Award, and lots of tips and repeat customers."

Sook Cha was grateful when customers arriving early cut Madame's tutoring short. The three other working girls eyed Sook Cha suspiciously. The fairest skinned one, Min, was beautiful, but hardened looking. The heavier one, Sun, was younger and quite jovial, and surprisingly successful with the customers despite the fact that she was the least attractive. The smallest girl looked far too young to be working as a prostitute, and was the first to befriend Sook Cha, complimenting her on her robe and helping her repair a failing hair extension. Her name was Hei, meaning 'Grace,' and, though her size and features were not the same, her youth and innocence made Sook Cha think of her friend, Ling, when last she saw her alive. Sook Cha was surprised to learn Hei had worked for Madame for over a year, and then Sook Cha was a little shocked when Hei happily answered the summons of a black American soldier in combat boots, laughing as she disappeared down the hallway with him.

Each of the other girls welcomed and disappeared down the hall with two and three successive customers, while Sook Cha remained seated alone. She looked at herself in the narrow full length mirror in Madames colorful and slightly garish living room that faced the main street in Yeong Deungpo, and she had to admit she was at least attractive, possibly even pretty, but no man who had entered thus far looked at her more than fleetingly. In the back of her mind she knew it probably had something to do with the fact that she really didn't want to be here, and that fact was probably etched on her face, but she couldn't bring the thought forward enough in her conscious mind to help her manufacture even a fake smile.

Sook Cha reached behind one of the satin pillows on the sofa and pulled out a stack of magazines, mostly months old Japanese magazines filled with black and white pictures and ads for products which she hadn't seen since before the war began. A glimpse of color showed on the corner of one of the magazines near the bottom of the stack, and she pulled it out to find an American movie magazine with lots of color pictures printed on stiff shiny pages. She looked with growing wonder at all the ultra modern looking cars and elegantly dressed people, most of whom were very fair Caucasians and many of whom had red and blonde hair.

The only foreigners Sook Cha had seen before the war were Japanese and a few Russians in military uniforms with their red piped visored caps covering their heads. The recent Allied soldiers mostly wore visored caps and all that had walked through Madame's door this evening had black hair. Sook Cha was mesmerized by the magazine's color photos showing scenes from *The Greatest Show On Earth*, a Japanese film titled *Gate Of Hell*, and another film called *From Here To Eternity*. Though she could not read these titles, she could tell from the pictures who were the good guys and who were the bad guys. She touched one photo showing the most handsome man she had ever seen, a blonde haired God-like man in the movie *From Here To Eternity* who went by the name of Burt Lancaster. She moved her fingertip gently across his face, before being distracted by the shortness of her fingernails which Young Mamasan had tried to overcome with cleaning, filing, and applying mineral oil to hide the cracks in them.

Suddenly Sook Cha was startled by a booming bass voice saying, "Hello, Lassie. Looks like you and me are the only ones here," which belied the fact that Sook Cha could see the Madame across the room staring at her. The stocky fifty-ish Aussie non-com smiled down at her, revealing a missing lower front tooth, while he removed his black beret from his crew cut grey hair. He slapped the beret against his thigh and rocked back and forth on his heels, looking questioningly over his shoulder at the Madame, then back to Sook Cha. "Lady here tells me you're an expert sakahachi girl, is that right?"

Sook Cha looked past him to the Madame who glared at her expectantly. Sook Cha tried unsuccessfully to form words in her throat, then nodded her head up and down rapidly to answer affirmatively, only guessing at what he had asked her. The Aussie grabbed her hand and yanked her from the sofa so abruptly she almost lost her balance on the gata sandels, saying, "Okay then, Lassie, come on and show me what you got," as he dragged her stumbling toward the hall.

Sook Cha removed her gata and put them beside his boots outside the latticed paper door to the tiny room. She stood in the corner in her white tobi socks, folding her arms in the sleeves of Young Mamasan's robe while the Aussie completely disrobed, except for his black socks, and lay on his back on the tatami covered floor. The man smiled at her, saying, "Okay,

37

Girlie, you can start with me nipples. I like that," and he began to tweak both his nipples with his own fingers.

Sook Cha knelt beside his right hip and held her hands hesitantly above his body. He took her left hand and placed it on his right nipple as he continued to demonstrate what he wanted on his left nipple. Sook Cha dutifully began to roll his nipple gently between her fingers, feeling it grow turgid as she did so. With his freed right hand he attempted to go under the front of her robe to fondle her breast, but she moved his hand aside and he settled for cupping her left buttock through the fabric of the robe. She placed her right hand on the inside of his right knee and heard him suck in air deeply and say, "That's it, Girlie, now you got it. Work your way up, now!"

She traced her fingertips in small circles up the inside of his pasty white hairy thigh, her eyes closing and then opening to view his thick short penis slowly emerging from his black and grey colored pubic hair. He smelled a little bit like the caustic cleaning soap Old Mamasan scrubbed Sook Cha down with when she came home from carrying honey buckets. The purple glans of his penis began to emerge from multiple folds of his foreskin, looking somewhat like a newborn puppy emerging from the labia of its mother's vagina. Her right hand had arrived at his testes and, remembering the Madame's advice, she cupped his scrotum gently, manipulating the egg shaped contents one by one between her fingers.

The man stopped tweaking his own nipple and dropped his left hand to the tatami with a thud to emphasize his impatience as he said, "That's enough of that, Dearie. Let's get on with it, Lass!" She gripped his penis and began to stroke the foreskin up and down, but her technique was too slow for him and he brought

38

his right hand up to grip the back of her neck and, slowly but forcefully, lower her head to his penis. She closed her eyes and parted her lips, noting that she could now smell the co-mingled scents of sterilizing soap, musk scented after shave cologne, and the fetid odor of the now revealed inner lining of his foreskin. Young Mamasan's petroleum jelly formulated lipstick made the penis glide smoothly between her lips and left red clay streaks on it as it emerged. The man increased the tempo and the depth of his strokes with his right hand on the back of her neck, and his breathing grew more rapid as his penis grew larger with each thrust in and out of her mouth. His voice was punctuated by rapid intakes of air as he spewed a litany of instructions. "Keep your fingers on me nipple, Lass, and your other on me balls. Thassssssit, Girlie. Faster now. Deeper now. Oh, you are one sweet little bitch!"

Sook Cha was trying to repress flashbacks of her rape and how the North Korean soldier had forced his penis to the back of her throat repeatedly, as if he was trying to choke her to death, and she knew he would eventually kill her one way or the other. With this man she was sensing a repetition of that violence as the gagging turned to choking, while he seemed oblivious to her distress and danger, putting both his hands on the back of her head and forcing it down beyond the limits of her mouth and throat. If she had eaten anything that day, she would surely have vomited all over him by this time.

Madame and the other two girls in the living room were startled by the Aussie's screams. "What the bloody hell!" Another scream. "Jesus fucking Christ Almighty! You crazy fucking bitch!"

Madame called for her husband, "Chul, Chul!"

39

The two girls stepped back and gasped as the Aussie came down the hall into the living room in nothing but his black socks, his right hand tightly holding his penis as blood oozed out between his fingers. He screamed at the Madame, "She bit me. Your crazy fucking whore bit me."

****

The incessant banging at the gate alarmed Old Mamasan. She looked at Young Mamasan with concern, then went to Sook Cha's room and emerged with the sheathed machete which she held at her side as she approached the gate. "Who's there."

An angry woman's voice replied, "It's me, the Madame."

Old Mamasan unbolted the gate and was pushed aside as Madame entered forcefully, half dragging Sook Cha by her wrist, and pushed her to the ground before the two women. "The boy's crazy sister tried to kill one of my clients! One of my best clients! Where is he? I want to tell him how much his sister cost me tonight. I'm not surprised she's crazy. I always thought he looked a little crazy, too!"

Old Mamasan replied, "He's not here."

Young Mamasan lifted Sook Cha to a sitting position at the edge of the porch. She gasped as she saw the blood on Sook Cha's face and hands, and the front of Young Mamasan's one good robe. With concern in her face and voice she asked, "Are you all right?"

Madame screamed in reply, "Yeah, she's all right. I told Chul to beat her for what she did to my client, but he chased her all over the house and couldn't catch her. I finally caught her in the alley halfway here,

40

and wanted you to know what she did and how much it cost me!"

Young Mamasan hugged Sook Cha to her, saying, "Madame, you know we cannot reimburse you for your losses, but, if you want, I will come to work for you and reimburse you out of my earnings."

Madame glared at Young Mamasan. "Noooooo! Your housekeeper makes excellent kimchi, and I will continue to buy it when it is ready. But you girls think you're too good to work for me. You look down on us at the same time you ask us for favors. I don't need you. I have many girls who want to work for me. Girls prettier than her, and younger than you. You keep your precious Lotus Blossom," and she left, slamming the gate shut behind her.

Young Mamasan pulled Sook Cha away from her bosom and asked, "Are you sure you're not hurt?"

Sook Cha looked down and whispered, "Yes."

Young Mamasan pushed her roughly away, causing Sook Cha to fall to the ground. She spoke angrily, "Well that's good, because I feel like beating you myself. You went to all this trouble to save my 'honor,' and you succeeded in doing that at the cost of your earning potential AND mine." She threw up her hands. "Now she wont hire either of us." Then with renewed anger, "What the hell did you do to destroy both our opportunities, and to make all this blood?"

Sook Cha tried to wipe the blood off the robe with her hand, and looked up sheepishly. "I bit him."

Young Mamasan looked incredulous. "You BIT him?"

Sook Cha spread her hands in appeal, "Yes. He was choking me with it and he wouldn't stop."

Young Mamasan looked blankly at Old Mamasan, who stared back at her. Then both women

41

burst into laughter and helped Sook Cha to her feet. "Here, let's get you washed up and out of this once beautiful now ruined robe." As Young Mamasan helped Sook Cha out of the robe, something fell to the floor. Young Mamasan picked up the American movie magazine, looking at it briefly as she said, "What's this?"

Sook Cha snatched the magazine from her. "That's mine."

Young Mamasan smiled at her. "Where'd you get it? Did you get it from Madame's house?"

Sook Cha rolled up the magazine and stuck it in the waist of the pants she had just put on. "I earned it."

Young Mamasan snickered as she wiped the makeup off Sook Cha's face. "How'd you earn it? Did you bite somebody?"

Sook Cha struggled into her boys shirt. "Yeah! New sakahachi girl technique Madame never knew about before."

Young Mamasan patted the magazine under Sook Cha's shirt. "Enjoy it, Sook Cha. It will be the most expensive magazine you will ever own." Then, as Sook Cha stood up to go to her room, Young Mamasan added, "And you may have to eat it in the next few days."

Chapter Three
THE UGLY AMERICAN

In 1945 at the end of World War II, the Korean peninsula was divided at the 38th parallel into Russian supported Communist North Korea and American supported Democratic South Korea. On June 25th, 1950, North Korea invaded South Korea with a surprise attack, and the United Nations, which had been formed at the end of World War II, came to the defense of South Korea with forces from twenty six member nations, which were predominantly from America.

In 1953, twenty miles North of Seoul and about three miles South of the 38th parallel where the North Koreans continued a sporadic shooting war despite the intermittent peace talks under way, there was a tiny farming village called Kimpo. Adjacent to the village were two American military bases side by side; an Army Infantry base and an Air Force Fighter Wing which was to support the infantry and protect a squadron of reconnaissance planes and a squadron of weather detection planes. Aside from being the closest United Nations military installation to the North Koreans, the Air Base was most famous for being the site where a North Korean pilot surrendered a Russian made MiG fighter plane, which the American's had been wanting to study, in his bid for asylum. That had been the most exciting event the Air Force Base Public Information Office had dealt with since young Max had arrived in Korea.

Max had joined the Air Force in his early twenties in order to avoid being drafted into the Army where it was most likely he would end up in the front line of the infantry which had suffered heavy casualties since the beginning of what was tactfully referred to as 'The Korean Conflict.' Max's gamble had not paid off very well in being assigned to what was probably the most dangerous United Nations location possible in Korea. Despite the peace talks, the North Koreans strafed the base twice a day during the morning 'Revile' flag raising ceremony and the evening 'Retreat' flag lowering ceremony. Max, and the rest of the platoon standing attention before the flag post in front of the Headquarters Building, would have to run and dive for the nearby trenches, which usually had a foot of melted snow covered with ice, in order to avoid the fifty caliber slugs that traced across their footprints where they had stood moments before. 'Bed check Charlie,' as the Americans had nicknamed the North Korean pilots making that run, took advantage of the fact that radar was least reliable during sunrise and sunset. Of course, there was the occasional low altitude bombing of any buildup of arms on these two bases and at the nearby port of Inchon, which usually had its share of fatalities, and there were sporadic attempts to infiltrate the base by slitting the throats of unwary guards on duty.

Max considered himself patriotic and was certainly willing to bear arms in defense of himself and his country. What he objected to was his, and many others, perception of the strategy imposed by President Harry Truman on General MacArthur, who was in charge of the campaign. MacArthur, a World War II hero, had switched from the Democratic to the Republican party and appeared destined to become the next President, and it appeared that Truman, a Democrat, had killed MacArthur's presidential bid by saddling him with a no-win position in Korea, not

44

allowing him to go above the 38th Parallel to win a decisive war, and killing huge numbers of American military men to maintain a stalemate. This was the first American military campaign in the 20th century, if not in American history, where some of the troops doubted their involvement and their leader's motives.

It would be almost fifty years before atomic scientists like Alfred Einstein and Henry Oppenheimer would die and their papers reveal Truman's true motive for keeping MacArthur from becoming President. MacArthur believed in using the atom bomb as a tactical weapon, and, having carried the burden of employing the atom bombs that destroyed Hiroshima and Nagasaki, Truman agreed with Einstein and Oppenheimer that atomic and nuclear weapons should never be used again.

But in 1953, good looking blonde haired well built Max was not a happy camper having to trade a promising civilian career as a young entertainer for a military desk job that was frequently interrupted by bullets and bombs. His peripheral talents as a writer and photographer had landed him what most would consider a 'cushy' job, but, in addition to the bullets and bombs, there was another 'fly in the ointment.' The fly was his boss, Lieutenant Conweb.

Max regarded himself as a bit of a non-conformist, but reasoned that his limited contributions to mankind outweighed his parking tickets, his military demotions, his infrequent illegality, and more frequent immorality. When he goofed, he forfeited without complaint, and, when he could not always accept the value he transgressed, he at least tried to avoid the situation. That failing, he'd do his best not to get caught again.

Lt. Conweb, however, was an ultra conformist. The Lieutenant's problem was that his limited cup of

45

intelligence was filled to the brim in basic training, then capped and preserved for posterity; the perfect product of an imperfect civilization that continually refines itself, even if the Lieutenant didn't feel the need to refine himself.

A short, slight, almost handsome man in his late thirties, his nose was a little too sharp, his chin a little too weak, and the thin hairline mustache on his upper lip almost invisible as it was strawberry blonde flecked with premature grey. His hair was the same strawberry blonde with grey patches and styled in a severe crew cut, like a military man's should be, and his grooming immaculate, with possibly a shade too much starch in the khakis for comfort. Early in the Korean Conflict, he had been an enlisted man whose Platoon Officer had been wounded in battle and given him a battlefield commission which stuck, even after Conweb led his platoon into a no-win position where he was the only survivor. In the succeeding years, he had not risen above the rank of First Lieutenant, and his resentment at having been trapped at that plateau showed.

Conweb had all the stubbornness, the narrowness, and the stuffiness of his New England background, and his pride in his heritage was disproportionate to either fact or theory. His allusions to his 'Boston background' and visiting the Hamptons were ill staged affectations, and, behind his back, Max's co-worker Ned referred to Conweb as 'Shanty Irish.' He was the kind of man who would berate a clerk for wasting a paperclip, then turn around and tear up a months work in a rage before that same clerk's eyes. To his six man staff, each of whom stood a foot taller and fifty pounds heavier, he was a peon who mimicked his outdated peers.

Lieutenant Conwebs' high school level psychology consisted of giving each man a distinctive nickname, usually a boyish bastardization cf the man's first or last name, and was genuinely hurt if this did not instill both love and subjugation. They likewise had a pet name for him, 'Cagney,' for the Lieutenant aped that short movie actor's character in everything from talking through his teeth (with an added twang to his voice) to the gesture of hitching up his belt and clearing his nose. He once heard Kim, the Korean darkroom assistant, use the nickname, and threatened Kim with dismissal if he didn't tell where he had heard it. Kim was loyal to his co-workers, so Max risked his neck by telling Lieutenant Conweb that Kim had heard Max speak of the Base Commander's use of the name in reference to Conweb in a complimentary sense. Conweb believed this because he imagined Max was on familiar terms with the Commander.

This assumption was Max's first bad step with his boss. Lieutenant Conweb imagined it because Max was a cocktail pianist at the officer's club, a part time job he direly needed to augment his income, and the Commander was one of those gregarious guys who is more addicted to a piano bar atmosphere than to drink. But, in the conservative Lieutenants' eyes, the commander was a lush and Max a seedy character who most likely sold him dope and dirty books. The Lieutenant stood in awe of the Commander's rank and resented Max's apparent fraternization with a superior, so never questioned whatever was said of the Commander, content with his authority over Max.

That authority reached the heights of either ridiculousness or injustice when he felt responsible for the morals of his men. His first action when he arrived was to review each man's records and, despite Max's high IQ and aptitude tests, civilian history, and the letter of commendation on his work, the Lieutenants' only notation was that Max and Ned had received demotions. Ned's problem was obvious to his boss. After twenty years in the service, Ned had two stripes and cirrhosis of the liver.

But having five years over Lieutenant Conweb in both writing and the service, not to mention even more years in life itself, did not save Ned from his boss' sincere lectures on the evils of alcoholism. The Lieutenant had high hopes that Max would prove Ned's younger counterpart when he found him in the officer's club, but just being there was sufficient indication that Max had some moral problem. He quickly found tangible evidence of it in a picture Max had taken in Kimpo Village.

Strolling through Kimpo with his camera, Max had recorded the resourcefulness of rooftops shingled with flattened American beer cans, room heaters fashioned from fifty gallon oil drums, and a fighter plane wing tip tank sliced in half and used as a bathtub. Bathing in the orient is an uninhibited communal function, so the adolescent girl bathing in the wing tip tank while her mother poured water over her from a wooden bucket elicited only smiles and laughter when Max snapped their picture. But, to Lieutenant Conweb, it was an opportunity to lecture Max on morality.

The Lieutenant had a fantastic memory for cliches, but obvious practice had failed to give him any technique in delivering them. He considered the picture evidence that Max had visited a prostitute for whom he had provided military property such as the wing tip tank, not allowing Max any defense of the accusation. He mentioned Max's marriage and pointed to the framed wall picture of his own tall, thick, masculine looking wife. Max's wife was obviously prettier and his marriage was obviously none of his boss' business, but

48

Max wisely refrained from voicing this or any defense and stood like a schoolboy staring at the wall. To one side of the picture on the wall was the framed letter of commendation Max's efforts had helped earn for his boss, the second to go in Max's file, and to the other side of the picture was the placard with the 'military slogan of the week,' another of his boss' high school psychologies. Each man was expected to dream up a new one, the Lieutenant's brand of military therapy and thermometer of his staff's indoctrination, Kim mis-lettering the foreign English words with a brush. More often, the Lieutenant ripped off Ben Franklins' proverbs from *Poor Richard's Almanac.*

Max estimated the cure of his faint nausea as requiring a light dinner and one Bromo Seltzer, promised the Lieutenant he would not take any more 'dirty' pictures nor consort with any 'unclean' girls, and left thinking with more than usual compassion of how comical and pitiful his boss was.

But, two 'slogans of the week' later, Max saw Kim in the darkroom looking at some wet prints and shaking his head. As he showed the prints to Max he said, "Cagneysan mebbe catchee good time, but no can catchee good picture."

The Japanese girl in the pictures bore a definite masculine resemblance to Conweb's wife, right down to the horse smile on her face. The near two dozen pictures showed slight differences of angle and poor focus, but an unvarying attempt to apparently record the inside of the girl's womb. Max's bowels lurched with anger and disgust.

The little swinging gate that separated Conweb's desk almost flew off its hinges as Max marched over and plopped the wet prints in front of the Lieutenant. "Knowing how you feel about obscenity, Sir, I thought

49

you would want to know these prints were being made in our darkroom."

Lieutenant Conweb rose with such steady indignation that Max thought he would continue up to the ceiling. "You know those are my prints," the words hissing between Conweb's teeth.

Max could hardly find the breath. to speak. "You have the audacity to talk to me about....."

The Lieutenant poked the prints rhythmically with his finger as he interrupted with, "I wasn?t talking about some brief manly sport with a girl who bathes and lives in a clean hotel in Tokyo. I was talking about consorting with a diseased whore in a fly infested rat hole that's furnished with stolen military supplies."

Max was shaking with anger and tried to control the volume of his voice. "You were talking about morals."

The Lieutenants' hard anger changed to a hard smile. "Yes, I was talking about sins that aren?t too brief to be forgotten, but, since you must get personal, let's talk about consorting with prostitutes in Off Limits areas. Let's talk about stealing military property to supply your diseased whore. Let's talk about the years of military justice you could serve if you don't die of syphilis."

Ned stood just behind Max, his hands a breath away from Max's fists that repeatedly clenched and unclenched as he tried to control his shaking. Max's stomach leveled out into a flat pool of gastric acid, and the Japanese girl's crotch and Conweb's sharp smiling face were superimposed into one impossibly loathsome creature that wavered before his eyes, almost obliviating the light.

50

His boss' voice brought everything into sharp focus as the Lieutenant said, "Don't touch him, Ned. Let the kid stretch his own neck."

Max thought, "Kid? If you're a man, I'd rather be Peter Pan," but he didn't say it. As much as his facts were warped, they were founded on incriminating seeds of truth. Though Ned might enjoy Max's first assault, he would never let Max kill him, and his boss would derive satisfaction rather than education from the incident. Max steadied myself with a long intake of air and tried to think about a nice triple bromo.

The Lieutenant sat down and took his time while Max was obliged to remain at attention. Then his boss reminded Max of his promise to be good, enumerated all his duties that would help prove his sincerity, listed a few additional duties he might occupy his restless free time with, and bemoaned his lack of appreciation for the restraint the Lieutenant executed in the face of Max's guilt, and the efforts his boss had gone to help him save himself. He handed the prints back to Max with instructions to see to their washing and drying. The Lieutenant would not ask Max to apologize, but, if he ever felt so inclined, or if he ever wanted to discuss his problems with his boss, feel free at any time.

Max's mouth was so dry he could hardly unstick his lips to say, "Thank you, Sir." After returning the prints to Kim, he left the office and headed toward his tent, bypassing the chow hall, trudging through the light snow as the sun set behind the mountain that rose above Kimpo Village, the one everyone called 'Witches Tit' because of its slightly curved conical shape. On his way to his tent he picked up his mail at the Squadron Orderly Room, his mail consisting of one lone envelope with a New Orleans postmark.

51

He sat on his cot and opened the envelope that bore the return address of his best friend, Etienne. When he had left for Korea, he had asked his friend to make himself available to help Max's wife in an emergency. Max's last letter to Etienne had expressed gratitude for his assistance to his wife and for his friendship. Now Max's throat tightened and his heart began to ache as he read the closing lines of Etienne's letter which said, "I am so glad you consider me your best friend, now, because of recent events and more than ever, there is a great need for us to be best friends."

Max had fought with his wife over when they should start a family and, because of his doubts and reluctance, they had no children, and, now, he guessed they never would. Max laid down on his cot and drew his visored fatigue green cap over his eyes so no one could see the tears that welled there.

****

"Josan?"

"Josan?"

"Catchee josan, GI?"

"Gimme choon gum."

"Catchee ichi bon josan?"

"Gimme cigarette."

"Catchee ichi bon josan, GI? Ichi bon josan look like Mariwen Monwo."

There must have been a dozen of the ragged little urchins, their innocent, ivory, doll like faces in utter contrast to their unkept noses, their tattered clothes, and their incessant chant; the chant of the pimp.

"Catchee josan? Short time, all night."

A growing sea of children, mostly boys, all under ten, pressed around Max with the strength of their number so great he could hardly lift his arms, all because he had hesitated long enough to try to interpret one beggar child's pitiful song.

"Catchee Josan, GI? Catchee girl, makee lovey?"

A Military Policeman walked casually into the meelee, shouting and flailing loosely with one hand, the children sprawling, crawling away immediately.

"Gotta watch these Gooks. We just won the war for them, and yet they turn on us like a pack of rats. They're liable to pick your pockets."

Max made a quick inventory of his pockets and replied, "I think they did."

The MP surveyed the receding children quickly, "Which one?"

Max straightened a rumpled cigarette. "Doesn't t matter, just some small change. You got a light, I think they got my lighter?

The MP lit his cigarette and regarded the newness of the Airman's uniform with a smile. "Bet you just arrived in Korea. Better watch out, man, you're in Yeong Deungpo, worst suburb in Seoul. You can find most anything here, 'cepting a white woman. If the clap don't get you, I will."

"Thanks for the tip. I'll try to avoid both of you."

The MP thought about that as Max moved away, but he had to have the last say. "Well, good luck, and just yell for me if any little boys pick on you again."

Max inhaled the cigarette and could almost taste the smell of Korea around him. The human fertilizer, the tainted meats displayed in open air, burning charcoal, chief fuel and heat. The place was a shambles, the few remnants of oriental architecture were vastly outnumbered by makeshift dwellings, straw mat walls, and roofs shingled with flattened out American beer cans. Even quilted coats and mandarin caps were sparse,

53

most natives flapping around in converted GI clothing. The very economy of the nation seemed hinged on the GI's presence, and the young women did far more business than the souvenir vendors, these being the two leading markets for GI dollars.

He drowned the cigarette in the muddy sidewalk and moved on. A svelte looking girl in western dress carried on an unsolicited conversation with him from a doorway, her machine like English centered mainly around monetary terms and phonetic reproductions of endearing expressions. A moon faced girl with gold teeth and rumpled slacks clutched his arm and gave an obscene commentary of her offering, and girls in Korean dress cooed invitingly from windows and sent ragged little boys out to approach select prospects.

Max ran the gamut of this mile long flesh market which, ironically enough, stopped at some railroad tracks. There he hesitated while the last doorfull of girls chorused at him. The sun was setting and so were his feelings. He was lonely and had resigned himself to such an awkward meeting, but, while many of the girls were attractive, the desperation or hardness of their voices had deadened in him any pleasure he might find with them. He had decided to return to the base in favor of a sanitary meal when a sound stopped him.

A timid voice called, "GI, GI, over here," then another lower voice chattered in Korean. The sun was almost gone and he could barely see two figures down the railroad tracks. They were in an alley about a half block off the main drag, a. small figure in a white Korean shirt and black boys pants, and a bent, wrinkled old woman. The old woman pushed the white shirted figure toward him and he recognized the long hair as a girls. The girl looked over her shoulder at the old woman, then at him and repeated even more timidly, "GI, you come this way," and she retreated to the alley.

Max suspected that what was forthcoming would be either very pleasant or he would get a knot on his head and lose all his folding money, but his heart quickened to adventure and he followed. A long trek down a narrow alley brought them to the heavy wooden gates of a cobblestoned, courtyard. While the old woman clanged the gate shut, causing his eyes to search quickly but vainly for another escape exit, the girl beckoned him to follow her across the porch to a sliding latticed door. Before he could do so, the old woman restrained him by pulling on his shirt, then pointing to his shoes with a frown, indicating he should remove them before stepping off the cobblestone onto the wood porch floor.

The latticed door opened into a small though relatively luxurious room. The floor was carpeted with tatami, the walls adorned with oriental prints and an antique looking photograph of a young girl, and the room furnished with low black lacquered cabinets and tables. A woman in her late twenties or early thirties sat in the middle of the room, attired in a traditional Korean dress, her eyes concentrated on the embroidery in her hands. The white shirted girl said, "Mamasan, you speakee GI," then knelt in a corner of the room and stared at the floor.

Young Mamasan was an attractive woman with a classic face, and truly a mother of an infant son as he later learned, but obviously not the mother of the white shirted girl in her late teens. The title 'Mamasan? marked her as mistress of the house. She turned sparkling witty eyes on him, obviously sizing him up, then gestured toward the girl. and said, "This Sook Cha."

Max knelt and bowed his head toward the girl to acknowledge the introduction, which greatly impressed Young Mamasan, although the girl appeared petrified with fear. As if teasing a child, Young Mamasan asked, "You like spend night with Sook Cha?"

Max looked at Sook Cha. She was of average height. While Young Mamasan's features were classic and her skin light yellow, Sook Cha had a low bridged nose, handsome features and a dusky yellow complexion. Her hair was shiny black, soft and long, pulled straight back from her high forehead. Her recently cleaned clothes ill fitted her trim body. She was wholesome, healthy, and her large almond eyes, that timidly looked at him from beneath the long lashes, looked guileless. She had the honest beauty that clothes and makeup could not affect for any of the dozens of girls he had passed on the street, and the few words she had spoken in her throaty voice rang with a vitality and sincerity that paled the hollow phonograph sound of the streetwalkers.

Young Mamasan's blunt proposition was incongruous to the appearance of the two women. Max wanted to say, "Don?t shame the girl. If this is for real, I will gladly make any arrangement, but don't be cold and hard in her presence." But all he could think of that might be understood was, "Sook Cha no skivvy josan."

Sook Cha leaned toward him like a grateful puppy, but Young Marnmasan apparently took objection to his use of the Korean slang for 'prostitute.? She spat the words, "Sook Cha skivvy josan now. No other girl here. You no like, you go."

Max answered too fast. "I like. I stay."

Young Mamasan looked up from her embroidery with a cagey smile, then said, "How much you speakee?"

He did not want to insult the girl by bidding too low, so he passed the buck and said, "You speakee."

Young Mamasan looked at his chevronless sleeves. Max had been busted to Airman Basic and wore no stripes. She thought he was an officer. "Twenny dolla."

She pushed him too far, that was four times the top going price. He still went overboard by countering with, "Ten dollar."

Young Mamasan stuck to her price, even after he explained he was no officer, she would not lose face. Finally Sook Cha timidly interjected toward Young Mamasan, "Ten dolla."

Young Mamasan returned her eyes and hands to her embroidery and conceded, "Ten dolla," and for the first time Sook Cha looked directly at Max, his hands, his sleeves, his hair, his right ear, and then right into his eyes, and the beginnings of a smile illuminated her face.

Max and Sook Cha retrieved their shoes outside Young Mamasans' door, his stodgy brogans and her rubber slippers with the curled up toes, and crossed the courtyard to Sook Cha's room, Sook Cha accepting a brazier of hot coals from Old Mamasan enroute. The latticed sliding door to Sook Cha's room was papered with newsprint, and the entire room could not have been over six feet square. The walls and floor were plastered adobe and a huge hole in the center of the ceiling and floor marked where a dud bomb had fallen. Sook Cha lit a stub of candle and set it on the shell case that served as a bedside table, the only other piece of furniture being a GI cot with a quilt for a mattress and a single blanket for covering. Two nails in the cracked walls sufficed as a closet, one holding her auxiliary black pants and the other a blue sweater. The only other noticeable thing in the room was a motly collection of pictures from

Japanese and American magazines. Most prominent was a magazine photo of Burt Lancaster and a color print of an American girl in a white dress.

It was the photo of Burt Lancaster which had contributed to their meeting. After the fiasco of attempting to work for Madame two days before, Sook Cha attempted to become a street walker in Young Mamasan's clothes, but Madame and the other 'skivvy josans' chased her off the main street with stones and taunts. And the local police would not allow streetwalkers outside of that district.

Sook Cha next attempted to solicit at the very edge of the district by the railroad tracks, not dressing in usual feminine streetwalker attire so the other working girls wouldn't notice her, and with Old Mamasan to protect her if the other prostitutes attacked her. Unfortunately, none of the potential customers noticed her either.

On her second night of initiating her career as a freelance prostitute, she happened to see an American who resembled Burt Lancaster, the 'good guy' in the American movie magazine she had stolen from Madame, and a strange new feeling overcame her fear of the other prostitutes and of renewed contact with a male. His blonde wavy hair was unlike the other GI's with crew cuts, and he moved with grace and spoke with courtesy even when he declined the invitations of the other working girls. She spotted him as she hid between the last few buildings before the railroad tracks, then ran behind the buildings hoping to arrive at the tracks before him. Old Mamasan complained as she tried to keep up with her.

Now, at last, he was here in her room, a seemingly better candidate than the Aussie Sergeant, and definitely better than the North Korean soldier who had raped her and the South Korean farmer who had tried to.

Sook Cha shifted her clothes so his could rest on one of the nails. She handled his clothes like a valet, folding each piece carefully before she placed it on the nail where it immediately hung limp and shapeless. She began to undress in the far corner. Max's throat bubbled with nervous laughter, then choked with emotion, for she was wearing a man's tee shirt and jockey shorts. A girl's beautiful young body that circumstance clothed in man's unglamourous underwear. Ridiculous, pitiful, but literally so. At first glance her body resembled a young boys, for she was only seventeen, but it was completely feminine where it should be. In the candlelight, her skin was the satiny color of tea stained ivory, glowing all over without a single mar or sign of looseness. Her tummy was taut as a swimmers, her hips slim and firm, and her breasts were tight and still blossoming.

Her precise, silent movements were unhesitating, positive, but when her evasive eyes finally met his, they were watery with fear, the candlelight sparkling in the dormant tears. Max's mind searched vainly for comprehensive words of tenderness that might calm her and he feared even the movement of putting out his cigarette as seeming too brusque. The eerie sounds of a Korean flute from a distant bar filled the void of his silence and motivated a mutual smile as she slipped under the khaki blanket. As he leaned across her to blow out the candle, she cringed. He smiled and kissed her lightly on the forehead and eyelids before snuffing the flame. In the dark her timid hand touched his face and she swallowed hard before saying, "Prease?"

Max stroked her hair. "Please what, Sook Cha?"

"Prease.....easy."

He reassured her, "Yes, easy," though he had already guessed, Sook Cha was essentially and emotionally, if not literally, a virgin.

Chapter Four
WHEN WORLDS COLLIDE

Oddly enough, the moments that dwell in our memory most indelibly are usually not those we planned for with preconceived expectations, but rather those little unplanned pockets of time when unexpected joy or pain sensitized us to the moment when, as the song says, "time stood still." In the balance of his life, Max would not remember the dozens of romantic conquests he experienced as an entertainer, or even his honeymoon and the best moments of his marriage to a beautiful but demanding wife, as vividly as he remembered the night, the circumstances, and the feelings he shared with Sook Cha in a six by six foot room while snow fell lightly outside the paper latticed door.

He remembered the flickering candlelight that illuminated the beauty of her body, the delicate muscle of her back, the curve of her young breast, the hollows in her neck, the glistening of her moist teeth. Then, as the height of their passion exploded like the finale of a fireworks display, they lay exhausted in each others arms staring into only darkness, not the bomb hole in a sooty ceiling, but a black screen on which the image of ecstasy lingers like a brilliant picture retained on the sensitive retina of the mind. That broad timeless moment when the limits of the world are a narrow cot that cradles all the hope, happiness, and security one can possibly find in that given time.

The passing moon cast a beam of blue light across the room, and Sook Cha looked from the picture of Burt Lancaster on the wall to Max's face, then traced the outline of his face as she spoke in a soft husky voice, "Tauksan stecky."

Max murmured, "What."

Sook Cha smiled, "You, tauksan stecky, vewy bootiful."

Max lifted his hand that had cupped her breast, and traced the outline of her face. "No, you are truly very very beautiful," and he kissed her as their bodies turned into yet another passionate embrace.

****

The cold blue light of morning illuminated an adoring smile on Sook Cha's face as she knelt in her black pants and blue sweater on the floor beside the cot where Max slept. Her hands were folded in her lap as she stared at him silently, a posture she had held for almost an hour. Occasionally during that hour she would run her fingers through his tousled hair or replace the blanket over an exposed leg or shoulder, admiring his pectoral muscles or strong but shapely calf and thigh. The short blonde hairs that covered his body fascinated her and she would brush her palm lightly over them until he would flinch and turn in his sleep. She remembered his passion that had lasted for hours, how he had turned her in various positions she had never imagined as part of lovemaking, and how he had never once, even upon his initial entry, ever hurt her. She remembered a moment when his sweat dripped upon her face and into her open mouth, and she was surprised that its salty taste was pleasurable and exciting to her. When he slept later, just to be sure, she licked his chest and again experienced a pleasing taste she had never known before, and again it excited her. For a long time before she rose, she had lay with her head upon his chest breathing in the perfume of his body; not of soap or cologne, but the distinctive aroma of this man; the heroic man in the picture on her wall, the man in the street who was kind to everyone, the man whose lovemaking had fulfilled the girlish dreams she had last discussed with Kim so many years ago when their breasts had just begun to blossom.

Max woke to the sound of the courtyard gates clanging shut. He was pleased to see Sook Cha's face brighten into a broad smile. She immediately rinsed a washcloth in a bowl of clean water beside her and wiped and dried his face and neck, which felt chilling but exhilarating to him. Next she rinsed the washcloth and cleaned and dried his armpits, chest, and abdomen. Finally, she rinsed the washcloth and carefully and with tender detail washed his inner thighs, scrotum, and penis. As she dried his genitals, she looked him in the eye with a questioning expression, when, suddenly, there was a knock at the door.

Sook cha covered Max as she responded, "Hai!"

The latticed door slid open and Old Mamasan said, excitedly, "GI in alley, all run run home!"

Old Mamasan was referring to the regular morning exodus of military service personnel from the bordellos of Yeong Deungpo to the early morning military vehicles that shuttled them back to their respective military bases in time to get to work. Sook Cha's brow furrowed slightly and Max heaved a regretful sigh as he hurriedly pulled on his uniform and grabbed his brogans from Old Mamasan's hands as he raced through the gate she held open for him.

****

63

As time acclimated Max's physical senses to the sights and smell and cold of Korea, Sook Cha and he broadened their home life and even their social life such as stolen time and military supplies would permit. To the deep smile that blazed in their eyes each time they met, were added the lighter more audible smiles that came with adjusting to each others person and customs.

When he first brought insecticide bombs to combat the flies, they proudly showed him they were accustomed to such equipment and produced, from God knows where, an American can of hair spray that effectively annihilated flies, though it didn?t linger in the air long enough to do much good.

When he choked on the grounds in his coffee, a luxury he had brought from the PX (Post Exchange), they began to break an egg in the coffee to settle the grounds, until he learned it was Old Mamasans' daily egg ration which she had to retrieve from the coffee and spit the grounds out as she chewed it. He switched to hot chocolate from the military rations.

The first supply of toilet parer he provided, which was a rare commodity even on the base, lived a short life as covering for the sliding doors, until he secured some short ends of aerial film that he had cleared and applied to the doors and windows. This prompted an overture from black marketeers who offered $50 a role for unexposed undeveloped aerial film. Young Manmasans' eyes gleamed at the prospective revenue, but she commended Max for declining the offer and discouraging black marketeers from her door. Although he did cut down on his smoking and hoard all the cigarette ration stamps he could to increase the family purchasing power, cigarettes bringing five times their purchase price on the Korean market.

64

****

About a month after Max began his unstable residence in Yeong Deungpo, he had his first glimpse of the Jee. Sook Cha and Max were lying on their cot, the mattress of which now boasted lumpy pieces of horsehair packing from equipment crates on the base, plus an added blanket. Sook Cha was lying on her back and he was propped on an elbow facing her. Max had a little Korean-English pocket dictionary, and they were going through their language lesson. Max would point to her features and repeat the English term and she would repeat the Korean: eye - nun, ear - gui, nose - ko, mouth - eeb. At that point she failed to reply, but stared horrified at the ceiling while her mouth worked soundlessly as if she couldn't catch her breath. Finally she sucked in a gulp of air and screamed, "Jee."

Max thought she was ill and failed to realize the object of her hysteria until she pointed upward. Her shouts of "Jee" screamed in his ear as he turned toward the ceiling, a much too low ceiling he decided at that moment, to face the largest rat he'd ever seen peering at them through the bomb hole. The rat's front paws clutched the crumbling plaster rim of the hole and his long whiskered nose twitched nervously. Max was hypnotized by the rats' eyes, two shiny black beads, and was puzzled because he couldn?t denote any separation of white or iris or pupil.

By the time he had courage to even begin inching a blanket over Sook Cha and moving his body off the bed, Young Mamasan invaded the room with a broom she immediately poked up into the hole, spouting a line of jibberish at the rat that sounded like Gilbert and Sullivan double timing. Old Mamasan kneeled at the door and brandished a brazier poker toward the ceiling as if incanting voodoo rites.

After a stout performance, Young Mamasan stopped abruptly and turned a smiling face to the young couple to say, "Jee, he cold," shivering to illustrate the poor things plight. Somehow Max couldn?t feel as sympathetic to the Jee as he did to Mickey Mouse. He was a little amused, though, to think they had a pet name for him, until some time later he learned 'jee? simply means rodent. Max remembered that his sister, as a child, had developed a friendship with a packrat she named 'Oscar.? Oscar started the acquaintance by swapping their mother's jewelry for pieces in his sisters jewelry box, and his sister took to leaving Oscar little gift wrapped pieces of cheese and nuts. She thoroughly enjoyed the friendship until Oscar started walking off with some of her prized pieces of jewelry and leaving lumps of butter and old milk bottle caps in their place. In this Korean household, however, any reference to the 'Jee? was accepted as meaning that beady eyed super-rat and none other, for any lesser fellows didn't stand a chance with him around.

Max remembered hearing curious noises in the unlit privy, and after that he avoided its use as much as possible. He made several attempts to cover the bomb hole, and, each time the covering fell, he nearly jumped through the wall fearing the Jee would come down with it. The household more or less accepted the Jee, for any conventional trap (which would have to be handmade) would be unlikely to phase him, and poisoning was out because of the infant child. There was some consolation in the realization that he didn?t reside in their house all the time and theirs was cleaner than most. But the Jee became a personality and a byword typifying every dislikeable element from black marketeers to the MPs.

66

****

Max and Sook Cha took infinite pride in each other. To her, Max was an exceptional GI. He had good manners, even to acquired Korean customs. In the privacy of the house, he wore a monks robe, sans dragon and yellow sash. In those things he chose not to accept, he deferred politely, but never derided their choice. His demonstrativeness was the badge of Sook Chas' womanly success, yet always seemed in good taste, evoking sighs and smiles in every audience, but never laughter or resentment.

Young Mamasan berated Max for his gifts of K-rations and old shoes to the neighbors for it encouraged beggars and parasites at their door, so he cut it down, but Sook Cha loved him for it. As a provider, Max was monetarily poor, but very resourceful. The furnishings and paraphernalia he fabricated from military salvage were 'ichi bon (number one) stateside' caliber and unobtainable on any market.

As a lover, Max made Sook Cha's position enviable for he was not around often enough for her to grow too tired of him. The ladies of this house were of the opinion that gentleness was the exception in a Korean husband and overindulgence the rule among GIs. Max seemed the happy compromise in what they desired in a man.

Sook Cha's crowning social moments were their occasional trips to the operettas she called "Operas" or "Movies." She first invited him to these with timidity and misgivings, fearing he would ridicule what she guessed to be vastly inferior entertainment to his standards, but was overjoyed at his serious and interested reception of them, not realizing his interest was largely professional.

67

Max did not discourage Sook Cha's joy in being his interpreter of the obvious plots and actions of each play. Attempting to define the role of a character portraying a lion, she would stammer, "He, er, he, er," then mimic a lion in the same manner as the performer, and Max would refrain from identifying any but her own definition, suddenly brightening with grateful recognition. As a hunter waltzed offstage with his spear she would report, "Warrior go," and when the crowned hero arrived on a throne supported by a chorus of singing girls, she would announce, "Prince come." So, amid a balcony full of kimchie eating, nutshell dropping music lovers, she would battle or embrace his nearest arm in proportion to the respective drama on stage, then she would proudly be escorted out the front entrance by the rare cultured GI who was most often mistaken for an officer because he had no stripes on his arm (actually the lowest possible rank).

****

Sook Cha's past unfolded to Max slowly over a long period, in probing sessions of broken English, from bitter reminders of painful memories, and in the dark hours of the morning when the contrast of tenderness made her release in tears and awkward torrents of words the gift of her experience. The more he learned of her past, the more he marveled at the sanity of her values.

Max had an Air Force blue military raincoat dyed black for Sook Cha, and, when he gave it to her, it brought tears to her eyes because it reminded her of the black raincoat her father wore the day he died. Tears streaming down her face, Sook Cha relived in pantomime and broken English the details of that tragic experience, re-enacted within the confines of that tiny

68

six foot by six foot room, ending with her lying on top of Max and breathing on his eyelids as she had done for Ling to close her eyes in death.

On another occasion, Max stopped by the house while on a military mission to Seoul, and happened to be carrying a 45 calibre automatic pistol required in his role as a courier. Sook Cha removed his shoulder holster as he undressed, placing it on the nail in the wall and slowly removing the pistol which she stared at as if it hypnotized her. She asked him how it worked and what was necessary to make it fire, and the ensuing conversation revealed the story of her rape and her desperate efforts to kill the North Korean soldier. Max promised to eventually take her somewhere and teach her to safely and accurately use a variety of firearms.

When Max managed to barter his cigarette rations with friends on the base for a variety of luxury foods, including the rarity of canned ham, with which he gifted the household, Sook Cha was eager to reward him in turn. When he half teasingly half seriously asked if she would fellate him, something she only did rarely and reluctantly, she hesitated, frowned slightly, then said, "I no good at sakahachi."

Max tilted her chin up to him and said, "Well, you're not exactly bad at it. Maybe you just need a little more practice."

Sook Cha pressed her lips together tightly, then her frown turned into a painful smile and she encircled his hand with hers. "Dai jobi, okay, okay. Come, I do it now," and she dragged him by the hand into her room.

Max undressed and lay on the cot, Sook Cha kneeling on the cot between his legs. She began to attack his penis like a voracious animal, choking and gagging in her increasing efforts to swallow him whole. Finally Max gripped her head and raised her off of him, frowning slightly as he said, "Sweetheart, Sook Cha baby, you're hurting yourself. You're almost hurting me."

Sook Cha looked disappointed. "You no like? Dai jobi, I go deeper. You see."

Max smoothed the hair back from her face where saliva glued it to her temples and cheeks. "No, sweetheart. Let me show you. You don't have to hurt yourself. Just take it slow and easy." And Max gave her a tutorial in fellatio, then followed it up with an expert demonstration of cunnilingus, something she had evaded during his earlier attempts.

As they both lay sated from their mutual oral sex, Sook Cha started laughing. When Max inquired what was funny, she told him of her misadventures with the Madame and the Aussie Sergeant, ending with, "You know what Madame know, 'The hand is quicker than the mouth and doesn't wear out as fast.' You both right," and the two hugged each other as they laughed.

****

Bathing in the orient is an uninhibited communal function, so it was no great surprise when Max arrived at the house in Yeong Deungpo one day to find Sook Cha bathing with two of her girlfriends in the large round wooden tub on the hardwood porch floor. The girl friends were a young widow who operated a beauty shop and her thirteen year old daughter, both of whom were attractive and not inclined to fraternize with the GIs.

The beautician was Young Mamasan's friend, and she had bartered her letter writing and accounting skills with the beautician in order to maintain her appearance and keep her spirits up. She tried to get Sook

Cha to avail herself of the beautician's skill at hairdressing and makeup, but Sook Cha would have none of it. When Max arrived to find the three girls bathing, it was one of Young Mamasan's efforts to convince Sook Cha to allow the beautician to feminize her.

The beautician had brought her adopted daughter, Hye, who had been an abandoned child the beautician saved during the initial bloody invasion. Hye was thirteen, the same age Sook Cha's friend, Ling, had been when she had been murdered on that field of horror. Sook Cha was grateful to the beautician for being Blossom's savior, and therefore tolerated Young Mamasan's efforts to have the beautician help feminize her. The beautician stepped out of the tub and knelt behind Sook Cha who leaned her head over the edge of the tub as the beautician combed her long black hair. Sook Cha laughingly protested and Hye, seated facing her in the tub, encouraged her to cooperate.

When Max brought out his camera and asked permission to photograph them, Sook Cha and Hye just smiled and giggled. The beautician looked at Young Mamasan questioningly, and Young Mamasan smiled and closed her eyes briefly as she nodded assent. The beautician turned her handsome smile toward Max and continued combing out Sook Cha's long black wet hair with exaggerated strokes. Max shot two rolls of film of the process of communal bathing, the shampooing, the body soaping, and the rinsing as the three girls doused each other with buckets of fresh water, creating a human waterfall as berobed Young Mamasan emptied a bucket over the head of the beautician who simultaneously did the same to Sook Cha who did the same to Hye

At the airbase, Max processed the films of the girls after office hours to minimize any chance of Lt.

71

Conweb seeing them. It was not uncommon for Max and Blake, the other staff photographer, to use the darkroom after office hours when shooting nighttime events on the base. This evening Blake showed up while Max was finishing multiple sets of prints of the girls, the extra sets intended as gifts for them. Blake admired the prints and asked Max a lot of questions about the girls, Max answering minimally as he didn't want to advertise his off base activities. When Max wasn't looking, Blake pocketed a print of Hye standing in the tub alone.

Blake was the same age as Max, from upper state New York, and was a college graduate with a fine arts degree and the ambition to become an opera singer. He was married to his college sweetheart, a tall blonde girl with an athletic figure and the ambition to become an Olympic competitor in swimming. The two young men shared many interests in common; musical careers, photography as an avocation, and a concern about how faithful their wives were being back home. If Blake had any reason to doubt his wife, he had not shared it with Max, and Max had not shared the status of his marriage with Blake. Their friendship was more on a professional and cultural basis, not on a personal level.

However, after that night in the darkroom, Blake became more inquisitive about Max's double life in Yeong Deungpo, pressing Max for an invitation to join him there. Against his better judgement, Max succumbed to the bribe of several cans of lobster Blake had received in a care package from his wife which he offered to share with Max and the ladies, provided he could dine with them. As an afterthought, Blake suggested the beautician and her adopted daughter also be invited to dine with them.

At the dinner, Blake, Max, and Young Mamasan were the only ones who had ever tasted lobster before. Sook Cha, the beautician, and Hye were doubtful about it at first, their concern based mostly on the picture of a lobster on the cans, but delighted with the strange new delicacy swimming in garlic flavored butter for which Max had spent all his ration stamps at the PX.

After diner, Blake entertained by singing a capella the aria *Vogliatemi Bene* from Puccini's opera, *Madame Butterfly*. Young Mamasan was torn between being jealous of his upstaging her with his talent and the reality that she is impressed by his talent. But Max was concerned that Blake seemed to be singing directly to both the beautician and to Hye, and Max, other than Blake, was the only one who understood that the title translates as *Love Me, Please*, and the libretto paints a seduction scene. He was further concerned when Blake extracted an invitation to visit the beautician and promised he'd bring her more treats from the PX.

After Blake left on the evening shuttle bus, Max remained and confessed to Sook Cha and Young Mamasan that Blake is married, even though Max has not confessed that he himself was married. The ladies did not seem concerned, so Max added that he thought Blake was romantically interested in the beautician. Whereupon Young Mamasan frowned and said, "No way. Blakesan, him sameo sameo you, quality peoples. Him no hanky panky wit she. Him unnerstan' she no skivvy josan. You jus' jealous him sing sing tauksan ichi bon."

Sook Cha came to Max's defense, putting her hands on his chest and saying. "I know you no jealous, Maxsan. Hai (yes), him sing sing weary good." The she tilted her head to one side and looked off into space. "But I unnerstan', he no weal inside."

Young Mamasan smiled mischievously saying, "But him tauksan ichi bon lobster weary weal." She then imitated a lobster and playfully attacked everyone with raised arms and hands posed like pinching lobster claws.

Back at the base, Max sensed a mutual discomfort around Blake. When Max tried to inquire if Blake had subsequently visited Yeong Deungpo, Blake was evasive and uneasy. Although the two had never been chummy beyond occasional conversations about work or music or photography, now Blake went out of his way to avoid Max and Max thought it best to let the subject of Yeong Deungpo be forgotten in their mutual work environment.

Less than two months later, Max arrived at the house in Yeong Deungpo as the beautician was leaving. Max greeted her cordially, but the woman coldly ignored him as she exited the big red gates. Max approached Sook Cha and Young Mamasan with a puzzled look, noting their sullen expressions. "What's the matter? Did I say something wrong?"

Sook Cha put her arms around Max's waist and rested her head sadly on his chest. Young Mamasan looked past him toward the gates and said, "She have, how you say, missy-cawage."

Max put his arms around Sook Cha. "Your beautician friend had a miscarraige?"

Young Mamasan continued to stare at the gates. "No she. Her dotter, Hye."

Max kissed the top of Sook Cha's head, then looked up in surprise. "Hye? But, she's only thirteen, right?"

Sook Cha sniffled into Max's shirt. "You fwen, Blake. I say, him no weal inside."

Max held Sook Cha by her shoulders and looked into her tear filled eyes. "Are you telling me Blake raped that child?"

Young Mamasan remained as if hypnotized by the red gates. "No wape. Him speakee slicky slicky. Him sing sing pity pity (pretty pretty)."

Sook Cha clutched the front of Max's shirt and bowed her head against him. "I no wan' lobster, nevermore."

Max sat on the edge of the porch, pulling Sook Cha down on his knee as she rested her head on his shoulder. He spoke angrily. "Let's not blame the poor lobster. Let's blame the son of a bitch with no conscience, with no morals. God damn, I have to work with this bastard for another six or eight months. How can I face him every day without wanting to beat the shit out of him?"

Young Mamasan looked down, slipped off her red satin slippers, and stepped up onto the porch in her stocking feet. "You face him likee we face fo (four) yea (years) wo (war). Stay live one mo' day, den next day, den next day. Pity soon you find way home."

Max put his hand to his forehead. "She's only thirteen. It's like what that soldier did to you when you were thirteen."

Sook Cha put her cheek against his. "No sameo, Maxsan. Soldier, he wape me. Blake, he slicky slicky, but he no illegal."

Max closed his eyes. "In my country it is. It's called Staturatory Rape."

Young Mamasan lit the brazier. "You no stateside, Maxsan. You Korea. No law fo' josan here. Jus' fo'get wha hoppon. Jus' no mo' Blake my house. Dai jobi (OK)?"

75

Max pressed Sook Cha's body to his chest. "Dai jobi."

Sook Cha spoke softly into his ear. "She speakee twoo, Maxsan. You no speakee Blake. Jus' make bad thing for you."

For the first time since he arrived that night, he realized what an awkward position he was in with Blake. Blake now knew intimate details of his life in Yeong Deungpo, and, if Blake shared any of that information with Conweb, it could be disastrous. He wanted to confront Blake with his anger, but, Sook Cha was right, he dare not risk it.

But the aria from *Madame Butterly* wouldn't leave his head. In the libretto, CioCioSan asks if it is true that Western men pin a butterfly's wings to a table, and Pinkerton admits it is true. Max wonders if the story of *Madame Butterfly* motivated Blake to debauch this Asian girl, even though the character of Pinkerton is a cad.

Another realization occurred to Max. At that moment he felt alienated from his countrymen and his culture, and he felt all the closer to these three women.

Chapter Five
NO GOOD DEED
GOES UNPUNISHED

Streptococcal Pharyngitis (strep throat) was one of the more prevalent bacterial infections that were rampant in the dense postwar Korean population with inadequate water supply, sewerage, and medical services. Add to that years of starvation diet and malnutrition, and it was no surprise that both Sook Cha and Young Mamasan had succumbed to strep throat in the past. But, left untreated, strep throat can lead to scarlet fever. When Sook Cha once again contracted strep throat, this time it did not go away in one week as before. This time it advanced to scarlet fever.

For two weeks, Max had made the trip to Yeong Deungpo as frequently as possible to help the other two women care for Sook Cha. Max felt frustrated by the lack of civilian medical services or even pharmacies. He brought all the over the counter variations of aspirin and cough syrups the PX could provide, but nothing seemed to help.

Max knew what would help, and he risked Lt. Conweb's wrath by going on sick call with fake symptoms so he could get a prescription for penicillin. The doctor, however, saw through his ruse and denied his request for antibiotic medication. Desperate, Max reluctantly explained Sook Cha's plight and asked the doctor to make an exception. The doctor was only a few years older than Max and not a career serviceman. He bit his lip as he looked off into space and hesitated before responding. Then he started scribbling on a notepad, saying, "There's a clinic just outside of Yeong Deungpo. It's not exactly open to the public, but I have a Korean colleague there. Here's his name and the clinic address. Tell him I sent you, and they'll treat your Korean friend."

Max smiled gratefully as he took the paper, reluctantly having to ask the good doctor to spell some of the illegible words on the note, then saluted sharply as he backed out of the little canvassed cubicle that was the doctor's office. His heart sang with glee as he exited the sick call tent, relieved that soon Sook Cha's suffering would be over.

Max created a pretense that he needed a folding wheelchair as a prop to be used in a photo story, then struggled to get the awkward thing in and out of the shuttle bus on his next visit to Yeong Deungpo. As Young Mamasan stayed at home with the baby, Old Mamasan helped Max get a weak and floppy Sook Cha into the wheelchair and navigate the muddy streets the considerable distance to the outskirts of Yeong Deungpo. There they found an official looking building with no markings, but, when they entered and requested the name on the note, they were ushered into an office where an elderly Korean in a white coat introduced himself as "Dr. Park." After reading the note, he issued orders to a nurse who gave Sook Cha an injection, then he gave Max a plastic box with a syringe, additional vials of medication, and a card and several papers written in Korean. Dr. Park then politely ushered them out the door, adding, in his broken English, that Sook Cha must come back for "regular checkups."

The only thing that Max could read in the box was the English word "Penicillin" on the vials. He knew he could administer the additional injections, but he couldn't read the paperwork that presumably would have instructions as to dosage and frequency of injections. Back at their home, he gave the box to Young Mamasan and asked her to translate the instructions. He watched her face change from curiosity to confusion, and then to concern. She looked back and forth between the card and the pages printed in Korean. Then she looked Max in the eye and held the card up before him. "You know what this is?"

Max sensed she might be angry with him. He said slowly, "Nooooo."

Young Mamasan hissed her "S's" as she spoke. "This card speakee Sook Cha now skivy josan. This pwostitue's card." Then she angrily shook the papers in her other hand. "This papers speakee Sook Cha go every month, get checkup for V.D., doctor lookee lookee mebbe she catchee disease. My address on these paper. My house now skivy josan house."

Max watched in stunned silence as he saw her lower lip tremble. He said stonily, "I didn't know."

She sounded accusatory, "You speakee you doctor, Sook Cha skivy josan?"

Max answered emphatically. "No!"

Young Mamasan shook her head negatively. "He speakee you he make Sook Cha skivy josan?"

Max looked down at the floor, then back into her eyes. "No, he didn't. He should have, but he didn't."

Still holding the card and papers, she dropped her hands to her sides. "Well, she skivy josan now."

Max spoke defiantly. "No, she isn't! Sook Cha is not defined by that little piece of paper."

Young Mamasan raised the papers up to her eye level, clenched her teeth, then said, "Speakee here, she go V.D. clinic every month, or police come make her go."

Max sighed deeply. "What can I say? I had no idea it was a V.D. clinic. What's done is done. Maybe they'll provide future medical treatment, if needed. Does the paperwork offer any instructions for the penicillin?"

She shuffled through the papers. "Say one vial a day until all gone." Then her tone softened. "You teach me how sticky needle. I do for Sook Cha when you no here."

****

Indeed, Max was not perfect. While Sook Cha was ill, Young Mamasan and Max nursed her in Young Mamasan's room, spending long sleepless nights playing Korean cards, sipping tea, and alternately mopping Sook Cha's sweaty brow or pressing their bodies close to her when she would chill and shake.

Young Mamasan was an interesting person to know, and a dynamic person to be around. She was an aristocrat, bred in the niceties of Korean culture, but at heart she was a thespian, or, more accurately, a comedienne. In oriental tradition, pantomime was her favorite medium of expression. She bore her station with an exaggerated haughtiness and dispensed the responsibility of command like a general issuing battle orders, but, with the same ferocity, she would pounce on every opportunity to satire or evoke laughter. She rarely spoke English, too great a condescension to Max, and would watch with such a superior smile while her words were translated to him when, in fact, she understood far more English than she bothered to speak. Yet the intent of her machine gun like Korean speech was always comprehensible to Max, whether she was commanding, explaining, consoling, berating, placating, or, more often, simply entertaining. Like watching a good actor in a foreign movie, you always get the drift, with pantomime paving the way for her words. Her being as well as her mesmerizing speech would be a good study for any potential dictator, for all loved or feared her and none questioned her. Thus she had always been to Max, her vicious monotone ending on a high note like an outraged hens each time he did wrong, and only the sparkling of her eyes to ever give him the satisfaction of knowing when he pleased her.

But sharing the vigil by Sook Cha's sickbed and days with little or no sleep began to break down Young Mamasan's reserve. Sitting cross-legged with her head leaned against the wall, Max would see her thinking, staring fixedly into nothingness, that intimate repose she so rarely revealed, and, when she caught him watching her, the beginnings of reproach on her forehead melted into a willing resignation.

Max looked at the antiquated photograph of a beautiful young girl and her eyes followed the photograph, then met his again. She smiled and said, "Me. Skoshi josan (little girl)." She looked back at the photograph. "Pappasan professor university (she pronounced it 'uniwersity'). Him speakee me go uniwersity. Me speakee me go catch job opera house. Sing. Pappasan very (again 'weary?') sad." A half hearted pantomime of poor Pappasan worrying about his brazen daughter. "Pappasan marry me Mr. Tai. No opera house, no uniwersity." She leaned her head back against the wall and closed her eyes. "No more Pappasan, no more Mr. Tai."

Max suddenly became aware of Mamasan as a person instead of a dictator who played a hard game of casino with that stack of little wooden cards. The girl in the photograph was beautiful, and his eye transported

81

the beauty to the woman seated across from him, now tender with a sad smile on her sleeping face. Responsibility had changed her personality more than her looks, and, seeing her everyday with the child strapped to her back where he continually mussed her hair, the title 'Mamasan' made her a person with a duty rather than a woman.

But now the woman slept, a young beautiful woman, one and the same as the girl in the photograph. Her brows arched questioningly, the lashes fluttered on the flat seamless eyelids, the nostrils of her narrow high bridged nose dilated with each breath, and her small heart shaped mouth parted as if to cry out, revealing pearly teeth. The widow's peak and pointed chin gave her face a heart shape, and the shiny black hair was elaborately groomed save for one long wisp at the temples that curled past a fragile ear to her smooth ivory throat.

Max pictured her as she usually worked, her skirts tucked up above her knees, her sandled feet usually muddy, sometimes playfully dancing a barefoot jig or in a wide pidgeon-toed stance caricaturing a theatrical pose. Her body was always swathed in thick muchly patched street robes that made her look stout, but, remembering how her bare legs stepped down with pointed toe into her sandles, he wondered how his logic had failed to relate those trim legs to a young woman's body.

For all the heavy tasks it performed, the hand that clutched the thin clean houserobe about her looked delicate, and the narrow ankle and small foot that curled beneath the warmth of her skirts glowed pale yellow in the flickering candlelight. His eye moved slowly up, discerning the curve of her leg, the womanly hips, the narrow waist now undisguised by heavy robes, the rthymically rising full breast, the still open mouth, the sparkling black eyes that now surprised him with an intent stare, little candleflames reflected in their depths.

Her expression was unchanged. Surely she had seen his intimate survey of her body, surely she could see the passion of his thoughts, but he could not decipher the intentness of her eyes. Max tried in vain to find the courage to let his eyes travel across her body again. Even more impossible was to speak his thoughts.

"You are a woman whose last embrace has long been an old memory, but whose body and soul are far too young to ever be fully satisfied by the incessant labor of voice and limb you undertake. I wonder if it is your natural appetite or its starvation that has been fed a little by my presence in this house; the times you've tested my muscle as I labored, the reluctance and then eager contact as you scrubbed my back when Sock Cha was interrupted in bathing me, the little jealousy that at times has made you invent interminable conversation when you knew Sook Cha and I wanted to be alone, your excessive exuberance either when I was most demonstrative to Sook Cha or she was not around, and the times when you were most vicious or your eyes sparkled the most, neither intensity of which have I seen you display to any other man. Your health, your happiness, and your balance are in need of a man, and I am a man you would accept. Likewise, you are a woman I would desire; for beauty, intelligence, and your dynamic personality. There is more than lack of sleep that makes us stare at each other so; we are both sad because Sook Cha is ill, we are both haggard by our increased duties, we both need the revitalization of our body and ego, and we are both frustrated by the unfulfillment of this attraction that has grown for months without consciousness or expression. A moment ago I hesitated to touch you fearing you would at least slug me or at worst destroy my welcome in this house. Now I have but one doubt, whether you are rationalizing, as I am, the fidelity of your friendship with Sook Cha or your moral code."

The candle flickered out, though Max thought he could still see the candleflame in her eyes that never once loosed their grip on him. He listened, trying to hear her movement, the slightest rustle of her robe that would trigger him to approach her, even just her breathing, but all he heard was an almost inaudible moan from Sook Cha. Max leaned his face close to Sook Cha to hear if she spoke and heard a soft padding across the room. Young Mamasan's hand touched his face in the dark while trying to stroke Sook Cha's wet brow. She ran her hand down his neck and shoulder, suddenly clenching the muscle of his arm in recognition. His hand caught hers as she released his arm, their fingers intertwining tightly as she leaned down to hear Sook Cha hoarsely whisper his name between deep rasping breaths. "Maxsan, Maxsan." Young Mamrnasan freed his hand and placed it on Sook Cha's cheek, and he whispered reassuringly in Sook Cha's unhearing ear while his own heard the sliding door that marked Young Mamasan's silent exit.

Max felt shame at being oblivious to that delerious girl's tribute of calling his name, and how, though Sook Cha was unconcious of his words and presence, minutes later he left her side to follow Young Mamasan. On the porch he lit a cigarette and watched through the tattered sliding door of Sook Cha's room while Young Mamasan tested the softness of the unfamiliar army cot with her hands. How comical it was to see her place the quilt mattress on the floor and try to curl her body around the bomb hole, how graceful

84

her body as she stretched to view Max's clothes hanging above her head, how sad the moist eyes in her pained face as she fingered the sleeve of his coat. How guilty he felt for having looked inside this woman, and for his overwhelming lust for her in the face of Sook Cha's suffering.

The blanket flew behind the door, the candle extinguished, amid squealing and scuffling there was a piercing burst of Korean, only one word of which was familiar to Max. "Jee!" Young Mamasan exploded through the frail latticework of the door, crumpling in a heap on the porch while the giant rat shot past her through the demolished door into the courtyard straight at Max, squealing and shining like a greased pig in a country contest. Petrified, Max unconsciously flicked his cigarette at the Jee and the rat seemed to run right into it rather than it flying toward him. The Jee stopped dead in his tracks and, literally, did a somersault and a triple take like a comic in an old flickering movie. Probably because he landed in that direction rather than by choice, the Jee raced toward the gate, his sleek fat body seemingly moved by magnets like a centipede whose short powerful legs are almost invisible beneath its hulk. He scaled the gate like a cat, his claws scratching loudly and his body falling softly with each attempt, while Max gathered his wits and a brogan which he flung with great effort and little aim. Reaching the heavy wooden bolt, the Jee made a great hop, clearing the top of the gate like a miniature kangaroo and emptying the house of his fearful squealing. The old woman's sliding door flew back and she peered out to see Young Mamasan lurch across the courtyard to Max, sucking in great sobbing gulps of air until she collapsed in his embrace.

"Are you all right?"

"Dai jobi, dai jobi. Jee no catchee me," she said breathlessly.

The old woman exited her room and passively lit a brazier of coals while Young Mamasan staggered in Max's arms to the porch where the two lay down together, she clutching his bare chest under the robe. His arms tightened around her to still her shaking and the tears she choked down in great swallows, enjoying the tight press of their bodies from her burning forehead on his cheek to her cold bare feet locked under his ankle. Max brushed the stray hair back at her temples and lifted her face to kiss her closed eyes, now welling with tears. At the touch of his lips she shuddered and her fingers dug into his back, her open mouth emitting the sound of a whimpering animal. He tilted her face to kiss her mouth and she turned it, her hair caressing his cheek, her mouth working soundlessly, hovering over his throat. Max ran his hands tightly over her robed body, feeling the strong back and the curve of her hip, while her hands smoothed his back, then his chest, and bit into the muscle of his arms to stay his hands. Though her thighs seemed bound to his, her hands pressed against his chest, lifting her shaking body as if in great effort. When Max tried to speak she opened her eyes, pressed her fingers to his lips and whispered hoarsely, "No speakee."

She returned her face to his bare chest and began to speak in Korean, her whole body slowly relaxing against his. She spoke softly, her lips moving against his flesh, without the exagerrated drama of her pantomime, although he knew that was the nature of her words. Some phrases sparkled with the hint of laughter, making her smile sadly, and she would turn her head, causing her hair to dance across his neck. Some phrases she would close by saying in a resigned way, "Ne, Maxsan

86

(Is that not so, Max)?" Her talk grew lighter, interjected with giggles that shook her body against his, causing his chest to rumble with responsive laughter, and he dreamily ran his fingers through her hair and lifted her face to his.

Her eyes sparkled brilliantly, her cheeks flushed rosily in the growing dawn, her close-lipped smile broadened to a moist grin, Playfully she pressed under Max's chin with a closed fist, then she shook her hair free of his hand, drew her leg from beneath his, and knelt facing him. For a moment Max was on the brink again, praying she would remove her sash, unfold her robe and welcome him to her body, her beauty, her being, but she had already shared the latter with him and all he could ask now was in a wavering partially turned hand he lifted to her, half beseeching, half inviting. Her grin melted into a soulful smile and she took his hand. "Arigato, Maxsan." She kissed the tips of his fingers. "Domo arigato (Thank you very much)."

She folded his robe over his chest and tightened his sash, then looked indifferently into space as she tightened her own robe, smoothing it over her hips and thighs as she rose and walked silently across the courtyard to enter Old Mamasans' room.

Old Mamasan beamed a toothless smile and waited at the door, gesturing Max toward the room with eagerness. Her gummy grin sank into a perplexed frown as Young Mamasan closed the door quietly, leaving Max and the old woman staring at each other in disappointment.

****

As the rising sun made the lattice pattern of the bedroom door travel across to tatami carpeted floor to illuminate Sook Cha's sweat beaded brow, Max rose on one elbow and once again dried her forehead with the folded washcloth. He replaced the cloth with his fingers and sensed, with hope, that her fever was lower than the night before. He drew the blue Air Force blanket up over their bodies, closed his eyes, and inhaled the perfume of her hair upon which his cheek rested. He fought off exhaustion and tried to remember how many syringes of penicillin were left, and if he should administer the next one before he had to catch the shuttle bus back to his base.

There was a soft knocking at the door. Max rose his sleepy head and whispered a response, "Hai (yes)?" The door slid quietly open and Old Mamasan crawled in on hands and knees pushing a tray with a steaming teapot and one china cup. Still in his robe, Max slid out from beneath the blanket as the old woman waved him away. He stood, closing his robe more tightly and tying the sash before exiting and closing the door quietly.

As the early morning sun painted the courtyard with a blood red light, Max slipped into gata sandals to cross the courtyard rather than cross the porch barefoot and risk Young Mamasan thinking he was approaching the door she had shut the night before. Even so, he turned his head just enough that his peripheral vision could tell if she opened her door, but the door remained closed and the silence of the courtyard was broken only by the clacking of his sandals.

He picked up the broken pieces of Sook Cha's door and, entering her abandoned bedroom and stepping over the bomb hole in the floor, he put the pieces under the metal army cot before lying down and pulling his blue overcoat over his body like a blanket. But, as exhausted as he was, he could not sleep.

88

Finally he rose and dressed for work, resigned to sleeping at the shuttle bus stop rather than risk oversleeping and being late for work. As he approached the gate, he first hesitated to listen for the sound of a sliding door, but there was none. Then, as he raised his hand to remove the bar at the gate, he remembered the Jee jumping onto the bar and over the gate. He wondered if Old Mamasan, being the clean freak she was, had washed the bar clean. He bit his lip, shrugged his shoulders, raised the bar, and exited the gate.

****

As Max trudged toward the shuttle bus stop, he instinctively reached into his pocket for a cigarette. Finding none, he remembered that he had been cutting back smoking more and more in order to convert his PX cigarette ration stamps into household income by selling the unopened cartons on the market. He had tried substituting the less expensive Japanese 'Peace' cigarettes available on the civilian market, but they were unbelievably rough on the throat and induced a hacking cough after only one or two packs. The street vendors, children and ragged adults with a cardboard boxes suspended by neck straps, also offered 'homemade' cigarettes, cigarettes rolled in little manual pocket rolling machines made from 'roll your own' cigarette papers and tobacco salvaged from discarded cigarette butts. They were worse than Peace cigarettes and a great opportunity to catch some virulent disease.

The streets were fairly empty at this early hour. The dried mud of the rutted side streets was almost like concrete from the cold, the cobblestone of the main drag echoed his footsteps against the closed doors of the unopened shops. He tried to think of something positive to look forward to, such as breakfast at the base, but that was more than an hour away. All he could think of to lift his spirits at the moment was a cigarette. Then he smelled something that seemed to answer his need. It smelled like sandalwood.

At the incline where the cobbled stoned street met the blacktop of the main highway, there was a clearing with a small stone Buddhist shrine. In the sand filled bowl before the little stone seated Buddha, several sticks of burning incense sent grey streams of scented clouds into the cold morning air. Max stopped before the shrine, enjoying the scent.

Max was not religious. He believed in the possibility of a spiritual realm and hoped for the survival of the human spirit after death, otherwise how else could there be accountability for ones behavior and the motivation to live a good life. But he despaired of the hypocrisies of organized religion and refused to participate in the congregations and rituals of those around him.

Yet here he stood, lured by the stimulating scent of sandalwood, in meditative repose before a religious shrine. He smiled, wondering if anyone was observing him and assuming that this American serviceman had become a Buddhist convert. Unwilling to leave the calming scent of the incense, he closed his eyes in thought.

Max had been betrayed by the doctor he thought was his friend. Max's lust had almost led him to betray Sook Cha during her most desperate hour of need. These failings may be excused as having originated with good intentions, or rationalized as lack of communication or human weaknesses. But allowing them to fester into bitter resentment or self loathing guilt would only serve to worsen already dire circumstances.

He knew he had to eventually return to a base where he still had to work side by side with Blake and occasionally rely on the doctor's services. He knew that these three women still needed him and that Young Mamasan had shown strength and class in shutting the door the night before. He knew he had to accept the shortcomings in Blake, the doctor, and himself, and set aside anger, resentment, and guilt in order to make the best of each new day.

He knew he could resolve these conflicts in himself through his own resignation and adaptation. What he couldn't do was make Sook Cha well. He thought about his Catholic wife and her family's appeals to religious deities to support their material and self serving goals. And then he thought to himself, "Why not? What harm can it do?"

With eyes still closed, he parted his lips and whispered to the little stone Buddha. "To all the good and positive spirits who can hear me and are willing to support my cause, please strengthen and cure this innocent and worthy girl, ease her suffering and restore her health so that she and her two female companions may help rebuild their country and contribute to a kinder and better world."

Max wondered if he should offer to barter something like his wife's family did, give something to charity or make a resolution. He had already given what little he had. He thought about making a resolution to quit smoking, but then reasoned that he would benefit economically and healthwise, and such a resolution was not a true sacrifice. He parted his lips, hesitated, then whispered, "I ask this in the name of justice for all she has suffered, and in the hope that any higher power must possess compassion."

Max's eyes opened at the startling sound of a honking horn as the shuttle bus arrived up on the highway, and the sound of boots running on the cobblestones as a growing collection of GI's raced to meet it.

Chapter Six
TO CONFORM
OR NOT TO CONFORM

The 'shuttle buses' ran every hour on the hour from six in the morning until six in the evening roundtrip between the American Army and Air Force Bases near the DMZ (De-Militarized Zone between North and South Korea) and the heart of Seoul where the United Nations and the Republic of Korea administrative offices were in construction amid the rubble of the downtown district. Actually, the 'buses' were olive drab colored five ton Army trucks whose high canvas canopied beds had a metal bench seat on each side. Max was in pretty good shape, but it was a challenge to hoist yourself up the tailgate and swing into the bed where the benches were usually already filled. Sitting on the metal floor was not much worse than sitting on the un-upholstered metal benches because, with less than one ton of human cargo, the trucks' suspension had little give and the unpaved road was still pockmarked with bomb holes and ox cart ruts that made the almost one hour ride a painful experience. Max was glad he had a little padding on his butt. Sook Cha had told him the ladies admired his butt, and she lamented that it looked better than her own. Max had smiled and added, "Bigger, maybe, but certainly not better."

Kimpo was about fifty miles Northwest of Seoul and passed through a rural district mostly filled with rice paddies and fields of onion, garlic, hot peppers, and carrots, radishes, turnips, and parsnips that sometimes grew as big as a baseball bat. These crops gave off their own pungent odors which were occasionally accented by the human fertilizer ladled into the furrowed rows from the 'honey buckets' that Sook Cha had been employed to collect when the ladies first returned to Young Mamasan's pre-wear home. Yeong Deungpo was on the immediate West side of Seoul, so Max's commute was a little less than an hour each way.

His schedule was hectic, not just the prescribed 8AM to 5:30PM Monday through Friday, but Lieutenant Conweb managed to tack on five to ten extra hours every week in order to fill up the Lieutenants' own boring life. Some of Lieutenant Conweb's projects were designed to kiss up to the Base Commander or in the hopes of getting himself a Commendation, but often it was just 'busy work' designed to keep his men occupied because 'idle hands are the devil's workshop,' which was one of his favorite 'Military Slogans Of The Week.'

Max was also committed to, and desperately needed, five hours each Friday, Saturday, and Sunday from 9PM to 2AM when he was employed as a cocktail pianist at the piano bar in the Officer's Club. There he had to smile and make 'nice nice' while Lieutenant Conweb often sat nearby giving him the 'evil eye.' This is where he negotiated such fringe benefits as cultivating the doctor who arranged for Sook Cha to get penicillin, even though that turned out to have its down side.

Another young Lieutenant at the piano bar was in charge of enlisted men's entertainment, and he recruited Max to write, MC, and perform in a talent show which was so successful in the enlisted men's club that they got permission to take it on the road to both enlisted men's and officer's clubs in nearby UN bases in Korea and even some military installations in Japan. Belatedly, the Lieutenant decided that he would be the show's director in order to reap the glory and get a couple free rides to Japan. Max negotiated a sizeable donation from each base where they performed which would benefit the Korean Orphanage which the base sponsored in Kimpo.

The talent show included two enlisted men who impersonated the then popular comedy team of Jerry Lewis and Dean Martin, another enlisted man who usually brought the house down impersonating popular vocalist Johnnie Ray and all his emotional antics singing the song *Cry*, a nurse Lieutenant who was a passable amateur on her accordion, but who also brought the house down as soon as she walked onstage in her skin tight red satin pants suit, Blake who Max had to include because he had the best possible voice for Broadway show tunes, the Lieutenant Director who validated his inclusion in the roadshow by reciting *Casey At The Bat* in Korean dialect which mostly went over the heads of the audience and offended a few local Koreans, and Max who accompanied the vocalists on the piano and glued it all together with hip comedy patter and interviews with the performers.

The scariest performance was at an Australian camp on the front lines where a small inebriated but enthusiastic audience were so taken with Max's rendition of *Twelfth Street Rag* that they wouldn't let the show go on and made Max repeat the number interminably, even when motar fire began to surround the performance tent. While the rest of the cast dove under the tables for safety, the Aussies kept Max at the piano and two of them got in a fist fight over whether he should play *Twelfth Street Rag* yet again or whether Max should accompany them singing *Darktown Strutter's Ball*. When Max asked the handsome Aussie Captain in charge if maybe they should all take cover, the Captain tweaked his handlebar mustache and said, "Don't worry,

Mate, if it's got your number on it, you wont feel a thing when it hits. Carpe diem, son, and just keep tickling those ivories."

The height of the tour was playing a luxurious Officer's Club in Itazuke, Japan, where a 23 piece Japanese orchestra in tuxedos, replete with violin section, stayed on stage while the Talent Show was sandwiched in between sets. Max felt self conscious asking the pianist to surrender his grand piano so Max could accompany the first vocals, then was amazed when, one by one, the sections of the orchestra started to back him up. All the performers were thrilled with the fullness of sound they felt behind them that night, and the formally dressed audience were equally thrilled when the Johnnie Ray impersonator threw off his coat, tore off his tie, ripped open his shirt, and jumped on the center ringside table, ending up kneeling in a paroxysm of crying.

Later the cast celebrated in the Kokasai Hotel with an abundance of 'hotel girls.' They all brought their girls to Max's room to rehash and revel in the success of the Itazuke show, and, a little bit, to show off the beautiful Japanese girls they had paired off with in the hotel's nightclub. One of the most extrovert of the girls sat by Max, wrapped her self around him, and tried to kiss him. When he turned his head and her kiss accidentally landed on his cheek, she said, playfully, "Wot's amatter, you? You like boys?"

Max took her hand out of his crotch and placed it on her thigh. "No, I have a girl."

The hotel girl looked around mockingly. "I no see girl."

Max shook his head negatively, "She's not in Japan."

The hotel girl became coy. "Oh, you have girl stateside."

Max shook his head again, "No, she's in Korea."

The hotel girl froze. "She Korean?"

Max looked her in the eye. "Yes."

The girl narrowed her eyes into a hateful stare, rose, and hissed her words through her teeth. "You turn me down for Korean girl. You insult me," and she turned to continue her complaint to the other girls and cast members.

Blake had observed the exchange from a distance, then came over to Max and said, "Hey, man, she really dug you. If it's the money, I can lend you some."

Max shook his head again. "No. It's not the money. I just dig someone else, and you know who."

Blake handed Max one of the two beers he had in his hands, then, as he turned to leave, he said, "Who'da thought, the hippee's a faithful man."

****

Max returned from the roadshow with gifts from Japan for the household; colorful parasols for all three ladies, rare spices for Old Mamasans' kimchie jars, cosmetics for Young Mamasan that were unavailable in Korea, and a beautiful carved ivory decorative hair comb for Sook Cha. They listened intently to his tales of the outrageous Aussies and the fabulous Itazuke Officers' Club. He did not mention the hotel girls at the Kokasai, but Sook Cha was concerned about the description of the nurses skin tight red satin pants suit.

Later that night, as he licked the dimples on Sook Chas' lower back and tenderly caressed her buttocks, he said, "Your ass is more beautiful that any of

97

the nurses at the base, certainly more beautiful than mine. I love the shape, I love the color, and I love that it is as smooth and soft as a baby's. Most of all, I love that is part of you, because I love the whole package. Every part of you fits together just right, and every part of you fits together with me just right." With that he began to spoon her, turning her face sideways so they could taste each others kiss a he entered her.

****

Although most of the officers at the K14 Air Force Base near Kimpo did not like Lieutenant Conweb, there was a grudging loyalty among commissioned officers that did not extend to enlisted men. The Base Commander, the Doctor, the Nurse, and the Lieutenant in charge of entertainment, all liked Max much more than his boss, but felt obliged to listen to Lieutenant Conweb's complaints about Max and share information with him.

Through them, Lieutenant Conweb learned the intimate details of Max's problems with his stateside wife. This included the fact that his wife had a high paying job in her father's business, yet still received a $90 a month allotment from Max's pay, which left Max with only $30 a month, which is why he so desperately needed his piano bar gig at the Officer's Club. And, of course, the Doctor knew Max had a Korean girlfriend in Yeong Deungpo, even down to her address which was now on record as a known prostitute because Max took her to get the penicillin.

The Doc did not agree with Lieutenant Conweb that they should moralize about Max's private life or do anything to coerce him to stay in his marriage or stay away from Sook Cha, and all of them certainly did not agree that Max should lose his piano bar job as part of that coercion. But Lieutenant Conweb had his own agenda regarding Max, and his fellow officers had provided him all he needed to rationalize his actions.

****

Max wore his charcoal grey Korean robe as he sat cross legged on the porch at the house in Yeong Deungpo. He ate his midday meal, a can of smoked oysters with rice and a mild version of the kimpchie sauce they made for him, while the ladies sat in a circle with him eating the real stuff. Young Mamasan entertained, comically telling of her resistance to an amouress GI, which was understandable because she had recently blossomed since the night the Jee jumped over the gate. She used the old woman as a straight man in her story and injected more English now than before for Max's benefit, and, when Sook Cha would lean against him with laughter, Young Mamasan would smile at him and share a happy compromise.

Suddenly Young Mamasans' narrative ended abruptly. As Max looked up at her, Sook Cha held his head rigidly forward and he heard Young Mamasan whisper hoarsely, "M.P.." The M.P. Captain and the Korean National Policeman ambled through the open gate hesitantly, followed by two helmeted guards. Max's back was to the gate and Sook Cha sat close beside him to shield him from their view. Young Mamasan approached the policeman. He was apologetically asking if this were a house of prostitution, could he please see everyone's ID. Out of the corner of his eye, Max could see the Captain strolling around curiously, his gaze intrigued by the neatness and furnishings of Sook Cha's room, Max's drawings and photographs of her, the candlesticks and cookware fashioned from scrap metals, and Max's brogans in the neat row of sandles and slippers at the edge of the porch.

He looked up into Max's face as surprised as Max was to see him. For all the blondness of Max's hair, the Captain had failed to recognize him in a robe. The policeman handed the Captain Sook Cha's prostitutes VD card which had not been punched since she recovered from the flu, and added that there was only one such girl in the "very orderly and well bred house."

While the policeman importantly, but self consciously, told Sook Cha she would have to get her shots and have her card punched, the Captain said to Max, "I don't know what this is, but someone at K14 issued a report that it was a whorehouse. You couldn't have seen the 'Off Limits' sign we've just painted outside that gate, so I don't see how I can take you in, but I'm ordering you to get your clothes, er, your uniform on, get out of here, and don't ever come back."

One of the guards was a Sergeant who wore his 45 automatic pistol on a tooled leather belt, the elaborately tooled holster strapped to his thigh with a rawhide thong. He refused to let Max shut the door as he changed. "What's matter, boy, you 'shamed of that uniform?" All Max could think of was Sook Cha and the VD card he had cursed her with.

"Hey I'm talking to you, boy:" It sounded like 'I'm tarking to you, barh.' He followed Max to where the other three waited at the gate.

Max looked over his shoulder at Sook Cha, pointed the cap on his head and said, as he left, "I plead the 5th amendment."

****
100

The lowest three ranks of enlisted me stood guard once every ten days. It was the most grueling of duties, which was still a long way from being in combat, but occasionally there would be 'infiltrators,' be they North Korean spies or South Korean scavengers, and every so often a guard would be found with his corpse tied to the eight foot high barbed wire fence and his throat slit or garroted. Equal to the fear of what was on the other side of the fence was the cold, the damp, and the overwhelming desire to sleep. Technically, the war was still on, and deserting or sleeping on your post was a death penalty offense. Of course, there was also the possibility that the guy on the next post might be nervous enough to mistakenly shoot you in the dark.

Within days after the appearance of the MPs at the house in Yeong Deungpo, Max found himself on twelve hours of night guard duty every other day. Usually a man received a half day off after guard duty, but, by being scheduled every other night, Max worked a total of twenty hours every other day and eight or more hours the days in between, most of it in the cold of night. His sleep was at odd broken hours and his mealtimes at hours when the chow hall wasn't open. His office workload in no way slackened, rather it increased because he would sleepily double expose the same plate or find himself dozing in the acid smelling reddish pool of light in the darkroom.

Lieutenant Conweb's conscious reasoning was to save Max's marriage by destroying his relationship with Sook Cha. His unconscious jealousy found this convoluted rationalization a convenient excuse for breaking the spirit of a man who Lieutenant Conweb's superiors liked better and who had a more rewarding personal life than his own. Under military law, they

101

were still in a War Zone and the Lieutenant could legally work Max up to twenty-three hours a day, and, under military law, Lieutenant Conweb could make all his threats of 'fraternization' and 'theft of military property' bear dire consequences.

Not surprisingly, after several nights on guard, Max developed severe cold symptoms. Lieutenant Conweb informed the Sick Call Staff in advance that Max was falsely attempting to evade guard duty, and the doctor at sick call was the one who had betrayed Max. The doctor's sense of guilt led him to pass Max off to Paramedics who did not diagnose him properly, could not prescribe any serious medication, and, instead, shoved various colored pills at him which were too big to go down his swollen throat. Fortunately for Max, after two weeks on guard, his throat was so swollen that he feinted from hunger in the office, rather than on guard, before his illness could potentially kill him.

Max woke in the hospital to see the doctor who betrayed him looking down with a guilty expression. Max's inability to speak was interpreted as an accusing stare, which prompted the doctor to volunteer a noncommital sort of confession, beginning with his avoiding Max on sick call and regressing to his joking with Lieutenant Conweb about Max's quest for Sook Cha's penicillin. When he finally realized Max was just unable to speak, he lapsed into a lengthy medical explanation of Max's illness. Max had strep throat and potentially lethal bi-lateral inflamation of the mastoid bones. The result was that Max lost temporary hearing in one ear, both ears would be permanently slightly impaired, and he would be extremely uncomfortable for a few weeks. The latter understatement was the doctor's parting joke.

The next time Max woke it was prompted by a needle being jabbed in his fanny. Max suspected it was a foot long, square, and barbed. The red headed nurse rolled him over and jabbed another painful needle in his arm to feed him intravenously. She was in her blue pants uniform instead of her tight red satin pants, and she carried a tray of needles instead of an accordion, but she was the same Lieutenant who had let him bring in the Korean seamstress that sewed her into the red satin pants for the talent show. She was unquestionably the most attractive woman on the base and, in the officer's club, had her choice of any combination of looks, brains, money, and position. But the experience of having a thousand men staring at the outline of her body in silent appreciation as she walked onstage, then burst forth with thunderous applause was a life changing experience for her. The red pants became a little legend and the red headed Lieutenant became a little stage struck.

She regarded Max as 'show peep,' and she became a piano bar addict at the officer's club where he welcomed the prop of an attractive girl to help carry the conversation and distract the others from difficult and impossible requests. The fuzz headed pack of collegiate Lieutenants that always flocked around her quickly lost any resentment of her newfound musical interest and appreciated the advantage of having the most powerful man (the Commander) and the most attractive girl always available at a convenient time and place and, almost always, in good humor. Although Max could see Conweb, alone at a corner table, mentally adding a new crime to his list, that of 'pimp.'

"What's matter, get hold of some bad gook whiskey?" She unhooked the metal clip and watched the sugar water drip from the bottle into the tube that led to his arm. "I've been waiting two days for you to wake up so I could enjoy sticking that needle in your ass."

Max's tongue felt swollen and heavy and he labored over the two words, "I bet."

She sat side saddle on the bed and took his pulse from a limp wrist. "Yeah, Honey, you're under my direction now. I can't tell you when you blow a sour note, but I tell you when to eat and when to piss and when to sleep."

His chest labored to suck in some air before adding, "And when to roll over."

She threw his wrist back at him and wrote on the chart. "Your bottom doesn't hurt now, does it?"

Talking was becoming easier. "I don't mind. It's just that I'm so attached to it."

She laughed as she leaned over and hung the chart, then she leaned on her knee and looked at him seriously. "Doc tells me you're on somebody's shit list for being a bad boy."

"But I make a very well behaved corpse."

"You make a better fixture at the piano bar."

Max chafed, "Fixture? Thanks."

She pouted, "Now is that any way to talk to the director? I was just trying to say we missed you at the club. Since you've gone I can appreciate how much you contribute to the morale."

"I needed the loot, Honey, order yourself another fixture from Sears Roebuck."

She ruffled his hair. "Wouldn't have to if you'd behave. 'Ole Conweb may be chicken shit, but he is the law. Is it so Goddam hard to steer clear of trouble?"

With a little effort, Max shook his hair loose. "Get off it, will ya. I got enough people pounding sand up my ass."

104

She stood up with a straight face. "Well, don't get salty, Soldier."

Max sulked. "Well, don't get gung ho with the troops."

She stood undecided, then smiled and smoothed the hair back from his forehead. "Okay. See you later."

Max was too tired to turn his head, but saw the other men in the ward sit up to watch her exit. One of them called out, "Hey, Lieutenant, where are the red pants?"

Max had one visitor while he was in the hospital; Ned. Max had not thought of visitors until Ned arrived, and the visit made Max realize how few friends he had on the base. Ned summed his presence up when Max asked him if Conweb had sent him.

"Hell no. Cagney would crawl all over me like a bobcat if he knew I was here. He'd have to stop and think whether I was a bad influence on you or you a bad influence on me, but it would amount to a half hour lecture, you can bet. On my time, of course. But I get regular lectures anyhow. That's why I'm here. Nothing to lose."

At least Ned was honest. The only friends Max had were those with nothing to lose. Many were intrigued by him, but few ventured near him. When Max first arrived they were intrigued by the way he decorated his tent area. The armless chair he built and sprung with strips of innertube and upholstered with horsehair matting and Korean print material. The black enameled bed lamp fashioned from a tin can and shaded with the same material. The curved top black enameled desk covered with plexiglass and illuminated by an overhanging Korean lantern. Most popular were the later additions of nude charcoal drawings of Sook Cha, mounted on irregular red, white, and black mats against

105

the woven bamboo with which he lined the six feet of wall space beside his bed.

These were the first to disappear when Lieutenant Conweb held inspection. They were immoral, and, though the nude calendar girls in other tents had failed to offend him, he took notice of another man's calendar girl in Max's tent to justify his disapproval of the drawings. After that, the smaller things began to disappear as Max spent more time in Yeong Deungpo. and he didn't mind when the bamboo was stripped from the walls for being "against fire regulations."

He shared little in common with his military peers; as for the girl waiting back home, his wasn't waiting, and as for complaining about the 'filth and backwardness' of Korea, Max would reply, "Hey, Man, they just survived a war." The probable result of knowing Max was the possibility of losing too many games of chess and losing out on a good conduct medal. The Commander had nothing to lose, no one would question his friendliness and he already had his good conduct medal. The red headed Lieutenant had nothing to lose, no one would begrudge her anything, particular under the guise of 'show biz.' Ned had nothing to lose, he hated himself more than any other man and masochistically brought more hell on himself than any friend or foe ever could.

Ned handed Max a small glossy card. The base insignia and name were printed across the top, the word 'CORRESPONDENT' was emblazoned. in red in the middle, and at the bottom, in bold and colorful print, was the signature line, "Lt. John F. Conweb, Officer In Charge." The fine print inferred the bearer was Involved in some glamoress news gathering position in a war zone.

106

Ned chuckled. "Cagney did you a favor today. He gave me some of your work 'cause I laughed when he handed out these cards. Bet he'll look all over Korea trying to find a show girl or a ball game this will get him into free." He looked at the card and stopped laughing. "When I took a newspaper route more than thirty years ago I dreamed of owning a card like this. Now it's a laugh. I made more money throwing papers and never had anyone like Cagney to contend with. Did you ever throw a paper route?"

Max said he had and Ned continued.

"It's a good job for a boy; gives him incentive. I've got a boy that's the right age for a paper route. Maybe he already has one. I became manager over twenty three paper boys, and when we moved to Birmingham I applied for a reporter's job on a city paper and just wrote on the application, 'With Atlanta News for five years.' Ha! It didn't get me that job, but I became a clerk. Can't remember when I stopped being a clerk and started being a reporter. From running copy I went to rewriting other people's copy, and, between them not being able to spell or being too lushed to see the keyboard, I finally ended up writing complete stories. I never thought of myself as a reporter when some staff guy had too big a hangover and they'd send me out. But by then I was married and had too many problems to think of anything as being glamorous. Wasn't bad at it, though. Might have still been on the staff if Vera hadn't nagged hell out of me so much I joined the service. I had some rough editors that would make Cagney look like the pipsqueek he is, but Vera was worse than all of 'em combined. Boy, could that bitch scream, as if the kids didn't do enough screaming on their own. Enough to drive a man to drink."

107

This struck a chord in Ned's mind and he looked at his watch. It was time for the enlisted mens club to open. He rose to leave and pointed to the bottle that dripped dextrose into Max's arm. "Bet you wish that was hundred proof, eh?"

Max sallied, "If it was, I'd share it with you."

Ned held up a protesting hand. "No thanks. I may be a bottle baby, but I never take it in the arm."

As Ned turned to go, Max rose on his elbow and stopped him. "Ned?"

Ned turned back, "Yeah?"

"You know that money you owe me?"

Ned looked down and started tapping his thigh with his cap, "Yeah, Max, about that..."

Max tried to sound tactful. "I'll make you a deal. I figure it's over fifty now, but if you'll take twenty-five to a friend of mine in Yeong Deungpo, we'll forget about the rest."

Ned raised an open hand, "Oh, Max, I couldn't....I mean....I'll deliver the twenty-five, I understand about that, but I'll still pay you the rest."

Max smiled gratefully, "Whatever, it's just important you get it there as soon as possible. The name and address is written in English and Korean under the nameplate in the lid of my camera case in the darkroom. Can do?"

Ned smiled wanfully and pointed the cap on his head. "You bet, Max. Cagney didn't come up with any extra work for us this weekend, think he felt guilty about you, so I'll get it there tomorrow."

Max leaned back on his pillow. "Thanks, Ned."

A stout nurse nearby was looking with disapproval at Ned's stubbled face and stained teeth. On his way out Ned winked and gave her a lascivious look that sent her waddling to the other end of the ward as if he'd pinched her.

Max progressed from dextrose water to soup and Jello, and, by the time the red headed Lieutenant started personally supervising his walking exercises, he knew the rest of the guys in the ward were thoroughly jealous of him. With his arm around her neck, the two would explore the labyrinth of corridors all military hospitals seem to be made of. Max always suspected that some methodical but mischievous mind designed these hospitals consisting of many small equal sized buildings linked, as if by afterthought, with enclosed causeways. When it is difficult to walk, you resent the unused buildings along the way that might have housed your destination more conveniently.

At first, the destination of each exercise was a long circle leading nowhere, but one day, when Max threatened to vomit if made to take another step, she urged, "Don't stop now, we're almost there." Where? An empty room with a piano in it, one of those military olive colored Stienway spinets that, no matter how battered and out of tune, were always so rugged they were never completely unserviceable. Max cracked his knuckles and made a run on the keyboard that sounded like someone just tripped over a xylophone, but, after a week of counting the corrugations of a Quonset hut roof, it was a lovely sound that made him forget his uneasy stomach and remember the warmth of a girl's yellow skin.

His last night on guard he felt a burning need to write a love song, the burning feeling caused more by streptococci than the love bug. He sloshed through the snow to the next post and asked the guard if they had a pencil and paper. The other guard hesitantly proffered him a stub of pencil and must have really thought Max nuts when he scrounged through the dark looking for a scrap of paper. He peeled the label from a used tomato can, the back of which provided room for two stanzas scribbled in the dark. It was in his pocket when he was taken to the hospital, so he asked the Lieutenant to forget regulations long enough to retrieve it from the sealed envelope in the office.

She did, and he began putting the words to music on that broken down piano. Max must have given her a convincing performance of the finished product because her first impression was that she had inspired the song. When Max averted that idea, she was both relieved and offended, but thought it a beautiful way to remember the girl back home. Unwisely, Max pinpointed the emotion as being for a Korean girl.

Max pulled his hands off the keys just in time as the frowning nurse slammed the keyboard cover down, did an about face, and marched out of the room without a word. Max stumbled through the halls until he found an abandoned wheelchair and, with much effort and a lot of banging into walls and carts, made his way back to his ward alone. Thereafter he never saw the red headed nurse unless she was jabbing painful needles in him, her sneering expression saying more than her silence as she would twist the exiting needle.

The rest of his hospital stay, the two stanzas on the back of the tomato can label sang in his head, and he hoped he would somehow someday have the opportunity to play it for Sook Cha, even if she couldn't entirely understand it. The words on the back of the tomato can label read:

Verse:
Somewhere in Korea
*   as the snow came falling down,*

A soldier boy stood guard alone
    with silence all around,
Thoughts kept running through his mind
    as he shouldered his gun,
And as these thoughts swelled in his heart
    this is the song he sung,

Chorus:
To whom do I speak
    in the still of the night,
Who?s there in the dark
    for my arms to hold tight,
Whose presence can make
    all the cold turn to warm,
Whose hand can add strength
    to my cold tired arm,

Then when the sun
    starts to goldplate the skies,
Who's there to share
    this wealth with my eyes,
And with the dawn
    when my vigil is through,
Whose lips might I kiss
    as I last kissed you.

Chapter Seven
THE TIES THAT BIND

Prompted by the Doctor, Conweb had commuted Max's guard duty to the usual once every 10 days, but he confined him to the base for thirty days based on the fact that the MP Captain had reported Max's presence at Sook Cha's residence, even though he did not arrest him. When Max reported for duty, Conweb informed him that the thirty days confinement was a, "Disciplinary action for being in an Off Limits area."

Max was a little pale, but stood stiffly at attention and stared at 'Military Slogan Of The Week' above Conweb's head as he barked his response. "But Sir, I entered the residence before the Off Limits sign was posted."

Conweb placed the Disciplinary Action paperwork in Max's Personnel Folder on his desk and look up at him in a smile. "All the report I received says was that you were in the residence of a known prostitute which was posted Off Limits. I could bust you for that offense, but you've already been busted to the lowest possible rank before I arrived. We could argue that it was a Court Martial Offense for putting yourself and your fellow servicemen at risk of disease, but I think that would be going too far. No, thirty days confined to the base will give you a chance to renew your bonds with your comrades in arms, and possibly think seriously about how consorting with prostitutes might affect your marriage."

Max stared at the Military Slogan Of The Week which read, "There is no little enemy," and thought to

113

himself, "Obviously, Ben Franklin never met Conweb."
Conweb's dig about 'conorting with prostitutes' brought
up the image of the Japanese hotel girl's crotch that
Conweb had photographed and referred to as 'manly
sport,' but Max knew moral debates with this man were
pointless. Instead, he barked a minimal, "Yes Sir!"

Conweb's cheek twitched and his smile appeared
pained. "I'm providing you an opportunity to salvage
something of value, here, Airman. I would think that
deserves a 'thank you.'"

Max's continued to stare at the slogan, but one
eyebrow raised and there was a hesitant moment before
he responded mechanically, "Yes Sir. Thank you, Sir."

Conweb's pained smile softened into a satisfied
one. "Very well, then, why don't you go over to your
desk and start catching up on your backlog of work. I'm
sure your co-workers will be happy to no longer have to
do it for you. You're dismissed."

Max gave a snappy salute, made a sharp about
face, and marched through the little swinging gate that
separated Conweb's desk from the rest of the office.

****

Max sat on his metal cot, the only one of three
items that remained in his tent area, the others being a
foot locker and a pipe suspended by wires from the tent
rafters that served as a hanging rod for his clothes. His
hand made furnishings, wall coverings, and decorations
had all been stripped away by his 'comrades in arms'
during his stays in Yeong Deungpo.

He shuffled through the thin pack of letters from
his wife, a few of which included photos. She was
beautiful, often compared to the Swedish actress Greta
Garbo; tall, slim, long straight black hair, aquiline

features that could at times appear haughty and aloof. She had entered the nightclub where he played cocktail piano in the French Quarter to celebrate her 'coming out party,' a rite of passage for New Orleans debutantes known as a 'cotillion..' Max was impressed with the requests she made: *Habernera*, a popular theme from the opera *Carmen*; *Harlem Nocturne*, a classy jazz number; and *All The Things You Are*, a show tune by Jerome Kern and Oscar Hammerstein with lyrics that provided Max an opportunity to praise her beauty. She reciprocated by saying to her formally gowned girlfriends in a voice loud enough for all to hear, "Isn't he gorgeous? Wouldn't we make such beautiful babies together." Then she gave him her card with only her name hand engraved on one side, and her phone number hand written on the back.

Max did not come from a currently wealthy family. The Great Depression had wiped away the wealth and prestige of previous generations. But the history and the genes were there, and the girl who would become his wife was more interested in the genes, and her parents found his family history a reasonable compromise. Their courtship and marriage was orchestrated more by the bride than the groom, and only when their family plans were dictated solely by her did Max begin to feel he was merely a player and not a partner.

Max's widowed mother had allowed him to make his own choices in life, and he had been eclectic, adhering to no single philosophy, religion, or social identity. While these differences with his wife were viewed as colorful eccentricities in their personal relationship, they became deal breakers in planning their extended family. Max didn't want to leave entertainment and enter his father-in-law's business, he

115

didn't want to spend all his time in leisure pursuits, and, most of all, he didn't want his children raised within the confines of his in-laws business, social, and religious dogmas.

On the other hand, Etienne was the kind of man who was happy to be a 'player.' Their friendship was initiated by Etiennes' nightclubbing habits, the two carousing together after two in the morning when Max got off work and all the rowdier establishments on Esplanade and Decateur Streets remained open until daylight. Etienne was actually jealous when Max started going with his wife to be, ruefully complaining that Max was cheating on him with "that other brunette."

Max shuffled through the letters to Etiennes' last letter, opened it, and re-read the last line, "I am so glad you consider me your best friend, now, because of recent events and more than ever, there is a great need for us to be best friends." Max pictured the two brunette heads, his wife and his best friend, laughing as they clinked glasses at the club in which he played. Then Max pictured the two of them in bed together and it saddened him, but, somehow, it did not bring tears to his eyes.

When Max had first read Etiennes' letter, he thought of writing him, but decided his request for clarification should be sent to his wife instead. Her response was overdue, and he waited for each mail call like one waits for 'the other shoe to drop.' This day, the first day out of the hospital, a package arrived from his wife. He opened the box filled with excelsior packing to find the ivory ball he had sent her when he first arrived in Korea. It was one of those ball within a ball sculptures, an amazing example of the ivory carver's art, three elaborately patterned open work balls carved from

116

a single piece of ivory, one ball inside the other, sitting on a black onyx pedestal.   In his letter to her accompanying the ball, he had described it as a metaphor of how people are sometimes trapped within the larger constructs that surround them.

As he attempted to lift the ball, it broke into several pieces, no single ball remaining intact. At the bottom on the box amid the excelsior and broken ivory fragments were two items; her gold wedding band and her card, her name hand engraved on one side, and handwritten on the back the words, "Now you are free."

****

Ned made weekly deliveries of money and supplies to the house in Yeong Deungpo, but the verbal messages and explanations left something to be desired. Max could only hope they understood, only hope they believed in his return, and only hope Sook Cha would not feel the need to prostitute herself because of doubt or necessity.   This latter thought more than saddened him, it even inspired tears.

At night he would dream of walking through the red wood gates of the house in Yeong Deungpo, see Sook Chas' delighted smile, and hear that "Ah-ieeeeee" sound she made, like the cartoon strip *Terry And The Pirates*, when she saw him and ran to him to fling her arms and legs around him in a long tight sensual embrace. He dreamed of sitting cross legged on the narrow wooden porch in his robe eating kimchie and loving the pungent smell and burning hot taste of it, which in reality he couldn't stand. In his dreams Young Mamasan would tell her comical tales of their daily life, but in exaggerated Kabuki style with flamboyant costumes, makeup, and drum and cymbal musical

117

accompaniment. Old Mamasan would direct Young Mamasans' performance with her red hot poker from the brazier like a conductor leading an orchestra.

But the best of dreams were those in Sook Chas' tiny room. The bomb hole in the ceiling was like a skylight to a starry moonlit sky, instead of a hole in a ceiling below a roof that had long ago been repaired. The bomb hole in the floor was like a bottomless chasm in which falling pebbles made a hollow echoing sound as if they would never reach the bottom. The narrow metal cot was wider, newer with a pristine shiny fatigue green paint job, and the thick plush mattress was covered with fatigue green blanket that was trimmed in satin and felt like velvet. There, on a dreamy bed beneath a starry sky, Max clung to the soft sweet young body of a girl with yellow skin that smelled like flowers, and almond eyes that looked at him with desire. He tasted every crevice that might harbor a bead of her perfumed sweat, he nibbled at every protrubence on her body from her earlobes to her toes. He tried to enmesh himself into her body, again and again, hoping that with some eventual thrust he would pass completely through into somewhere, he knew not where, but somewhere where there was peace, and happiness, and fulfillment. Then he would wake on his narrow cot to find it soaked with sweat and semen.

A week after he received the box from his wife, someone mailed him a large kraft envelope from New Orleans containing a newspaper clipping of a gossip column written by a columnist who was one of his friends and admirers from his French Quarter days. This columnist had been very kind to him, perhaps in part because the columnist was gay and had been attracted to him, but an older man who had never made a pass at him. The clipping included a photo of Maxs' wife with Etienne and a caption circled in red saying, "Guess what new socialite couple dance the night away in French Quarter haunts while hubby fights the war for them in Korea?" There was no return address or letter, card, or signature to indicate who had sent the clipping. He doubted it was his wife who was not referred to kindly in the caption, nor Etienne who was not so unkind, particularly to his best friend and under the circumstances. Perhaps the columnist who might think Max should be informed, or perhaps some jealous woman he had a one night stand with and who always resented his subsequent marriage. Max decided to believe it came from a well meaning friend or patron who simply thought he should know.

That night he had the first dream about his wife since he received Etienne's letter months before. She hung by her wrists from the barrel of a monstrous sized Civil War cannon in Jackson Square Park before St. Louis Cathedral in the heart of the French Quarter, the cannon five times as big as the one that actually existed there. Her wrists were tied with black velvet ropes and her naked body, clothed only in black opera hose and black stiletto heeled shoes, turned slowly and gracefully like a ballet dancer pirouetting in slow motion. Before her, seated in old fashioned wooden folding chairs on the grassy lawn of the park, was an audience consisting of her parents, Etienne, Max's deceased mother, the columnist, several of the women he had affairs with before his marriage, and a large number of his friends and patrons at the night club. Max stepped into the dream dressed like Zorro, replete with shiny black pork pie hat, a narrow black satin mask over his eyes, and a period costume mostly made of satin and including shiny black leather knee high boots and whip. As he appeared, the audience applauded.

Her father was the first to speak in Max's dream. "Strike her for marrying you. You know she was foolish to do so." And Max was surprised to see himself raise the very long whip, make it rotate and whistle several times, and see the barest tip of it paint a thin red line across her breast and rib cage. She writhed and convulsed, but only emitted a muffled whimper through her voluptuous closed lips.

Then Eitienne spoke up enthusiastically. "Strike her for tempting me. You know she did." And again, the whip sang through the air, painting another diagonal thin red line across her hips and pubic region.

With a pained frown on her face, his mother, who had died before he met his wife, said sorrowfully, "Strike her for hurting you, son. She did not need to do that." Tears welled behind his Zorro mask as he reluctantly lifted his arm and weilded the snake like whip. This time her body had pivoted somewhat and the whip painted its thin red line across her beautiful buttocks that he had so admired and enjoyed. Finally, tears began to fall from her eyes and she emitted a plaintive wail.

The audience in his dream now became excited and each in turn requested he strike to avenge the memory of some unkind act of which they felt his wife was guilty. He tried to raise his arm fast enough to comply with their demands, but it became harder and harder and the whip became heavier and heavier until the crowd rose up and began to surround him shouting for her blood.

Max woke from this nightmare in a pool of sweat, but no trace of semen.

****

Guido smiled as Max brought the box into the supply tent. The little Italian Corporal actually ran the Supply Depot whose Supply Officer was always off base chasing girls in On Limits or Off Limits areas because his limitless merchandise resources enabled him to bribe any MPs that caught him. Guido had been the source of the aerial film that covered the windows in Yeong Deungpo, and the horsehair packing that served as a mattress for Sook Cha's bed, and a great variety of luxuries in war torn Korea such as toilet paper and fabric and much much more.

Max lifted out the ivory ball sculpture, his efforts to glue it together revealed in thin grey lines that hid among the open work pattern of the balls. Guido's bushy black eyebrows raised with interest as Max spoke. "Guido, this cost over a hundred bucks new, and I've managed to repair it to a presentable state, if not original condition."

Guido's pudgy fingers lifted the ball very gently off its pedestal as he inspected it carefully and critically. "Go on, Max. I'm interested."

Max looked around to make sure no one was within earshot. "I need a white dress for a girl about size three. Maybe a nurse's dress uniform that I could have an off base tailor modify into a street dress."

Guido looked around to make sure no one was within earshot, also, then gave Max a 'come hither' smile and affected a woman's voice. "I'm a size three, you know. Thinking of playing some fantasy doctor and nurse sex games with me?"

Max half smiled and half frowned. "Behave, Guido. It's for a girl I know."

Guido's smile faded. "Oh well, who's the lucky girl. I know it's not the red headed nurse because she's got her own white dress uniform. Speaking of which,

121

why didn't you ask her? You two are chummy." The latter brought the smile back to his face as he wiggled his eyebrows up and down suggestively. Max started to put the ball back in the box. "Not any more."

Guido pulled the boxed ball towards himself to keep Max from removing it altogether."Whazzamatter? Trouble in paradise?"

Max kept his hand on the box so they were both holding it on the counter top. "No. It's just that paradise is not on this base, and I need the dress for someone off base."

Guido pursed his lips and said, "Well, I've been told I'm about as off base as you can get." Max frowned. Then Guido patted the box with both hands, saying,"All right! All right! You want a size three white dress, nurse or whatever, and you're willing to give me your poor broken balls for it."

Max patted the box with both hands and said, "Right!"

Guido pulled the box out of Max's hands and put it under the counter, then leaned on one elbow and blinked his eyes at Max with another seductive smile. "Done! Of course, you know, Sugar, if you played your cards right, you could get anything you want from me. Balls or no balls."

Max patted the counter with both hands. "Guido, you know I don't play those particular games."

Guido pursed his lips again. "That's what they all say, Honey. Is there anything else I can do for you?"

Max pointed the cap on his head and answered, "Not unless you can get the rest of my confinement to the base commuted."

Guido smiled mischieviouly, "Funny you should ask. I'm having a very private party in the supply tent tonight after bed check. You'd be surprised who you

122

might meet there, including some of the powers that be, the powers that wanna be, and the weaklings that grovel under the powers that be."

Max pulled the screen door open. "No thanks, I don't think I'm up to any party."

Guido reached across the counter and grabbed Max's arm, then noticed the lack of stripes and stroked the un-faded area where two stripes had once been. "Oh, poor baby. You haven't got those back YET?." Before Max could answer, Guido continued, "Now listen. How'd you like to get some bling bling to go with that white dress, and maybe even a off base pass to help you deliver it. Some of my party goers could make that happen. They're fans of yours 'cause they saw your tent area decor and wanted to meet you. Whad'ya say, Sweetheart?"

Max pulled his wrinkled sleeve down to straighten it. "Thanks, Guido, but, as I said, I don't play those particular games."

Guido looked at Max pathetically. "I know, Baby, you only play solitaire. Remember, I'm the one that collects your stinky sheets for the laundry." Guido shifted back to coyness. "But seriously, Honey, come to the party. No strings. Off base pass? It could happen!"

The screen door clicked shut as Max exited without responding.

****

Max realized he was practically tip-toeing through the darkness of the starless overcast night. When he reached the supply tent, he guessed Guido had played an elaborate joke on him because the tent was pitch black and silent. Just to be sure, he knocked softly at the storm door. A foot square black cloth panel flew back and Guido's face peered through the screen. "Ohhhhh, you came." Then Guido looked down at Maxs' chest. "And you wore your uniform. I guess I forgot to tell you, this is one place where you don't give your name, rank, and serial number." Max felt foolish and started to go when the door flew open and Guido yanked him inside, shutting the door abruptly behind him. "But that's okay, Sweetie. Everybody here knows who the hell you are anyhow."

He dragged Max over to a makeshift bar and ladled him a drink into a Dixie cup from a galvanized wash tub being used as a punch bowl. "Here, Baby, you'll have to catch up with everyone else. They're about ten drinks ahead of you." Guido put his fingers to his mouth and made a shrill whistle to get everyone's attention. Max wondered if the whistle would attract attention in the tent area, then noticed the tent walls were all draped with heavy matting to restrict light and sound. Guido gestured toward Max and said, "You all know our talented musician photographer. This is his first visit, so be gentle. I lured him here with the promise that no one would bite, so behave yourselves." Guido raised his Dixie cup and everyone followed his lead as they all chorused, "Welcome!"

There were about a dozen people, half of them known to him, most of them enlisted men, all of them in casual civilian clothing. Most servicemen knew each other by their last names, partly because that was the name tag sewn above their left breast pocket, and partly because few of them developed close enough friendships to ever learn the others first name. Max was standing next to a young black Sergeant who worked in Headquarters Building, and a nondescript fellow in his early thirties with a brunette crew cut who looked familiar, but he couldn't place him. The crew cut

124

extended his hand to Max saying, "I like your work. You have style." Max shook his hand, but looked confused by his remark. The crew cut chuckled and said, "I mean your music. I'm a fan at your piano bar."

Maxs' smile relaxed and he responded, "Thanks. It's a little difficult to recognize people out of uniform."

The crew cut smiled and nodded affirmatively. "Well, that's the whole idea. What happens in the supply tent, stays in the supply tent. Right?"

Max smiled and nodded affirmatively. "Right!"

The young Sergeant extended his hand and, when Max shook it, it was very soft and very limp. The Sergeant spoke in a soft but husky voice. "I like your work, too, and your style. But I'm talking about your photography. Guido showed me some of your pictures that you bartered with him. Your work is so artistic, and you obviously have an understanding and compassion for the Korean civilians."

Max tried to remember which of his photography he might have bartered with Guido and which Guido might have confiscated from Maxs' tent area. Max smiled and bowed his head modestly. "Thank you. I do appreciate Korean culture, and feel that, despite whatever inconveniences, we are privileged to observe these people and this moment in history."

Guido had sidled up to Maxs' elbow and interjected, "See. I told you he was an intellectual." Guido poked Max in the ribs gently. "Incidently, Intellectual, the Sergeant here is the one who passes out passes, I mean 'Off Base' passes. You might want to talk to him about that."

Other partygoers circulated past Max, most offering varying degrees of praise for his 'work' in one medium or another, none behaving as flamboyantly as Guido, and all avoiding any mention of their military

125

position or identity. After an hour, Max thanked Guido for inviting him and headed for the door. The Sergeant followed him saying, "I'm leaving, too. I'll walk with you."

Max hesitated, saying, "I thought you were in Headquarters Squadron?" Then realized he wasn't supposed to identify name, rank, or serial number.

The Sergeant continued behind him unruffled. "Yes, but that's on the way past your tent."

Max felt uncomfortable. Other than the softness of his hands and the limpness of his wrist, Max did not see any effeminate traits in the Sergeant. When they stopped to let a jeep go by, he caught himself checking out the Sergeants figure. The young mans torso was straight and slim, and he did have a provocative derriere, but his gait and speech revealed nothing gay about him. The Sergeant broke the silence. "Guido said you're in need of an Off Base Pass."

Max looked down as he crossed the road. "Yes, but I've been confined to base for thirty days and still have sixteen days to go. Using an Off Base Pass would be risky to anyone who used it or who issued it."

The Sergeant spoke matter of factly, "Not so. The risk would be all yours because I'd deny any knowledge of it. But the risk is minimal. Unless there's some unusual base wide security issue, nobody's going to look closely at your Pass. You biggest risk is if you get caught for some infraction by the MPs off base. Then you're in deep shit."

Max thought to himself that he would be at risk regardless as long as that 'Off Limits' sign remained outside the house in Yeong Deungpo. "But I have no money, I couldn't compensate you, even if there is no risk to you."

The Sergeant responded without emotion. "No problem. I like you, I like your work, we could work something out."

Maxs' brow furrowed in thought. "Well, I can't get you into the Officers Club piano bar, but I could offer you some of the prints you admired."

They were passing the line of latrines that divided each squadron's tent area and the Sergeant said, "Wait for me, will ya. I'll just be a moment," and he ducked into the nearest latrine building.

Max felt awkward waiting, then opened the door and said, "I'm heading back to my tent. I'll talk to you tomorrow."

He heard the Sergeant's hushed voice say, "Hey, I'm stuck. Come give me a hand."

Max entered the latrine and didn't see anyone. "Where are you?"

The Sergeant's voice whispered, "I'm in the shower room."

Max walked toward the shower room. "How can you be stuck in the shower room?" As he entered the darkened room, the Sergeant wrapped one arm around him and kissed him on the mouth, at the same time grabbing Max's hand which he placed on his buttock. Max struggled with him briefly, finally managing to push the man back until the Sergeant fell on the floor with a thud. Wiping his mouth with his sleeve, Max yelled at him, "Jesus, Man, are you crazy?"

The Sergeant pulled himself into a seated position on the floor and bowed his head onto his knees. "I'm sorry. I just thought...."

Max straightened his clothes and angrily interrupted him. "Thought what? I didn't say or do anything to... I just went there to barter a deal, and I don't mean barter sex!"

127

The Sergeant wrapped his arms over his bowed head. "I know that. It's just that I told Guido some time ago that I was madly in love with you, and he thought.....I thought....maybe...."

Max started to back toward the door. "Enough! Let's just forget tonight ever happened. Okay?"

As Max exited the room he heard the Sergeant whisper, "Okay." Then, as he exited the latrine, he thought he heard sobbing.

****

Max was afraid to go to sleep that night. He tossed and turned for a long time on his narrow cot and, when sleep finally came, it ushered in the nightmare he had been hoping to avoid. He dreamed he was walking down the main street in the red light district of Yeong Deungpo. The girls in the bordellos solicited him and, as he passed by the open living rooms where the girls congregated, he was aware that the Sergeant in his crisp blue uniform was in the company of the girls, standing talking to them in one brothel, seated on the sofa with them in another. Then, as he was approaching the railroad tracks where he would turn to find the alley where Sook Cha lived, he saw her ahead of him. Sook Cha was dressed in her black pants and blue sweater, but she wore exaggerated makeup like the prostitutes did, and she was soliciting the servicemen who passed by her. He could hear her entreaties, "You want good time, GI? Short time, long time. I makee you feel vewy vewy good."

Then the handsome Aussie Captain from the base where the show was interrupted by mortar fire strolled by her, stopped, and twirled his handlebar mustache as she tempted him. "You like saccahachi

128

girl, soljer, me number one ichi ban saccahachi girl. Max teach me real good.," and she pulled the willing Captain by the arm toward the railroad tracks.

In his dream Max stood stunned beside the open parlor of a brothel and the girls there started to taunt him. "Maxsan, she no wait for you. She skivvy Josan now. She bad for you. Come! We have number one ichi ban girl girl for you," and they ushered forth a very tall figure wrapped in a beautiful embroidered robe with a crowned hat like the operetta heroines wore. Suddenly they pulled the robe and hat from the figure to reveal the naked Sergeant looking coy and turning his provocatively shaped black buttocks to Max."

Max woke drenched in sweat. He quickly looked at the middle of his cot for any signs of semen, and sighed with relief when he found none.

****

Two days later Max was typing captions for pictures he had taken which were to accompany an article they were sending to *The Stars and Stripes*, the weekly distributed to all American servicemen serving overseas. One of the pictures was taken in the base hospital and included the red headed nurse and another nurse who happened to be an attractive young black woman. The red headed nurse still subjected him to snide remarks at the piano bar and dirty looks when their paths crossed at sick call, but she could manage to smile when he included her in any journalistic pictures.

The black nurse in the picture started Max to thinking about the one and only black woman with whom he had ever slept. Shortly after he began working in the French Quarter nightclub, he had been tuning the baby grand piano in the afternoon when no one was there but the beer delivery men and the cleaning lady, who happened to be a young attractive black woman. When he had finished tuning the piano, he sat at the keyboard and began practicing an abbreviated version of *Rhapsody In Blue* which he was adding to his repertoire. After completing his third attempt, which had improved slightly from the first attempt, he looked up to find the cleaning lady sitting at a ringside table staring at him intensely. A little embarrassed, he asked, "Was the last effort better than the first?"

The young woman looked at him raptly, saying, "It was beautiful. You are beautiful."

Maxs' chick radar suddenly turned on. He looked her up and down and decided she was beautiful, too. She was tall, slim, darker than Lena Horne, but with similar features in face and figure. Her white uniform, despite a few smudges, contrasted beautifully with her coloring and helped define her conical bust, flat abdomen, slim hips, and athletic legs. He joked, "I don't know if you qualify as a music critic."

She suddenly sat erect and spoke confidently. "Actually, I'm an opera student at Howard University."

Max teased her. "Really, I thought you were the cleaning lady."

She raised one eyebrow and matched his sarcasm. "I am, but I know my music, and you're good." Then she smiled seductively and added, "And I know my men, and you're beautiful."

Max stood, stepped down from the dias on which the piano sat, and stepped toward her at the same time that she rose to meet his embrace. The two wrapped themselves around each other and competed to see who could swallow the other's tongue. As they wrestled in an upright position, knocking over chairs and unsuccessfully attempting to find a table that would support their combined weight, the middle aged Cajun waitress who lived in the rear courtyard entered the back door. Seeing them, she casually walked over, handed Max her keys, and said, "I'm going to the French Market for tonights' lemons and limes and stuff. Make sure you lock my apartment and put the key under the potted palm before you leave," then she exited.

Behind closed eyelids, Max remembered the image of the young womans' slim hipped chocolate brown body on the white sheets of the waitresses' squeaky bed. At the time, despite the existence of segregation and growing racial strife, her racial identity was meaningless to him. Her complexion only affected him as novel in his experience and beautiful in its combination with white sheets, the cream colored walls of the waitresses' apartment, and the chartreuse color of the large potted plants in the courtyard. It wasn't of any consequence until after they lay still on the rumpled sheets and she said, "I'm appearing in *Aida* at Howard University. Would you like to see a performance?"

Max raised on one elbow and began to run his extended fingertips across her nipples, delighting in seeing them become tumescent and rise into hard dark cherry pits. "Yes, of course, I'd love to. And you should hear me add *Rhapsody In Blue* to my repertoire tonight."

After a few seconds of silence, she removed his hand from her breast, sat on the edge of the bed, and said, "I don't think so."

Surprised, Max asked, "Why not?"

She rose and reached for her white uniform draped over the nearby chair. "Are you kidding? Where are you from? You're in the segregated South, Dum Dum."

131

That's when the double standard dawned on him. He would be welcome at an opera at Howard University, but she wouldn't be welcome as the entertainer's guest at a French Quarter night club. His reverie concluded as he recalled her slim hipped high thrusting buttocks which dissolved into the image of the Sergeants' derriere in his dream.

Maxs' daydream evaporated as he opened his eyelids to see Ned shaking him and saying, "Max, there's an officer her to see you." Then added under his breath, "And thank God I caught you before Conweb found you napping."

At first Max didn't identify the brunette crew cut officer from the party, but remembered in time to extend his hand in greeting, then, as the officer extended his hand, Max withdrew his as he remembered to salute him as required. The officer returned the salute, began to extend his hand a second time, then looked around the office and withdrew his hand to retrieve a small white envelope from his pocket which he proffered to Max, saying, "The Sergeant over at headquarters asked me to deliver this to you. Apparently there was some misunderstanding." The officers' brow furrowed slightly. "I hope everything is okay."

Max felt awkward. "Oh, yes sir. No problem. Everything's fine. Nothing to be concerned about."

The officer slowly smiled and put his hat on. "Well good. I'm glad. Look forward to seeing you at the piano bar."

Max snapped to attention and smiled. "Yes sir. Thank you, sir." Max saluted and the officer returned the salute and left.

Ned rolled himself in his office chair over to Max and whispered hoarsely, "What was that all about?

132

Looked like you two were playing patty cake for a while there."

Max looked down at the envelope in his hand. "Nothing. He was just delivering something."

Ned inquired, "What?"

Max put the envelope in his pocket and frowned at Ned. "Nothing, Nosey. Now get back to work before Conweb catches us gabbing."

Ned rolled back to his desk as Max sat at his and pulled the envelope out of his pocket. He pressed his lips together tightly, tapped the envelope on his desk blotter three times nervously, then opened it. There was an official Off Base Pass with his name on it and signed, apparently, by one of his fans, the Base Commander. Max wondered if the signature was a forgery. A small note dropped out of the envelope that read, "Sorry. A peace offering. No strings. Honest."

He pulled a note pad over intending to write an angry response, then stopped. He started to tear the pass in half, then thought about the ivory ball he had received. Max sighed deeply, put the intact pass into a new unmarked envelope, then wrote a note saying, "No thanks. I appreciate the gesture, but I think I'll just wait it out." He put the note in the envelope with the pass, sealed it, walked over to Headquarters and asked one of the clerks to deliver it to the Sergeant.

Chapter Eight
CAMELOT

Max   walked out of the main gate with a shopping bag filled with PX goodies, some of them gift wrapped. His feet stirred little clouds of yellow dust on that long narrow ribbon of road that led to Yeong Deungpo, and he headed for the nearby intersection where the shuttle bus picked up passengers from his base. The base was surrounded by irregular shaped rice paddies that looked like a crazy geometrical drawing from twenty thousand feet in the air.   Little hills feathered at the top where rare amounts of green jutted the landscape, clusters of adobe type farmer's houses sprinkled in the tiny valleys between. Close to the base you could see where military vehicles had forged an impromptu road to a cluster of houses, usually with an 'Off Limits' sign marking the consequence, but farther from the base these tentacles of military contagion grew less.

The shuttle bus arrived and he labored to get himself and his shopping bag over the tailgate before the five ton truck roared ahead, spilling the bag, the contents of which rolled across the metal floor. An Australian soldier picked up a package of toilet paper and handed it back to Max, saying, "Oiii, Yank, setting up housekeeping in Seoul, are yeh?" Max retrieved the package and silently started stuffing the fallen items into the bag, his thoughts dwelling on the dream in which Sook Cha lured the Aussie Captain to her house. The soldier assumed Maxs' silence indicated he had taken offense. He added in an apologetic tone, "No offense,

Mate. Just thought how lucky you are to have a friendly place off base to wipe your bottom. Wish I were so lucky."

Max smiled at him. "No offense taken, Mate." He mimicked the Australian's accent pronouncing it 'might.' "If you're going to Seoul, I'm sure you'll find a friendly place where your bottom will be well treated." Two Turkish soldiers sat between Max and the Australian, one interpreting the conversation to the other who began to snicker as his eyes darted back and forth between the two men.

About halfway to Seoul, an old farmer was attempting to repair a wooden wheel on his ox cart which blocked the road. The military driver braked too hard and the five ton truck skidded sideways and down the embankment at the side of the road, becoming hopelessly mired in the yellow muddy ditch at the bottom of the embankment. Everyone clambered out of the truck and up on the road in hopes of flagging a ride from some vehicle that might return to Seoul or their original military base because of the road block.

Max sat at the side of the road viewing the patchwork quilt of rice paddies that carpeted this valley between two mountain ranges. About a mile from the side of the road he saw a small hill surrounded by rice paddies, a small cluster of adobe type structures dotting its leveled top, and a narrow road, too narrow for a big truck, connecting it to the main road with a small half moon bridge halfway to allow irrigation of the paddies. It was still early enough in the morning for patches of fog to drift down from the mountains and hover over the paddies surrounding the little hill.

Max thought that, despite the geometric pattern of the rice paddies, the cluster of houses on the little hill resembled a mediaeval castle in Scotland surrounded by an immense moat. He imagined the Loch Ness Monster raising its dragon like head above the misty waters of the paddies. But no monster appeared. It was a totally peaceful scene, hidden away from the military, inaccessible to most of their vehicles, without a sign of any kind in sight, particularly no 'Off Limits' signs.

From the other side of the ox cart he heard the Aussie, "Aye, Mate (might). Hurry ('urray) up. We're off to Seoul, we are!" Max gathered his shopping bag and tried to get around the ox cart, arriving just in time to see an olive green personnel vehicle racing toward Seoul with the Aussie waving out the back window and shrugging his shoulders.

Max turned back to the view he had been watching, then started walking slowly toward the junction where the narrow road to the little hill met the main road. As he descended to the narrow road, he could hear more plainly the sounds of crickets, the guttural communication of frogs, and the occasional bird singing to his friends about all the delicious crickets and frogs that abounded in the rice paddies. As he crossed the little moon bridge, he remembered the calendar picture on Sook Cha's wall and her tales of survival beneath such a bridge.

He began to trudge up the little hill and noticed that the pungent odor of the paddies diminished with the height, and understood why as a breeze was felt at the higher elevation. There were two houses and several smaller farm structures, one certainly a chicken coop as evidenced by the small but colorful chickens that roamed freely. He approached the larger of the two houses first, which appeared to be abandoned, its open door revealing hardwood floors, probably once polished by bare feet, and interior adobe wails smoothly finished and occasionally illuminated with pale Bhuddist paintings reminiscent of American Indian wall drawings. There was a large central room and three smaller rooms. Max felt like Little Red Riding Hood intruding upon the home of Papa Bear, Mama Bear, and Baby Bear.

Behind the large house was a smaller residence and, as he approached it, a boy about seven years old, stick in hand, stepped through the door as if to challenge him. Max greeted him in Korean, "Annyong haseyo!" Then asked, "Pappaasan? Mamasan?"

The boys frown did not change as he replied, "No Mamasan. No josan (No mother. No girl)."

Max read his mind and regretted that, even in this comparative isolation, a five year old knew how to disinterest a GI. Max stood his ground. "Dai jobi, no josan. Me speakee Pappasan. You likee candy?"

The candy softened the boy a little and, when Pappasan arrived, the more mature PX goodies paved the way for business. Pappasan was a GI shy, but genial handsome man around a healthy forty. He invited Max to share tea with them as he answered Max's questions about the land, such as gestures, broken English, and Max's poor Korean vocabulary allowed. Formerly the owner of surrounding lands that were farmed by sharecroppers, Pappasan lost his wife in the war and now tilled the remaining few paddies himself, living alone with his son in the little house, saving the larger house for the wealth and wife its maintenance required.

Max looked around the lonely hill populated by a lonely man and his motherless seven year old son. Max knew what he had to do, but he didn't know how he would be able to pull it off. He asked Pappasan if he would sell the large house to Max, but Pappasan was not inclined to sell. Max then posed some hypothetical questions; how much would the house be worth if he

138

were to sell it (100,000 yen, about $330 American), how much would the lost paddies he wanted to recover cost (20,000 yen for each of the five paddies, about the same as the price for the house). He had seen how Papasan had looked at the paddies he lost when he pointed them out to Max, and he suspected Papasan was weighing his need for the house against his desire to recover his lost farmland. The farmer confessed he would consider selling the house, but, regardless, he would be Max's friend and Max would be welcome to call at any time.

As he left, he gave Papasan the remaining PX goodies in the shopping bag, except for the three gift wrapped packages.

****

As Max exited the jeep that had given him a lift to Yeong Deungpo, he regretted arriving so late at sunset. Although his exile was over and despite the fact that he had the weekend before him, he did not want to walk through the red light district to the railroad tracks at the beginning of its busiest hours. He knew his vision of seeing Sook Cha soliciting as a prostitute had only been a dream, but he also knew how tenuous survival was for those three ladies. Added to that, he knew they knew his days in Korea were numbered.

His heart rose ever higher in his throat the closer he got to the railroad tracks. The 'skivvy josans' on all sides coo'ed and sing songed their fleshy wares, reaching curiously for the shopping bag which he hugged to his chest for protection. Then, his heart stopped as he saw Sook Cha stepping out of a brothel.

She wore her baggy black pants, blue sweater, no makeup, and her hair was hidden beneath a knitted skull cap. She was dressing like a boy again. For a moment,

Max wondered if she were prostituting herself as a boy, as the Madame had once suggested.

Then Sook Cha turned around and gripped one side of a wicker basket, backed further out the brothel door, and Max saw the other side of the basket gripped by Old Mamasan, the basket containing a five gallon size lidded earthen jar which probably contained kimchie, as indicated by the tin ladle that hung on the side of the basket.

They hadn't seen him, and he continued to follow some distance behind them, feeling guilty about stalking them, but not wanting his arrival to be in the midst of this flesh market. He could not turn the corner at the railroad tracks until they entered the alley and, as he peered around the corner into the alley, he saw the red gates closing with the 'Off Limits' sign still posted on it. He walked slowly, taking long deep breaths as he approached the gates. Heaving a big sigh, he rapped sharply on the gates with his knuckles.

There was no response. He knocked again. Old Mamasan's angry voice screamed, "Aniyo, aniyo (No, no)!" Then in broken English, "Go way, go way. No skivvy josan here!" Max felt both regret that his presence had caused the 'Off Limits' sign to be posted as a beacon to drunk Gis looking for a brothel, and relief that the ladies did not appear to have resorted to prostitution.

Max cleared his throat and called out loudly, "Sook Cha?"

The gate opened a crack to reveal Old Mamasan, her ferocious frown melting as she recognized him, opened the gate wider, and stepped to one side to let him enter. He stepped inside and saw Young Mamasan at the far end of the porch kneeling outside her door looking at him in surprise. He looked to the right and saw Sook Cha kneeling beside one of the large kimchie jars, ladle frozen in hand as she stopped transferring kimchie into the lidded earthen jar they had carried. She moved in slow motion, setting the ladle down and removing her skull cap to let her long glossy black hair fall down her back as she rose and moved toward Max, tears streaming down her face.

There was no scream as in the past and in his dream. Just the sound of gulping air because they had both held their breath from the moment they saw each other until their bodies collided. Old Mamasan caught the shopping bag that dropped from Max's hand as he threw his arms around Sook Cha and felt her arms surround him. There was no immediate kiss, just the pressure of their tear stained faces glued check to cheek, and the long sustained crush of their bodies from head to toe. Finally she gulped in air and sobbed out his name, "Maxsan,." the word causing her body to vibrate against his.

He sucked the tear induced drainage back into his sinuses and echoed her name. "Sook Cha." She felt the rumbling bass of his voice pass through every part of her body and a pained smile began to form on her face as she opened and closed her eyes, unwilling to let go of their embrace. He moved his face away and brought one hand up to brush away the strands of hair glued by tears to her temples. He kissed her eyes, her tears tasting salty and, yet, magical, as if he could taste her sincerity, her fidelity, and her love.

She tilted her head back and opened her eyes. In a hoarse whisper, she said, "Maxsan. Take me. Makee lovee. Prease?"

Max picked her up in his arms and, while the other two women remained mute like statues, Max

141

carried Sook Cha into her little room with the bomb hole in ceiling and floor.

****

The 'U' shaped courtyard of the house in Yeong Deungpo started, as you entered the gates, with the privy on the immediate left, then Sook Cha's room, at the end of the 'U' was Old Mamasan's room, at the far end of the right side next to that was Young Mamasan's room, then the roof continued on the right side over an open area devoted to food preparation and dining, and, to the immediate right of the gates, the large kimchie jars buried in the ground with only their earthenware lids showing above the hardwood porch floor. The hardwood porch floor extended completely around the 'U' shaped layout and provided about four feet of depth in front of the rooms and about twelve feet of depth in the kitchen/eating area and for the kimchie jars. Sook Cha's room was about 6'x6', Old Mamasan's about 6'x9', and Young Mamasan's about 9'x9.' The walls were an offwhite plaster over mud bricks, known in Southwest America as 'adobe block,' and the plaster was in ill repair, particularly on the exterior around the double red painted wood gates. The roof was originally curved red clay tile, known in Southwest America as 'Mission Tile,' but had been repaired in some places with tiles of different colors and shapes, and even a few places where metal flashing was improvised from flattened out tin cans.

All in all, from the exterior, the house gave the appearance of a Hacienda in Mexico, except that it was butted on both sides by similar houses forming one continuous residential complex along a secondary alley only wide enough for foot traffic and handcarts. Space was at a premium in all of Korea, be it living space in crowded cities like Seoul and its suburbs like Yeong Deungpo, or be it arable land for farming, which included even the terraced hillsides with rice paddies at the valley floor and earthen crops on the rising terraces.

In the kitchen/dining area of the house, food was cooked over cast iron braziers set on large adobe blocks topped with large red kiln fired tiles, an arrangement that protected the wooden floor and raised everything to a convenient height for the kneeling cook along the outside wall. These same braziers provided rather inefficient heating for the living areas in cold weather, and dangerous when some people placed them under their sleeping blanket in an effort to retain the heat.

Dining was at a twelve inch high four foot square table around which the family of four sat cross legged, usually with Old Mamasan hobbling between brazier and table on her knees. As Max exited Sook Cha's room the next morning, he saw the other two women already seated at the table eating their morning meal of rice and hot tea.. Max began to regret that he had given Pappasan the coffee from his bag of PX goodies, the bag with the remaining gift wrapped items now sitting beside his place at the table. As he joined them, Old Mamasan set a small bowl of hot rice and a cup of hot tea before him, then a lidded bowl of kimchie in the middle of the table knowing he would probably not add it to his rice.

Young Mamasan was the first to speak, "Nedsan speakee you takee 'moki' (sore throat), ne (yes or is that so)?" Max smiled and nodded assent. She continued, "Maxsan now 'dai jobi' (Japanese cognate for okay)?"

Max negotiated a clump of rice into his mouth with the chopsticks. "Ne, dai jobi."

Young Mamasan maneuvered her rice faster and more skillfully. "Long time moki, ne?"

Max stopped eating and stared her. Old Mamasan eyes darted furtively between the two as each spoke. During this brief silence, she averted her eyes to her food., pouring the remainder of her tea into the remainder of the rice in her bowl and noisily slurping it from the bowl shoveling the rice with her chopsticks into her mouth, as is she was trying to make a distraction in their conversation.

Max took a deep breath, "Didn't Ned tell you.....?" Max hesitated, looked down at his half eaten rice, then back at Young Mamasan. "Ned speakee you, me Honcho (boss) speakee me, 'No leave base thirty 'deo' (days)!'" Max flashed ten fingers three times, then continued, "Honcho speakee, 'No go Yeong Deungpo!' He speakee, MP catchee me Yeong Deungpo, Honcho put me in jail!" And he emphasized 'jail' by crossing his wrists and shaking them as if he were handcuffed.

Young Mamasan listened intently, her chopsticks frozen halfway to her mouth, little grains of rice falling from them back into her bowl. She set the chopsticks down, looked down, then back up at Max impassively, tilting her head to one side. "Ned no speakee Honcho, no speakee MP." She shrugged her shoulders, raised her hands palms up, and raised her eyebrows inquisitively. "Ned no speakee dai jobi. Ned speakee drunkee drunkee."

Maxs' irritation subsided as he nodded assent, realizing Ned had not adequately communicated Maxs' situation. Then he asked, "Ned bring twenty-five dollar each weekend, ne?"

Young Mamasan smiled broadly. "Ne, every week, twenny dollar, five dollar, he gib Sook Cha," and

144

she slapped one hand into the other palm twice, as if receiving the bills. Then she lowered her head and furrowed her brow. "Twoo, MP catchee, you go hoosegow?"

Ned laughed, wondering where she had picked up American slang for jail. "True, true!"

Sook Cha approached and sat down, "What twoo?" Young Mamasan excitedly explained in Korean all that Ned had failed to communicate, Sook Cha's eyebrows rising higher and higher. Sook Cha took Max's free hand and held it in both of hers, looked at him sadly and said, "Mianhamnida (I am sorry), Nedsan no speakee you hab bad Honcho, you go hoosegow. Him speakee beero beero, go catchee skivvy josan."

Young Mamasan took a deep breath, looked straight at Max, and said, "Ne, Maxsan. Mianhamnida. I vewy sowey."

Max added his other hand to Sook Cha's, looked from one woman to the other, and said, "No sweat."

Young Mamasan looked at them slyly, then said, "Sook Cha vewy sad. She no like mebbe you catchee good time wit noose wit wed hair." Sook Cha frowned at her, broke her hands free of Max, and threw her china spoon at Young Mamasan in playful anger while Old Mamasan cackled with laughter.

Max shook his head negatively. "No worry. Red head nurse no good time, only very bad time, believe me," and he leaned over to hug Sook Cha who buried her face in his chest, embarrassed.

Then Sook Cha sat erect, poured herself a cup of tea, and said, "Young Mamasan speakee you catch good time wit noose wit wed hair. No me. Old Mamasan, she speakee you hab stateside wife, she come beat you up, speakee you no more see Sook Cha." She set her teacup down and looked him in the eye. "I know you

145

hab bad time, some'sin hoppon. I know you good mon, you come back to Sook Cha."

Max leaned over, held her face in one hand, and kissed her lips, ending the kiss with a noisy 'smack,' saying, "And you were right!" Then he opened the shopping bag and removed the first gift, handing it to Old Mamasan. She opened it with care to save the brightly patterned gift wrapping paper, her wide toothless smile changing to confusion as she lifted the box lid off a matched set of stainless steel kitchen knives with hardwood handles. She frowned at Max, then looked questioningly at Young Mamasan and said something in Korean.

Young Mamasan suppressed a giggle and replied in Korean, which made Old Mamasan's expression change from confusion to disbelief as she looked back at the knives. Young Mamasan said to Max, "Mamasan speakee, 'Why gib stab stab, Mamasan no soljer.' I speakee, 'No stab stab, go chop chop, makee kimchie.'"

With one hand Max plucked a large parsnip from the kimchie and with the other he took the French chefs knife from the boxed collection and proceeded to expertly slice it into thin discs on the wooden trivet beneath the kimchie bowl. "I know you do magical things with that battered old Chinese meat cleaver, but, believe me, you can do a lot more things with this set of knives."

No one understood what he said, but Old Mamasan took the knife from him, playfully poised it to stab him, then returned it to the box where it would remain for weeks before she condescended to employ them in her daily routine.

Max handed the next box to Young Mamasan who opened it eagerly, Old Mamasan helping her salvage the wrapping paper which began to tear in her haste. Inside the box were a set of different sized embroidery rings, needles, and a variety of colored threads and bottles of colored Indian beads. The instruction book was in English, but it didn't matter and the patterns in it were all Young Mamasan needed. Her mouth opened and her eyes lit up as she opened the box, taking a hank of bright red embroidery thread out, she rubbed its softness against her cheek, her eyes closing. Then she returned the thread and removed a bottle of gold beads, shaking it near her ear and smiling delightedly at the trio before her. She set the box down, placed both hands on the middle of the table, leaned across the kimchie bowl, and, after looking sideways at Sook Cha for permission, kissed Max on the forehead three times rapidly, emitting a shrill cry like a banshee. She calmed down as she sat again, wrinkled her nose, and said with a smile, "I likee! Kamsa hamnida (thank you), Maxsan."

Sook Cha's box was the biggest, providing a wealth of wrapping paper for Old Mamasan to carefully fold and salvage. As the box lid came off and the white tissue paper was folded aside, Sook Chas face registered amazement as she beheld the white dress so like the one in the magazine picture on her wall. No one would recognize it as a nurses uniform after Max had taken it to the off base seamstress whose daily chore of shortening mens pants cuffs and sewing stripe patches on sleeves was challenged by his project. He had made a drawing traced from the magazine picture on Sook Cha's wall and he had instructed the seamstress in how to make pleats and sew a scallop around the neck, showing her where to salvage extra material from the skirt hem and the epaulets that had to be removed from the shoulder tops. Max found the white thigh high stockings at the PX which stocked them for nurses, and, from somewhere, Guido had found a pair of women's white high heeled shoes the right size. The PX only stocked nurses white sensible shoes.

Sook Cha lifted each piece up like it was a sacred object, inspected it like it was something from outer space no one had ever seen before, while the other two women "Ohhhhhhed" and "Awwwwwed." She set the box down and stood before Max, her mouth open and smiling, tears welling in her eyes, then threw her arms around him and whispered, "My white dwess. You lookee lookee. You knew."

Young Mamasan said, "Show Maxsan. Give lookee lookee new dwess," and Old Mamasan echoed the same sentiments in Korean. Sook Cha sniffled back her tears, gathered the box of gifts, and retreated to her room. Soon she reappeared looking radiant in her new white dress, stockings, and high heels that she had never worn before. She took hesitant steps onto the porch in front of her room, decided not to risk attempting the one foot step down to the courtyard, and paraded slowly around the 'U' shape of the porch to reach the dining table, making each step carefully like a centenarian in a nursing home who lost their walker, her arms held out at her sides for balance. She reached down and removed the shoes before sitting beside Max, tapping the shoes on his chest and saying, "We go opera, me wear slipper, carrying white shoe for inside opera, ne?"

Max responded, "Ne," and kissed the top of her head.

****

That night, as Sook Cha removed her tee shirt and black pants before getting in bed, she asked,

148

"Maxsan, you like me catchee white dress, you fuckee movie star girl?"

Max lay on the cot and pulled her legs closer to him, caressing the backs of her calves and thighs. "Just the white stockings."

Sook Cha half heartedly tried to stop his roving hands, swooning as they traveled over the backs of her knees. "Just stockings? Too cold. You tear."

Max kissed the inside of her thighs. "Dai jobi. I brought you two extra pair, and I'll keep you warm. I promise."

Sook Cha sat on the edge of the bed and began to don her stockings. "You bad boy. Fuckee movie star girl in just stocking. Movie star girl catchee cold, you fault!"

****

Monday morning, as Max exited Sook Cha's room and headed for the alley where the exodus of GIs sounded like cattle being herded toward the shuttle buses at the main road junction, Young Mamasan stopped him. "Maxsan, Old Mamasan need....need....," then she made a sawing motion. Max looked puzzled, so she tried again. "Mamasan need, chop chop wood."

Max took a guess. "Don't worry, I'll teach her how to use the kitchen knives."

Young Mamasan pulled on his sleeve to detain him. "No chop chop food, chop chop wood," and she made more sawing motions.

Max nodded affirmatively. "A wood saw. Dai jobi, I'll see what I can do."

Just then Old Mamasan came through the gate, slammed it closed, and bolted it. "MP in alley. Catchee tauksan GI."

149

Young Mamasan pulled Max away from the gate. "No can go, Maxsan. MP catchee, go hoosegow."

Max threw up his hands. "I have to. If I'm the least bit late for work, Conweb will restrict me again."

Sook Cha had exited her room, putting on her blue sweater on top of her black pants as she listened to the conversation. Both she and Old Mamasan went to the privy and came out with a rickety old ladder, its three inch diameter dried up rungs tied with old packing cord to the three inch diameter eight foot long stiles. They placed it against the rear tile roof and gestured for Max to mount it. Sook Cha spoke in a loud stage whisper, as if the MPs outside might hear her, "You go over two, three house, lookee lookee, no MP, you run chop chop to shuttle bus."

Max reluctantly mounted the ladder. The second rung broke beneath his weight. He clung to the sides and continued gingerly, testing each rung before he reached the tiled roof. The tiles were difficult to negotiate insasmuch as they were not all properly secured, some were cracked and broke under his weight, the pieces sliding down and narrowly missing the women on the ground. From the rooftop, he could see the white helmets of the MPs as they escorted Off Limits violators to a waiting personnel carrier. Max slid on his belly across two more rooftops until he reached another alley where there was no foot traffic. He dropped feet first the ten feet to the hard ground, twisting his ankle as he landed. He hobbled the half mile to the shuttle bus and thanked the two British soldiers who pulled him over the tailgate, which he could never have made without their help.

****

150

When Max visited the house a few days later, his Ace bandaged ankle was back to normal and he brought with him the wood saw Old Mamasan had requested and a topographical map of the area that included Kimpo and Seoul. The map was labeled in English, which complicated his efforts to show them where Papasan's hilltop house was located, but Sook Cha figured it out and concluded that she had never traversed that area because it had been occupied by North Koreans prior to their arrival at Yeong Deungpo.

The three ladies sat around the table with confused frowns as he tried to describe the two houses atop the hill, touting the virtues of a less crowded more serene environment free of lusting service men, black marketeers, and which provided a plentiful food supply. Reluctantly prefacing his next statements with the probability that, when he left Korea in the coming months, Max would have to serve two more years stateside before leaving the service, Max proposed that he purchase the big house on the hill for Sook Cha and that the other two ladies join her there.

The suggestion of such a gift did not meet entirely with smiles. To Sook Cha, leaving the city meant the loss of such luxuries as the operetta, and entering the country was a re-association with her war experiences. To Young Marnmasan, leaving her house was a loss of prestiege and entering a house that would belong to Sook Cha was, in a way, a loss of security. Old Mamasan liked the idea, but would obviously defer to the two younger stronger members of the household.

Max was puzzled how they could be so thrilled and grateful to receive the relatively inexpensive gifts he had brought them, yet hesitate and frown over the prospect of this gift costing hundreds of dollars which he didn't even know if he would be able to raise. He

151

finally wrested a promise from them that, if he could commandeer a jeep, they would at least visit Papasan's farm and look at the house.

That night, as Sook Cha undressed for bed, she looked down at Max's frowning face as he lay on the cot. "Maxsan, you like me catchee movie star stocking, you fuckee movie star girl?"

Max smiled and pulled her nude torso down on top of him. "Not tonight. Tonight I makee lovee to tauksan stecky Korean josan. I love her so much I'm willing to buy her a house that she doesn't even know if she wants." He buried his face between her small breasts and kissed a trail from one nipple to the other, eliciting squeals and giggles that echoed through the house in Yeong Deungpo.

Chapter Nine
THE MOTHER OF INVENTION

When Max had suggested a photo story around the U.N. buildings in downtown Seoul, emphasizing that they would have no contact with U.N. personnel or photo 'ops' for Conweb to strut his stuff, Conweb insisted Ned accompany Max in the jeep as an older higher ranking (Corporal) more responsible party who could monitor Max and keep him out of trouble. Max spent half his weekly income to park Ned in a brothel with some drinking money while Max chauffeured the ladies to Papasan's farm, planning to return to the office with a U.N. picture layout he had previously shot of which Conweb knew nothing.

It had been a pleasant enough outing. The handsome farmer had been extremely gracious and, even if Young Mamasan had not been softened by his obvious attraction to her, her comical aggressiveness toward him was a clue to some rare responsiveness in her. Sook Cha had been awed by the potential security and respectability owning such a house might provide, and Old Mamasan's eyes lit up at the prospect of farming so much land. All the women had enjoyed the interaction between Papasan and his son with Young Mamasan's baby boy. The PX canned goods and packaged snack foods Max brought provided a rare picnic lunch for everyone.

The return trip, however, had been made in silence. Max made sure Ned was sober enough to drive before having him return to the base alone with the warning to avoid Conweb until the next day. Then Max and the ladies sat down to a somber evening meal. Max's attempt to query them on their thoughts about moving to the hillside house ignited an eruption of mixed feelings.

Young Mamasan led with ridiculous and totally irrational arguments, the others following in the wake of her contrariness. She thoroughly annoyed Max by finally painting the farmer as a lecherous old sex fiend she would not want to be exposed to.

Max sulked as he changed into his house robe and wouldn't touch the tea they proffered him nor aid their awkward attempts at conversation to fill the silence Young Mamasan's outburst had provoked. Max was successfully subduing his exasperation until Young Mamasan herself lost control and blew the lid off.

After Max declined her second offer of tea, she banged the fragile cup down in front of Sook Cha and blurted angrily, "You go live farm house with husband. Me stay here. Him likee watch farmersan catehee me, make lovey, make work like farm josan. Nevah happen. Me like big house, Yeong Deungpo. Plenty people, plenty store, plenty opera."

Then Max exploded, gesturing toward the subjects of his discussion like an orator. "Sure, plenty of flies, plenty of mud for babysan to play in, plenty of people like skivvy josans and black marketeers. Tell me there's as much food here as there is in the country, that it's as clean here and that you couldn't go to the opera if you lived in the country. Tell me about your big beautiful house here with bomb holes in it, a house that shakes every time a train goes by and looks out on skivvy houses on all four sides. Does it make your baby healthy, does it make you that happy? Do you think you would be unsafe living in a house I bought Sook Cha in the country? Do you think I want you to move only so

154

that Sook Cha would follow? Do you think that it is an easy thing for me to do to buy that house, or that I will be here forever to make such an offer? You don't think at all. The muscle of your quick tongue is so big it leaves no room for brains in your pretty head. Stay here in your big house and live with the Jee."

Young Mamasan was trembling with anger. Sook Cha was trembling with tears at the sight of the two people she loved fighting. Old Mamasan sat by the brazier with a smile disguising the premeditation of her wrinkled hand that toyed with the poker in the coals, ready to subdue Max with it if he became violent.

Max waited for Young Mamasan's retort, hoping she would give him the provocation to slap her senseless, and Old Mamasan too if she made one false move with that bent yellow hot poker. Young Mamasan had not comprehended all of Max's tirade, only enough to be infuriated. Her ivory complection turned as ruddy as Sook Cha's and she emitted a long low hiss through her clenched teeth which might, in another tone of voice, have been meant complimentary, but, at the moment, it had every connotation of a healthy American obscene curse.

Still frustrated by the desire to slap her across the courtyard, Max turned abruptly towards Sook Chas's room, seeing Sook Cha out of the corner of his eye rise and look from Young Mamasan to him with indecision as to whom to console. Max jerked the sliding door shut behind him so viciously that it came out of its runners and, before he could wrestle it back into place, he heard Sook Cha's sing song voice call, "Maxsan," through her tears. Not knowing, but thinking to himself that she had waited for a nod from Young Mamasan before turning to him, he kicked the door into place and refused to open it or answer her husky pleading voice. "Maxsan,

155

prease, Maxsan," until her hoarse whispers faded into silence.

After what seemed like hours of silence, Max changed into his uniform with the simple intent of going out to get something to eat. He slid the door back, noticing that he had cracked the frame slightly with his last kick, and found Sook Cha curled quietly like a kitten on the porch in front of the room.

With the same questioning curiosity of a kitten, her open eyes traveled up his uniform with growing alarm while her lean body, now clothed in a thin house robe that could hardly protect her from the coldness of the night, rose to a kneeling position. By the time her eyes met his, her brows were knit in unrestrained fear, her body leaned forward and her arms embraced his thighs tightly. She sobbed into the wooly frabric of his uniform, "Maxsan, no go, Maxsan. No go now. Tomorrow I go with you, I leave Mamasan. Maxsan, no go without me."

The darkened courtyard bore no light from Young Mamasan's room. Sook Cha's sobs woke Old Mamasan from her squatting sleep before the now cold brazier. The old woman's sleepy eyes recognized Max with a frown, the savage American who was the cause of her poker in hand vigil and who would soon be pacified by a girl who had lowered herself to crawl to him. Old Mamasan yawned, she was too learned and wise to be moved in any way by the little drama before her and, accordingly, shuffled off on all fours into her little cubicle, sliding the door shut matter of factly.

Max lifted Sook Cha into his embrace, guided her into her room and gingerly slid the door shut, guiltily noticing it had begun to disintegrate from the crack. He sat her on his lap and rocked her in his arms like a child. She kept repeating the same lines over and

156

over until he touched her lips with his finger and said, "Shhhh. I'm not going, so you don't have to lie to make me stay."

Her brows knitted until her mind translated 'lie,.' then she blurted, "No, Maxsan, no speakee lie. You want go country house, me go, too. Me leave Mamasan."

"But I don't want you to leave Mamasan. You are good for each other, and the country is good for all of you, and I want you all to go."

Sook Cha pushed Max down on the bed and stood up, saying, "I go speak Mamasan."

Max pulled her down onto the narrow cot and smothered her protests with a kiss. "No, I'll speak to Mamasan some other time, but dont you get into the argument."

She put her small hands at the top of his shirt front and, her brows curling into a question mark, she queried, "And you no leave?"

Max kissed the tip of her nose and replied, "I no leave."

Her eyes closed, her mouth came up and caught his lip in her teeth, her brow moved ever so slightly into something very pleasant to see, and her hands quickly and quietly unbuttoned his shirt.

**********.

Lieutenant Conweb was so pleased with Max's UN picture story, Max pitched another location story about Korean farmers using U.S. supplied farming equipment to revitalize their industry. Max talked Conweb out of visiting the locations with him by explaining he would need hip boots to traverse the rice paddies that smelled of human fertilizer. The Lieutenant

157

settled for shots of himself handing farm tools to a make believe grateful Korean farmer who was actually a Korean civilian that worked in the base laundry. For the location shots, however, Conweb still required Ned to chaperone Max and 'keep him out of trouble.'

Once again, Max paid to park Ned in a brothel with a drinking allowance, then used the personnel carrier to take Sook Cha on another visit to Papasan's farm. The larger vehicle was needed to carry the farm supplies. These included a huge compost bin, which required assembly, and sacks of chemicals with instructions printed on the side which Max had to read and interpret to Papasan. These items were an effort by the UN to wean Korean farmers away from the use of nightsoil and its attendant health risks by introducing them to a combination of ancient composting techniques and the modern chemicals that could accelerate the process. Papasan was delighted to receive farm tools and supplies in exchange for posing for pictures, and Max shot enough beautiful scenic photos that day to illustrate a number of subsequent picture stories.

He also fulfilled his promise to Sook Cha to tutor her in the use of firearms. Max brought a .45 Colt automatic pistol like the one she acquired from the North Korean soldier, a Webley .455 revolver he borrowed from one of the Aussies, and both Maxs' own semi automatic M1 standard issue carbine and a bolt action Mauser Ned had come by in his many years in the military. At Papasan's remote location it was possible to set up a safe firing range that would not draw any attention. Max drew targets on the empty cardboard boxes in which the farm materials had been transported, then demonstrated and tutored Sook Cha in the use of each type of firearm.

Initially, Sook Cha was under obvious emotional stress in handling, mastering, and firing the 45 caliber automatic pistol, the same model of weapon she had desperately tried to fire and accidentally succeeded in firing into the temple of her rapist. Despite her hands that shook at first, the sweat and reddening of her face that revealed her discomfort, and the tears that filled her eyes as she finally managed to pull the trigger, the moment the deafening roar of the shot subsided and her arm and shoulder recovered from the recoil, she turned to face Max and she was smiling through her tears. She offered to return the pistol to Max, but he said, "No, try again. You didn't even hit the target. Keep trying until you at least get one within the biggest circle." As she lifted and repeatedly fired the weapon, he photographed her.

As Max showed her how to load each weapon, deal with the various safeguards built into them, and handle and fire them safely, Papasan watched with keen interest and obvious approval, recognizing that Max was teaching Sook Cha to defend herself. By the end of the day, Papasan showed a newfound respect for Sook Cha and a deepened rapport with Max. He announced that, if Max still wanted to buy the house, Papasan was willing to sell.

****

After they had sent Ned back to the base in the personnel carrier, Max and Sook Cha walked through the gates of the house in Yeong Deungpo. Despite the fact that the other two women had declined to visit Papasan's farm, they were seated on the porch with a dinner all prepared and welcoming smiles on their faces. As they all sat down to dinner, Young Mamasan spoke

159

to Sook Cha in rapid Korean with a conspiratorial smile on her face, then the three women jabbered between each other, all in Korean, all with gleeful smiles. When Max inquired, "What's up? What are you three up to?"

Their only answer was repressed giggles and Young Mamasan's cryptic explanation, "After dinna, Old Mamasan show you why she need chop chop saw," followed by more giggling.

The conversation over dinner was mostly devoted to Sook Chas' narration of her target practice which, because it was accompanied with bits of pantomime and "boom boom" sound effects, Max could follow with little or no translation. He was aware, however, that the other two women looked at him with growing approval, sometimes nodding affirmatively at both the description of the farm implements given the farmer, and the description of Sook Chas' firearm training.

The only time Young Mamasan appeared to slightly frown was when Sook Cha described how Max made her pose as the farmers' wife in some of the pictures. The little Max understood of Young Mamasan's response was her reference to "skoshi josan (little girl)," "nohng boo (farmer)," and "Nuuhl guuhn (old person)." Could it be that she was jealous that Sook Cha had posed as the farmers' wife? Yet, Max was certain, if Young Mamasan had gone with them, she would have objected to being asked to pose as the farmer's wife.

After dinner, Old Mamasan went and ceremoniously sat by the cooking brazier which had uncommonly been placed on one side of a tatami mat a short distance from the low dining table. Young Mamasan stood and formerly bowed to Max. Then Sook Cha looked at Max, as he finished his cup of tea, and said, "Mamasan speakee you skoshi opera. Me speakee you for her." Whereupon Young Mamasan began a dramatic recitation in Korean, pausing after each sentence for Sook Cha to translate. "Mamasan speakee, mebbe...," Sook Cha paused and rolled her eyes skyward as she searched for the English words, "What if MP come 'bang bang' on gate?" The 'bang bang' was emphasized with increased volume and dramatic guttural pronunciation, then immediately repeated by Young Mamasan who demonstrated by striking the air with an imaginary baseball bat impersonating MPs battering the outside of the gates. She stopped and looked into space above Max's head, as if there were a greater audience seated behind him, and delivered the next line of her recitation.

Sook Cha continued the translation, beginning to adopt the dramatic spirit of Young Mamasan's performance, "MP crash through gate, lookee here, lookee there, lookee all round." Young Mamasan danced around Old Mamasan, stopping at all four sides of the tatami mat to look away from her toward the walls and courtyard, finally stopping to face Max and deliver her next line. Sook Cha translated in similar dramatic tones, "MP lookee for GI, lookee ebery where, but no find GI."

Young Mamasan extends both arms with upturned palms and looks skyward with closed eyes, letting out a plaintive wail, "Eeeiiiiyeeee," before delivering her next line. Dropping her arms to her sides and looking down dejectedly, she takes ten solemn steps towards the gate, as if in a funeral procession, then turns and closes the imaginary gates in front of her, then turns again away from her audience, kneels, and bends her body down into a ball.

Sook Cha stirs herself from her hypnotic appreciation of Young Mamasan's performance, then translates, "MP tauksan mad, no can find GI. MP sad, lose face, go out gate, go far away, neber come back Young Mamasan's house."

Suddenly Young Mamasan jumps up and faces her audience with outstretched hands and an elated smile. This time her, "Eeeiiiyeeee," is a happy sound. As she delivers her next line, she advances toward Old Mamasan, her hands gesturing toward her with each step, she dances around her, stopping and facing her at each of the four sides of the tatami. Now the placid old woman appears to wake up and gives Young Mamasan a mischievous smile each time she stops in her dance.

Sook Cha smiles and her voice reflects her happiness as she translates, "Old Mamasan trick MP. Old Mamasan no let catchee GI. Old Mamasan and chop chop saw outsmart MP!"

At this point, Old Mamasan rises and, together with Young Mamasan, they set the brazier to one side, pull back the tatami, open a barely discernible two foot square trapdoor in the floor, and pull out the geisha doll that normally resides in a glass enclosure on Young Mamasan's makeup table. Holding the doll high, Young Mamasan triumphantly announces, "GI okay! MP no catchee! Eeeiiiyeeee!"

Maxs' jaw dropped. He rolled onto all fours and crawled over to the trap door, admiring the precision with which Old Mamasan had constructed it down to the brass hinges which he suspected came from some piece of Young Mamasan's furniture. With admiration in his voice he exclaimed, "Son of a bitch! You are some clever sneaky broads."

The smiling women knelt around him as Sook Cha asked, "You likee, Maxsan?"

162

Max noted that the porch joists held the floor barely ten inches above the ground, and the hole they had dug was probably not quite big enough for him to squeeze into, but reasoned he could easily excavate it to a more realistic size. Max smiled up at them, "I likee tauksan." Then he slid over to Old Mamasan, hugged her to him and kissed her forehead. "Domo arigato, Mamasan, arigato, arigato." Whereupon the old woman reached for the brazier poker and, jokingly, raised it over her head as he backed away in mock fear amid everyone's laughter.

****

Max was paid twenty-five dollars a week for his piano bar job at the officer's club, and he was paid thirty dollars a month Air Force salary after his wife's ninety dollar allotment was deducted. If he didn't spend a single cent, it would take four months of his income to raise enough to buy the farmer's house. When he went into the service, his wife had given up their beautiful French Quarter apartment and moved back into her wealthy parent's home. She had given up her high paying job with her father's firm when they were married, but she had returned to it when he went overseas. The little ninety dollar Air Force allotment was really inconsequential to her, but, when Max asked her to waive it, she refused. Max's personal belongings, his grand piano and car and jewelry, were now in his wife's possession and, despite his request, she refused to sell them for him or give up her possession of them.

As Max entered the supply tent, Guido was busy stacking boxes that made a rattling sound like a tambourine. As Guido stretched his petite torso to place a box on the top of the stack, it fell and broke open to reveal a large quantity of gleaming silver empty tin cans with no tops, sounding like a bunch of drummer's cymbals as they rolled in every direction. Guido cursed in Italian, and Max thought it might not be the best time to do business with him.

Max tried to make small talk to lighten Guido's mood. "So, what's with all the cans? Are you really the heiress to the Campbell Soup fortune?"

Guido tossed the cans helter skelter into the open box, then kicked the remainder into the corner. "I wish. Just some overflow from food service. Some genius at Headquarters in Japan decided we should can local fresh foods so they don't have to airlift so damn much to us."

Max set the box he carried on the counter. "Sounds logical."

Guido started to pat the box Max set down, eyeing it curiously. "Yeah, but, so far, none of the local stuff passes health inspections." He picked up the box and shook it. "So what's in the box. Did you bring me your balls again, Honey?"

Max frowned and smiled simultaneously. "Noooooo. However, once again I need money so..."

Guido shook his shoulders side to side impatiently. "Don't we all. Okay, so what did you bring me, Honey?"

Max started to open the box. "All my worldly possessions."

Guido finished opening the box for Max and began to remove a few pieces of jewelry, clothing, and a small 35mm rangefinder camera. Guido looked up at Max sadly. "Such a small world, Max, a small poverty stricken world you live in."

Max glumly started to return the items to the box. "Yeah, I guess so. But I still need money. Any ideas?"

Guido outlined a number of distasteful options. Max could prostitute himself to rich gays in the military, mostly commissioned officers. He could exploit his access to photographic equipment and supplies by dealing on the black market. And, the one that surprised Guido the most when Max declined, he could employ his photographic talents and become a pornographer with both a military and civilian market. Guido frowned at Max. "Well, Mary, I just don't know what to do with you. For a maverick who manages to get himself in hot water all the time, you've turned out to be a boring goody two shoes. It's not as if there is a legitimate market for your chosen profession, photo journalist, given the circumstances you're in."

Guido's words rang in Maxs' head as he returned his belongings to his foot locker in his tent. If not these pathetic belongings, what were his assets? His only assets were his talents. In his present situation, the most he could make selling his musical skills was twenty-five dollars a week. The only offer for his photographic talents was pornography. But, in his civilian past, he had sold his photos and journalism for considerable profit. Now, however, his photographic talents were owned by Uncle Sam and dictated by Conweb.

But, what if his photographic talents were once again his own?

Max went to his work office, even though it was after hours and there was no one there. He went through the small bookcase of reference books until he found the English Edition of the Korean phone book. There, in the commercial pages, he found a Western Union office in Seoul and wrote down the address.

Next he went through the filing cabinets of his past work and reviewed all the photo stories he had written and illustrated since he arrived in Korea. All of them had been published, and all of them would constitute plagiarism if he attempted to resell them.

The next weekend, he left the base early and rode the shaky shuttle bus all the way to downtown Seoul. In the Western Union Office, he stood before the little counter filled with yellow tablets of Western Union forms and yellow pencils and, tapping the pencil against the tablet in frustration, tried to think of what he would write. He didn't even have an exact address for the gossip columnist, but would have to gamble that, if he wired him at the newspaper office, it would get to him.

In his mind he again reviewed all the picture stories he had seen in the file cabinets the night before. What subject had he not already covered that was acceptable for military dissemination? Wait! Who said it had to acceptable to the military?

Max began to scribble furiously, ending his message with the question, "Will you agree to be my beard?" He sent the message with the Seoul Western Union Office 'will call' as a return address.

From Seoul he went to Yeong Deungpo, carrying his little 35mm camera that Guido had felt was worth nothing. He began taking candid pictures surreptitiously from the moment he got off the shuttle bus. The duck carcasses hanging in the shop window, the beggar children that surrounded him, the closed doors of the bordellos which occasionally opened to tradesmen delivering food and drink for the evening trade. As he approached the red gates of the ladies home, he photographed the stenciled 'Off Limits' sign on the outside wall.

That evening he was in good spirits and, at the dinner table, encouraged the ladies to tell him stories about Yeong Deungpo, the changes from pre-war to

166

post-war days, the daily routines and struggles for employment, even anecdotes about the skivvy houses.

Sook Cha told him about how the prostitutes studied American magazines in order to learn how to appeal to the GIs. One girl dyed her hair red and renamed herself Rita Haworth, dressing in what she hoped passed for the black satin dress that actress wore in the movie *Gilda*. Another girl adopted the technique of flattering potential clients by asking each GI with black hair who passed, "Awe you Fwank Sinatta (Frank Sinatra)," and each GI with blonde hair, "Are you "Mawon Bwando (Marlon Brando)?"

Young Mamasan warmed to Maxs' new interest in Korean culture and mimicked the various tradesmen, black marketeers, and bordello madames who provided a wealth of anecdotes; mostly humorous, some dramatic, a few even tragic. As a part time accountant for some of them, she knew too well the disparity of rewards between the businessmen who produced a legitimate and needed product or service, in which she included the bordellos, and black marketeers and gangsters who preyed upon them and did business indiscriminately with North or South Koreans.

Old Mamasan's contribution, despite the awkwardness of translation, was most profound and directly relevant to the questionable status of women's rights in Korea at that time. She had lived through the thirty-five years of Japanese occupation. In 1932 the Japanese established 'comfort women' stations throughout their Asian occupied territories, forcing between 80,000 and 200,000 women from the conquered populations, mostly Korean, to serve as slave prostitutes for the Japanese military. They were treated inhumanely, beaten to death for the slightest infraction, and many committed suicide to escape the horror of

167

servicing dozens of men daily with inadequate food, shelter, or medical treatment.

A married woman in her late thirties living in a remote farming area during the occupation, Old Mamasan still recalled being hidden by her family each time the Japanese forcibly recruited 'comfort women.' The memory that brought tears to her eyes was the day the Japanese found her fifteen year old daughter hiding in the barn and, when her husband tried to stop them, seeing him casually shot to death while soldiers forced her daughter into a truck and drove away without looking back. That was the last she ever saw of her daughter. The memory that staunched her tears was when, at the end of the war, a Japanese soldier tried to rape her and she stabbed him to death with her wooden pitchfork.

****

The next day and during his mid week visit, Max continued taking candid pictures of the persons in the anecdotes and even the nighttime activities in the red light district. He bribed permission to photograph them with the promise of providing free prints to everyone photographed, and explained away having them sign model releases as a means of keeping track of to whom he should deliver the free prints.

Later, when he set down his camera bag in Sook Cha's room and began to place his clothes on it as he disrobed, Sook Cha shut the repaired sliding door and stared at him sullenly. "Why you click clik skivvy Josan? You want catchee good time in skivvy house?"

Max was speechless and his only response was a quizzical frown?

Sook Cha picked up his shirt and threw it at him. Her words were hurt and angry. "Okay, go catchee good time in skivvy house, but no come back here!"

She resisted as he encircled her in his arms and pressed her face to his chest. "Sook Cha, Sook Cha, I don't want any other girl." He turned her face up to his. "I am taking pictures for a story. I don't care romantically about those girls or anyone I photograph. They're simply part of my picture stories."

She brought her hands up to his face as tears welled in her eyes. She didn't understand all that he said, but his embrace and the tone of his voice eased her fears.

He wiped the tears from her eyes with his lips, then kissed her mouth long and tenderly before saying, "I love only you. Sah-rahng tahng-sheen (I love you)."

She gripped his face in her hands as she kissed him forcefully, molding her body to his.

****

In the remaining two days before the next weekend, he went through his picture files in the office, selecting the out takes from previous published stories which he had not actually used, and poring over them to see if they would fit his new story line. Whenever Conweb was not in the office, he set aside his military work and typed furiously on his new project.

Finally, he set out for Seoul on a Saturday morning, arriving at the Western Union office just as they opened. His face dropped when they said there was nothing for him in 'will call,' but his expression of disappointment prompted the clerk to say, "Wait a minute, let me check the 'dead letter' box." The clerk came back with the folded yellow page, explaining,

"This came Tuesday, but we only hold them three days in 'will call.' Lucky you this was held in the 'dead letter' box."

Max almost snatched the paper out of his hand, then remembered to smile and thank him. He tore the page open and read with relief, "Max - Happy to be your 'beard' - Story line sounds great - Will submit for you with pseudonym - If successful, will forward any advance or final payment upon receipt - Take care." His gossip columnist had come through.

Max returned to the base and went straight to Headquarters Building. As Guido had promised, the black Sergeant was working the weekend and sat alone at his desk. He looked up surprised as Max approached him and said, "I need a favor."

The Sergeant smiled, shrugged his shoulders, and said, "You need a pass, you got it."

Max set the thick manilla packet down on the Sergeant's desk. "Not that. I need you to get this into the mail service without going through the censors."

The Sergeant froze. He looked at the packet as if it were a bomb. He even appeared to Max to be a shade lighter. He slowly shook his head side to side. "Unh unh. No can do. This is still a war zone. Censorship still applies, particularly to something that size."

Max raised both hands. "This is totally civilian stuff. Nothing military. I promise."

The Sergeant rolled his eyes. "Then why can't it go through the censors?"

Max clapped his hands together. "Well, Lieutenant Conweb, for one. He would knitpick this to death."

The Sergeant wasn't satisfied. "And for another?"

Max sighed. "And for another, it would probably get shot down by every conservative gung ho asshole in the system."

The Sergeant slammed a desk drawer shut and started to rise. "I'm convinced. Absolutely no can do."

Max put his hands on the Sergeant's shoulders and gently guided him back into his seat. The Sergeant looked wistfully at Max's hands on his shoulders as Max spoke. "Wait. Hear me out. This is nothing more than a magazine story submission to a stateside publication. It contains no reference to any specific U.S. military entity; no numbers, no names, no classified or even unclassified information whatsoever. It's about the Korean people and the aftermath of the war."

With his fingertips, the Sergeant removed Max's hands from his shoulders and spoke in a wavery voice. "I dunno. It's still against regulations. And you're asking me to take your word for all this."

Max picked up the package, tore open the top flap, and pulled the contents out onto the desk. "Here. Read it. See for yourself. If you think it poses any risk to the United States or the U.S. Military, I'll leave you in peace and you can report me to the authorities. But...," here Max's voice spoke with emphasis, "...do me the favor...of reading it before you decide."

The Sergeant looked back and forth between Max's face and the papers in front of him, then picked it up and started to read the following.

SURVIVING THE PEACE

Sook Cha had survived being raped, survived having her body treated as a commodity to be bartered, and survived starvation, but, at wars end, could she survive the peace? Enemy soldiers had been pushed

171

back behind an imaginary line, but soldiers in many different uniforms still occupied her country. Her government was in shambles, its infrastructure was non-existent, and she had no assets other than the clothes on her back, a pistol with which she had shot her rapist, and the will to live. There was no food, there were no jobs, and there was too little rule of law.

The Sergeant read on through all fifteen single spaced typewritten pages, then shuffled through the two dozen black and white photographs, chuckling over the picture of the girl who called herself Rita Hayworth, and almost crying over the photo of an eight year old carrying two honey buckets almost as big as himself on a pole across his shoulders. The Sergeant stacked the pages and pictures together, handed them to Max, then said, "Okay. Reseal them. I'll get them into the mail system without going through the censors." Then he folded his hands on the desk, looked up at Max, and said, "I guess I owe you one."

Chapter Ten
THE G.I. AND THE JEE

Max made weekend pilgrimages to the Western Union Office in Seoul, cautioning the clerks there to hold anything for him in Will Call for at least a week so he'd have time to retrieve it before it was sent back. This added a special burden to his routine, first catching the earliest possible shuttle bus to Seoul, then returning from Seoul to Yeong Deungpo to spend a few hours with the ladies before having to get back to the Officer's Club on the base for his piano gig. He spent more time traveling than he did with the ladies. He couldn't return to Yeong Deungpo until the earliest Sunday morning shuttle bus passed the main gate of the base, and often he was so sleepy he would miss the first or second one.

The third weekend there was a wire saying, "Story arrived - Powerful stuff - I am very impressed - Will begin submissions this week."

The fourth and fifth weekends there was nothing for him at the Western Union Office. Like every creative artist, Max began to doubt his usual confidence in his work, wondering if the gossip columnists praise was mere flattery and viewing the lack of response as possible rejection.

Every other Sunday he would visit the farmer briefly with some token gifts for him and the little boy, then continue on to Yeong Deungpo to be with the ladies.

On his way to the house in Yeong Deungpo, he would deliver the prints he had promised his model subjects, carefully side stepping any offers from the prostitutes to repay him in trade or pose for pornography. He did not even mention his story submission to Sook Cha and Young Mamasan, not wanting to admit to them that his offer to buy the farmer's house was not based on money in the bank, but rather on sheer hope and speculation that somehow something would augment his meager income to make it possible at the last minute

He busied himself excavating the hole beneath the trap door to more readily accommodate his size. He brought more tools and materials to refine the trap door and provide more scope to Old Mamasans' carpentry skills; hammer, chisels, screwdrivers, and various expendables such as sand paper, wood screws, and brass hinges to replace those from Young Mamasans' furniture which had been donated to the trap door project.

He also brought Young Mamasan extra embroidery supplies, larger sheets of sizing to embroider upon, and line drawings he had made from his photographs of Kimpo Village with the mountain behind, and of an American jet fighter plane against a sunset background. He promised her constant replenishment of her embroidery equipment and supplies if she would embroider these drawings for him.

****

Back at the base, Max had a moment of panic when Lieutenant Conweb called him up to his desk and said, with a slight frown, "I heard about that picture story submission."

Max tried desperately to suck air into his lungs. Had the Sergeant ratted him out? He couldn't believe that either the Sergeant or, perhaps, Guido, learning

174

about the picture story from the Sergeant, would betray him. Finally managing to gulp air into his chest, Max barked out, "Sir! What picture story submission, Sir?"

Lieutenant Conwebs' frown deepened, "You know, the U.N. and Korean downtown reconstruction story." Then he smiled and handed Max a copy of the international U.S. military weekly publication. "Thought you might like to know they accepted my story and now your photos will be seen world wide."

Max exhaled slowly and was so relieved he didn't take exception to seeing the Lieutenant's name appearing as a byline on Max's story, or the fact that none of his photos accompanying the story were credited to anyone. He really wanted to remind his boss that Max's past journalism and photos from this office had run in this and other national and international publications even before the Lieutenant had arrived at this base, but usually with Max's byline and photo credits. Instead, Max adopted a pained smile and said, "Thank you, Sir. That's good to know."

The Lieutenant grinned broadly. "Yes, well, you're welcome. Maybe I'll have as much luck with my Korean farm equipment story." There was a pause as he tapped his pencil on the paperwork on his desk, then looked up at Max with questioning raised eyebrows. "Now, do you have any ideas for future stories? If you do, type up a proposal and I'll see if it deserves the ole' Conweb spin and polish. Who knows, might get some more of your pictures immortalized in print."

Max sighed deeply. "Yes Sir. I'll see what I can come up with. Wouldn't want to pass up an opportunity like that."

Lieutenant Conweb looked back down at his paperwork. "Good man. That'll be all. Dismissed."

As Max passed Ned's desk, Ned swivelled in his chair and, with his back to his boss, whispered to Max, "Did you see that byline. Boy! He really gave you the...," and Ned finished his sentence by slapping his right biceps and raising his right fist to Max.

Under his breath, Max replied, "Isn't the first time, wont be the last."

As Max sat down at his desk, Ned rolled his desk chair over to him and said, "I was at the Airmans' Club and that Sergeant from Headquarters, you know, the black one, he was asking about you."

Max busied himself with paperwork. "Yeah, what was he asking?"

Ned looked down at the pencil in his hand and began tapping it against his thigh. "Oh, nothing much. Whether you came there often. I told him you didn't come much since the end of that talent show you put together."

Max didn't look up from his work. "Uh huh."

Ned stopped tapping the pencil and stared at Max. "You know he's a faggot, right?"

Max stopped working on the papers, turned his head sideways to look at Ned, and said, "Yeah, I know he's gay. He offered to do me a favor, and I let him. And, no! I didn't fuck him, not in any way, shape, or fashion."

Ned looked skyward and flipped his hands up so fast the pencil flew back to his desk. "No, of course not. I didn't mean..., that is, I just thought you should know. And you do!" Then Ned rolled his chair hastily back to his desk.

****

Max picked up his mail during lunchtime at the Squadron Orderly Room and sat on his cot in his tent. There was nothing from the gossip columnist, although he had requested they correspond through Western Union as the mail could take three weeks going through processing and traveling across the Pacific. There was a letter from a New Orleans lawyer, and Maxs' guess proved accurate as he opened it to find divorce papers from his wife. He felt strangely detached as he read the words "irreconcilable differences," thinking to himself how appropriate those words were in this case. There had been romantic love, and there had certainly been a lot of genuine lust. Their origins had been compatible enough to satisfy her parents. But there were indeed profound differences in the purpose of their union; to raise a family within the confines of a social and religious framework, or to raise children to be independent thinkers and chose their own destiny.

Whether it was the culmination of Lieutenant Conweb's plagiarism and the divorce papers all in one day, or the realization that his marriage was officially and finally over, Max began to feel a lump in his throat. He began to view the dissolution of his marriage as news of the death of a friend who had suffered a long lingering illness. It was no surprise, it had been expected, but now it was a reality, and whatever joys had been shared there would be shared no more. His eyes burned, and he expected tears to fall from them, but the tears never came.

On the way back to work, he stopped at the Provost Marshall's Office and had his signature notarized on the divorce papers. Back at his work office, he typed out a return envelope to his wife and inserted the notarized papers. Then he took one of his Public Information Office business cards with his name on it over the title 'Correspondent' and wrote on the back, "Now you are free." Inserting the business card in the envelope with the divorce papers, he sealed it and threw it in the 'Outgoing Mail' bin on his desk.

At the piano bar that evening, Max found himself playing sad songs of past love. While one of his loyal fans, a buxom middle aged nurse, watched him with adoring eyes, he sang one of the few songs he knew in French, *Les Feuilles Mortes (Autumn Leaves)*. As he sang the last lines of the song in French, "et la mer efface sur le sable, les peds des amants des unis (and the sea erases on the sands, the footsteps of parted lovers)," both he and the nurse had tears streaming down their faces.

The red headed nurse walked over to the piano bar and banged her highball glass down loudly, demanding, "Hey! What's this shit? You're bringing the whole place down. How about something lively like *Twelfth Street Rag*?" As the red headed nurse walked back to her table of young crew cut officers, Max and the buxon nurse smiled through their tears at each other as Max began a romping rendition of *Twelfth Street Rag*.

****

The sixth weekend, the morning shuttle bus to Seoul broke down at Yeong Deungpo before Max could get to the Seoul Western Union Office. He knew that when he visited the ladies, he would have to struggle to keep the news about his divorce to himself. He did not want his divorce to raise false hopes for Sook Cha about their relationship, because he had ambivalent feelings about marriage, raising children, and dealing with American attitudes about non-Caucasian immigrants.

178

Max arrived earlier than expected and in time to don a cloth mask and help Sook Cha chop up the horseradish which was a principal ingredient in Old Mamasan's kimpchie. The two got in a giggling match watching each others eyes tearing from the caustic fumes of the powerful hot seasoning. By early afternoon, when Max left for the Western Union Office in Seoul, his eyes were so red that a Turkish soldier on the shuttle bus asked him if he had been smoking hashhish, and where could he get some.

At the Western Union Office, the clerk brought him a folded yellow paper from the dead letter box. Max's hands shook as he opened it, tearing the bottom of the page in his eagerness. While his heart pounded, he read, "Everyone agrees it's a great story - Placed with Star Agency - Initial sale to Washington paper $250 - Possible future sales, but payment takes months - Will personally advance each sale whenever needed, just ask."

Tears welled in his red eyes, despite the smile on his face, as he penciled a reply, "Thanks more than I can say - Please forward $250 - Sook Cha and her family thank you."

Even though he knew the money would take a week or more to arrive, he knew he was three quarters the way to buying Sook Cha the farm house. He wanted to celebrate, but, had to wait until the next day when he would again be in Yeong Deungpo. Then he would again have to struggle to keep the sale of the story to himself because he did not know how they might feel about the picture story, even though they would probably never see it and, if they could understand it, they would probably appreciate it. He also did not want to admit to them that, until the sale of the story, he had no way to finance his offer to buy the farmer's house.

179

He managed to keep his exuberance bottled up until he arrived in Yeong Deungpo Sunday morning. The ladies could see he was in high spirits and Young Mamasan said, "Why you so hoppy? You bad honcho go stateside, mebbe MP catchee bad honcho in skivvy house, he go hoosegow?"

Max laughed. "No such luck."

Sook Cha stroked his face and smiled. "Mamasan speakee twoo. You lookee tauksan hoppy. Wha hoppon?"

Max smiled like a Chesire Cat. "Oh, nothing." He paused and then added, "There's an old saying, 'never count your chickens before they hatch.'"

Young Mamasan looked at him quizzicly. "You likee chicken? Old Mamasan go catchee chicken for you!"

Max chuckled. "No."

Sook Cha chimed in. "You likee egg? I go catchee egg!"

Max laughed. "No, no, no. I just likee be with you ladies. Let me take all of you to dinner this evening."

The two women looked at each other, then Young Mamasan shrugged her shoulders and said, "Dai Jobi. Tank you, Maxsan. I go speakee Old Mamasan and Babyan."

In 1953 war torn Yeong Deungpo, dining out options were neither plentiful nor luxurious. In Max's economic bracket and to avoid the red light district and its inflated prices intended for unknowing foreign servicemen, dining out meant selecting dishes from one of the dozen or so street vending wagons that surrounded the small park in front of the opera house.

The park centered around a crude concrete bust of South Korean President Syngman Rhee on a concrete pedestal that was obviously a segment of a Doric column salvaged from the building rubble that still dotted some areas of the city. The park was laid out like a Korean flag with Rhee's bust sitting on the Yin Yang symbol at the center poured in concrete, and concrete park tables and benches placed in the pattern of the four trigrams that appear in the four corners of the flag representing a variety of four polarities including; earth-moon-sun-universe, the four seasons, the four points of the compass, and other more esoteric concepts. The white field of the flag, representing the purity of the Korean people, was compromised by a carpet of green grass, the only grassy area Max had ever seen in Yeong Deungpo. The park was sparsely populated at this early evening hour, but there were still two white helmeted uniformed MPs, one American and one ROK (Republic of Korea), walking slowly around the perimeter with their eyes darting in every direction.

The family made their selections from the wagon Old Mamasan recommended, in part because the wagon owners were one of her kimchie customers, and retreated to one of the unoccupied concrete tables. Old Mamasan passed out the chopsticks she had brought from the house, and each person unwrapped their selection which had been served in a stiff waxed version of brown butcher paper. Most of their choices were delicacies rarely prepared at home; stuffed won ton, pickled fish, crispy duck, and a variety of noodles similar to Japanese soba (buckwheat) noodles and Thai glass (rice) noodles.

Conversation centered around past operetta performances they had attended in the Opera House facing the park. Young Mamasan and Sook Cha re-enacted their favorite parts while Old Mamasan and Max gave them a percussion accompaniment by tapping

181

their chopsticks on the brown paper that had served as their plates.

A rare GI, the only one in the park other than Max, weaved a slightly tipsy path toward them and, supporting himself on the end of their concrete table, said, "Hey, Man. Why so greedy. Looks like you've got more than you can handle. Why don't you let me take one of those ladies off your hands?"

The ladies did not understand him and realized he was slightly drunk, but they weren't sure whether they should take offense, fear him, or tolerate him because, like Max, he was an American. Max was trying to decide if his accent was from New York or New Jersey when the GI solved his indecision by saying. "Never had a Gook whore before. Don't have many Gooks in Detroit. Got lots of niggers, though. But a Gook is just a high yaller nigger, right?"

Max bolted out of his seat to stand beside the GI and, putting his arm around his shoulders, tried to steer him away from the table, saying, "Hey, Man, trying to have a peaceful meal here. What you're looking for you're gonna find two streets over there. Lots of girls. Lots of booze. Lots of fun!"

The GI beamed a smile and said, "Great!" Then he spun out of Max's grasp and lunged toward Sook Cha, saying, "But first, I want to kiss this one!"

Sook Cha rose and took three rapid steps backward, landing in a sideways kung fu posture while glaring at the GI and pointing a chopstick at his face with which, although he would never have anticipated it, she could have rendered him great harm. Max stepped forward immediately and pinned both the GI's arms behind him, bending him face down on the concrete table while the drunk GI complained, "Hey, Man, that's no way to treat a fellow American."

182

Max was wondering if he would have to forcibly escort the GI to the red light district and deposit him in a bordello to avoid any physical combat, when he felt a tap on his back. He looked over his shoulder to see the two MPs beside him. The big beefy American one said, "Okay, Buddy, back off."

Max stepped back, releasing the GI and saying, "I think he's had one too many."

The MP ignored the drunk GI's complaints and began to handcuff him, saying to Max, "You guys shouldn't be fighting over whores in this part of town."

Max cut him short. "Excuse me, Officer, but these ladies are not prostitutes."

The MP surveyed them meanacingly. "Okay, then what are they?"

Max narrowed his eyes at him. "They are my family."

The MP laughed, then rubbed a finger on Maxs' cheek. "Don't see no yellow on you, Fella, and don't see no blonde hair on that little boy."

Max struggled to contain his anger. "Am I free to go, Officer?"

The MP pushed the drunk in the direction of the street and answered, "Don't need to go. Stay with your 'fam-i-lee.' Just keep your nose clean and don't rough up any more drunken GIs."

The ROK MP had stood silent throughout the incident, his hands behind his back as he stared intently at the ladies. As he turned to join the other MP, his upper lip curled into a sneer of disapproval before he took his eyes off of them.

Although the ladies did not understand all of the American MP's English, they got the drift of the conversation. When the two MPs were barely out of earshot, all three hissed and spat out the same Korean curse, best interpreted as, "Bastards!"

****

Entering the courtyard of the house, the ladies were still enjoying their replay of the incident. Young Mamasan was the drunken GI and Old Mamasan was the rude MP. Young Mamasan kept trying to grope Sook Cha who, in turn, posed in a variety of exagerrated defensive kung fu postures. Then Young Mamasan crossed her hands behind her back and backed up to Max, saying, "Etii, etii (ouch, ouch), you hurt me, Maxsan! I no touchee josan no mo. I no kiss kiss Sook Cha!" Whereupon Old Mamasan grabbed Young Mamasan by the collar and dragged her off, the two of them laughing and giggling all the way to their rooms.

Sook Cha helped Max undress in her room. He sat on the edge of the cot and she knelt beside him, stroking his shoulder. Then she took both hands and encompassed his upper biceps, her fingertips straining to complete the circle around them. "You strong strong, Maxsan. You, how you say, you bwave man. You fight fight drunkee GI."

Max took one of her hands and kissed her palm. "Fortunately, I didn't have to fight anyone."

Sook Cha's eyes widened and she excitedly corrected him. "No, you fight fight MP. You speakee tough guy to MP."

Max took her other hand and kissed its palm, then looked into her eyes. "I'm sorry you all had to see Americans behaving like that."

Sook Cha shrugged her shoulders. "'Mewican, Korean, all sameo sameo. Some good, some bad." Then she pushed him down on his back, straddled his

184

pelvis with her own, and lowered her face to his. "You good man, Maxsan. No 'Mewican, no Korean, jus' good good. Tauksan ichi bon good."

Their lovemaking that night was more passionate than usual. During his refractory periods, she begged him to perform the cunnilingus that used to embarrass her. And each time he recovered, she would initiate all the unusual postures an techniques to which he had introduced her. She was insatiable and, more than ever, totally uninhibited, and Max was delighted, grateful, and accommodating.

After all the moans and sobs and sighs, when the candle had extinguished and both lay listening to the others breathing, then the words of love are uttered in husky dreamy tones.

"Maxsan?"

Softly, slowly, do not waken, "Yes?"

"Are we weally you family?"

Max had not anticipated such a question, but he did not hesitate to answer, "The four of you are more family than I have ever known."

"Maxsan, what something you want?"

"What do you mean?"

"Somethin you want most, somethin mebbe you neber hab? Somethin catchee store, somehow makee lovey, go lib country house? I gib. I do anything you say."

Max felt a lump in his throat. He knew he would remember these words in broken English for the rest of his life, "I do anything you say." For the first time in his life, in this one electric moment, he knew he was truly loved. Completely. Unconditionally.

"You already gave me."

"What I gib you?"

"Cherry josan."

"Can only gib once. What somethin can gib now?"

"Give me the color of your skin. Give me the perfume of your body. Give me these tears I kiss from your eyes."

"Want catchee picture me makee lovey?"

"Already have. Lots of 'em."

"Where?"

"Here, in my mind."

"Oh Maxsan, I want gib you somethin tauksan stecky (very beautiful) so you never leave me."

Max closed his eyes and felt a weight upon his chest. "Oh, Sook Cha, you know I'm going stateside in a few months."

"No, Maxsan. I know skoshie month you go stateside, you be tauksan hoppy. I want you be tauksan hoppy, Maxsan. You catchee tauksan stecky josan have long gold hair, give you ichi bon boysan. She make you tauksan happy. I want you be tauksan hoppy. Just here, just now, never leave me. I want make you tauksan hoppy. I do anything you say."

The weight lifted from Max's chest. He kissed a trail up her arm and across the snow cone of her breast. He heard her husky voice crooning, "Na nun dang sin ui (I love you)."

His lips traveled up the hollows of her neck to her fragile ear, and his own ear heard her whisper, "Salang hap ni da (darling)."

He tasted the salt of her tears as she continued to whisper, "Salang.. .salang.... salang," before he covered her mouth with his.

The door flew back and died instantly of multiple fractures. Robes flying, Young Mamrasan leaped into the room like a Samauri dancer to the accompaniment of what sounded like a Korean rhythm

186

band in the courtyard. She held a candle in her hand and, pointing it toward the courtyard like a sword and, assuming a Samauri's fighting stance, she screamed a flood of Korean at the couple on the bed, only one word of which Max understood. "MP!"

Max threw back the covers and scrambled to get into his jockey shorts, into which he stuffed his wallet, watch, and dog tags. Sook Cha donned her blue sweater, then bundled Maxs' clothes into a ball which she hid behind a box under her cot. As Max crossed the courtyard, he heard a banging on the gate followed by a dictatorial voice yelling Korean outside the gate, then English. "You GIs in there. Tell them to open this gate because we have the authority to break it down if they don't."

Young Marnasan stopped in the middle of a run to assume a sleepy attitude to match her sleepy voice as she stalled them in Korean. Old Mamasan spread a tatami mat over the trap door on the porch, then sat on it, then got up and opened the trapdoor for Max as he ran across the courtyard. Max crouched in the dark shallow hole, wishing he had excavated it a little more, and the trapdoor lowered over his head, but not completely. Through the open crack, he saw Young Mamasan open the gate and the uniformed men storm in. Suddenly someone's weight pressed down painfully on his back, crushing him into cold, moist, darkness.

Max heard their loud voices in Korean, then English, the doors sliding open and slammed shut, a few pots and pans rattling around him. Then he was only conscious of the immediate space around him, and of terror, for he was not alone.

A light moved overhead and briefly illuminated the cracks in the floor, but little else, save two pinpoints of yellow light that burned hardly two feet away from

187

him. The Jee! Max realized he was trapped between the police looking for him overhead and a monster rat two feet away from him below. He sucked in air and stifled a scream.

The light passed, but the two tiny yellow orbs continued to stare at him, then moved laterally with lightening speed, and he felt dirt fly in his face. Flicking the dirt out of his lashes, he found the two yellow dots were farther from his face, but closer to his body. He felt goose pimples rise so enormously on his body, he feared they might touch the Jee and frighten the animal into action.

He tried to think of something funny to lessen his terror. His epitaph, "Max, born nothing, lived nothing, died of a rat bite in a Korean whorehouse while not fighting for his country." The attempt did not calm him. He realized he had been holding his breath a long time and tried not to make a sound or breath in the direction of the Jee as he released the air from his bursting lungs and sucked in another breath.

He remembered when he was a kid and used to catch snakes and make hat bands and belts of their skins. Ignorant that some were poisonous and of the danger of those known to be poisonous, he used to place the forked stick over their heads and pick them up in his free hand just behind the head, amazing his younger friends by forcing the venomous jaws wide while the fangs unfolded in all their pink glory, then whipping the snake to death with one quick magic twist and dropping it into the box to be skinned, never to be feared.

But Max was a big boy now and wise enough to be scared to death of those dear little reptiles and rats and even some insects whose contaminated mandrills he had seen turn human flesh into black swollen pain and even death. Would he have to kill the Jee with his bare hands? If he could just get to his dog tags, he might strangle the Jee with the chain. But how could he, he was in a dark, shallow, cold, damp hole with a huge rat that he couldn't even see to avoid.

Heavy footsteps thundered overhead. He heard the latticed doors to the rooms slide open and slam shut, he heard English and Korean male voices barking commands, and he heard the three women's high pitched voices complaining in Korean and broken English.

Max prayed silently, "Please don't scare the Jee." Something touched him. A tail, a whisker, a foot? He jerked away involuntarily, and pandemonium started. The Jee squealed and Max thrashed about, scraping his back sorely on the overhead boards. The footsteps increased. Max felt the fur, felt the foot, felt the pressure of an animal as large as a small dog, but ten times as strong, ten times as mad and frightened. Breathless, without the time to scream for help, Max heard the slow motion conversation overhead.

"What's that?"

It's coming from underneath the floor."

"What are those women looking at?"

"There's a trap door here!"

"Open it!"

Max's skin felt. frozen. It seemed to contact the squealing Jee every where it turned. He dug with his hands, trying to catch the Jee by the throat. His hands closed on nothing but cold damp earth. His back was raw and bleeding and it was a tremendous relief when the trap door lifted from it, but it dropped back with such a sudden force that the pain went to the bone.

There was a sudden stillness in the hole and the squealing seemed far away. There was a stamping overhead, men shouting, women screaming, then four thunderous explosions, gun shots, and little sprays of dirt around Max trickled into the hole. The Jee was outside. Max tried to determine if the pain in his back was from the trap door or a gunshot. He couldn't figure out why they weren't removing him from the hole.

"Put that weapon in your holster, Sergeant. You want to kill somebody?"

Young Mamasan's voice was shrill and angry. "What you think this is, North Korea? Get shoots gun outta my house." Then she bombarded them in Korean until the voices were out of Max's range. He was too weak to lift up the trap door. When would they stop arguing and get him out of there.

Tick, tock, tick, tock. The luminous dial on his wrist watch glowed in front of him and its echoing gonging sound rattled through his head. Did they forget about him? What was that?

A light showed on the dirt in front of him and a rush of cool air replaced the trap doors weight on his back. He tried to straighten, pain stabbing his back, and saw the frightened faces of Sook Cha and Young Mamasan while the old woman stood behind their crouched figures giggling.

Sook Cha held the candle toward him. "You dai jobi?"

"Don't know. Think so." He forced himself upright, little droplets of blood trickling down to the band of his jockey shorts, and looked around at the deserted courtyard. "Where are the MPs?"

Young Mamasan's pale face remained unchanged as she spoke, "No see you. Jee scare MP off."

Sock Cha touched his raw back, "Jee no catchee you?"

Max raised his arms painfully and flexed the muscles of his back. "Jee no catchee me."

The old woman brought scalding water from the brazier, giggling nervously in the aftermath of the excitement. Young Mamasan took the water from her, poured some in the teapot, then poured the balance in the large wooden tub, already half filled with water, where she invited Max to enter.

Sook Cha softly sponged warm water over his back while he noticed two of the gunshots that had ricochetted and shattered the plaster of one wall. The other two shots had gone dangerously close to the trap door. The Jee had escaped. Max was almost glad. Possibly the Jee had saved him, and he resented the MPs too much to let them kill even such an unwanted member of this household.

As Max sat soaking in the wooden wash tub and felt the caresses of the sponge in Sook Cha's hand, he decided the Jee had forced recognition of some cold logic. For all the love and happiness he found in the house in Yeong Deungpo, staying there would only lessen its survival. Even though he really didn't have the total amount to buy the country house, he could rent it and see Sook Cha there less frequently, yet much more safely. Max felt as if he were deserting them in considering it, but it would be better than Sook Cha severing her more permanent alliance with the two women for a relatively temporary one with Max.

Sook Cha was slowly rinsing him off, faint dimples in her brow marking her premonition that he had something unpleasant to say. He stared hard at the three women, trying to screw up his courage to broach his idea to them.

The two other women began to prepare some food, the old woman holding up the French Chef's knife

191

and smiling at Max as she chopped the vegetables. Young Mamasan worked with swift precise movements and began to speak casually, without looking at anyone.

"Mebbe MP follow us fom pok (from park)."

Max shook his head doubtfully. "They wouldn't have waited so long."

Young Mamasan focused intently on her food preparation. "Mebbe they wait see if GI go 'Off Limits' skivvy house wid wed gates."

Max stepped out of the wash tub. "Yeah, I feel guilty each time I see that 'Off Limits' sign."

"This house make ichi ban skivy house. Much room for josan. Heavy gate no can bake. Twap door for GI." Young Mamasan unfolded Max's robe while Sook Cha gingerly dried him off, concentrating on Young Mamasan's voice. Young Mamasan held Max's robe for him and continued, "Madame speakee me, give tauksan GI dollar (much more negotiable) fo this house. Tomorrow I sell house."

Max wanted to protest, but she handed him a bowl of food so hot he burned his fingers. As he pursed his lips to talk, she interrupted, looking up at him and sounding as stern as she looked. "I buy half country house. We make paper, Babysan and me own half country house, Sook Cha own half."

Max and Sook Cha stared at her in amazement. They hadn't touched their food. Young Manmasan looked at Max's untouched plate, then into his eyes and queried, "Dai jobi?"

Max nodded agreement and began shoveling rice into his face with the chop sticks. "Dai jobi!"

Young Mamasan bit down on a hard piece of gristle, extracted it from her mouth and looked at it, saying, "We live country house. Skivy josan and Jee live Yeong Deungpo house." Uncharacteristically, she

192

flicked the gristle into the courtyard and Max stared at it, half expecting the Jee to brazenly retrieve it now that Young Mamasan had conceded the rat's part ownership.

Chapter Eleven
AUTUMN LEAVES

Max had to create another picture story for Lieutenant Conweb to plagiarize in order to commandeer a personnel carrier to transfer the household belongings. The Lieutenant bought a story line about the Korean orphanage the base supported, a story which Max could illustrate with past photos taken when the talent show proceeds were donated, and augment with photos of Young Mamasan's and the farmer's little boys, and Young Mamasan and Sook Cha posing as prospective adoptive parents. Ned was again appointed chaperone and ensconced in a Yeong Deungpo bordello until the end of the moving day.

The move was made in multiple trips during the one day the vehicle was available, the canvas top to the personnel carrier being temporarily removed so furniture and boxes of belongings could be piled mile high and lashed down, looking like a gypsy caravan. A handcart was borrowed to transport everything from the main road down the narrow pathway between the rice paddies to the cluster of little buildings on the hill.

The most challenging items to transport would have been Old Mamasans' giant kimchie jars which, at first, she stubbornly insisted had to be excavated and transported to the farm. Young Mamasan renegotiated the sale of the Yeong Deungpo house to include generous compensation for the kimchie jars, and Old Mamasan was mollified with sufficient payment to procure two smaller new jars to take to the farm and a remaining cash nest egg for her to hide under the floor of her room in the new house.

Of course there was some transitional strife. Young Mamasan felt obliged to put the farmer in his place and establish her ownership and authority regarding the house purchase. He took her imperious behavior with good natured patience, even showing some admiration for her assertiveness. Max and Sook Cha watched the two of them sparring with the same curiosity with which Young Mamasan had observed their own relationship develop.

Old Mamasan delighted in having the two young boys around her. She and the two younger women provided a quality of life and nurturing atmosphere the farmer's boy had never known, and the farmer was obviously grateful for their presence and help.

At first the women started taking treats for the boy back to the farmer's little house in the rear. Then the treats became meals for the boy, then the meals became meals for both boy and father, and, ultimately, the farmer and his boy were invited to share meals with the three women in their newly acquired house. The farmer reciprocated by providing food from his larder, and Old Mamasan expanded this by creating a kitchen garden which they both tended on the farmer's land. In the course of the first few weeks, the two families were informally integrated and Young Mamasan became more tolerant of and amicable with the patient farmer.

In the country, everyone turned pink and gold with confidence and security. No longer was there need to feel crafty and guilty in order to survive the daily economics of life. No longer was there fear of the MPs who never patrolled the farm areas. No longer did Max fear that Sook Cha would have to resort to prostitution to survive.

Max researched the very unreliable civilian transportation which, once or twice a month, enabled the ladies to visit the city and see their operettas. Max and the two young ladies made their first trip to the opera together and, when Max offered to take them to dinner afterwards in their old red light district, both Sook Cha and Young Mamasan declined with emphatic hissing denouncements of their former neighborhood. As they settled for refreshments from a street vendor, Young Mamasan said, "No likee see skivvy houses nevah mo. No chug chug twain twack shakee house. All that million miles away."

Then Sook Cha added, "We split from Jee. He dead to me," and the two women laughed between bites of food.

On the next visit to the operetta, they took the farmer and his son, neither of whom had ever seen one of these performances. Young Mamasan explained the progress of the action on stage to the boy and his father, both of whom sat entranced and amazed. Max and Sook Cha cuddled together as they watched them, remembering how Sook Cha had explained the stage play to Max, and reliving the thrill at having discovered and explored each others worlds.

While they all shared a picnic lunch in the tiny park across from the opera house, the farmer and his son conversed with Young Mamasan at great length. Sook Cha leaned toward Max and whispered, "He think city tauksan scary, but boysan likee opera, farmersan willing take Mamasan opera sometime." Then Max and Sook Cha smiled at each other and suppressed their giggles.

****

Lieutenant Conweb called Max up to his desk and announced, "My farm equipment story and orphanage story both got selected for publication. As a result, I've come to the attention of Air Force Headquarters in Seoul and they're reassigning me to become Air Force Pubic Information Officer for all of Korea. Lucky you, I'm taking you with me. So get ready to move to Seoul as soon as I can get them to cut our orders."

Max looked at the 'Military Slogan of the Week' over the Lieutenants head which read, "God Helps Those Who Help Themselves." He wondered if Ben Franklin ever expected his saying to license plagiarism. Max barked a response. "Sir, I didn't request a transfer."

The Lieutenant didn't look up from his papers. "Don't have to. I requested it for you."

Max swallowed hard. "But Sir, I didn't volunteer to go to Seoul."

The Lieutenant looked up with an aggravated expression. "You don't have to. I'm volunteering you, Airman."

Max attempted to respond. "But Sir...."

The Lieutenant raised his voice. "Don't 'but Sir' me, Airman. This is a great opportunity for you. I'm getting your photography immortalized in the annals of military journalism, and you're giving me a hard time. You're going with me, and that's it." Before Max could respond, the Lieutenant shouted, "Dismissed."

As Max passed Ned's desk, Ned slapped his biceps and raised his right fist, saying, "You were right. It ain't the last time."

At lunch time, Max went over to headquarters, but the black Sergeant was not in the building. Then Max tried the mess hall with no success, and finally

198

looked into the Airman's Club where he found the Sergeant with Guido sipping bottled soda. As soon as Max approached them, Guido rose to leave, saying, "Toodle-ooo. I know when two people want to be alone."

Max was about to protest when the Sergeant said, "Let him go. He was getting so campy he was embarrassing me. What can I do for you? An off base pass, or a censor by-pass. Seems like you're always getting passes from me, no pun intended."

Max sat down. "Yeah, I have asked favors of you, at least once."

The Sergeant sipped his soda. "Twice, actually. You originally asked me for a base pass, but you passed on the pass." The Sergeant smiled. "Pun intended."

Max smiled weakly. "Yeah, well. I was hoping you could give me some information. Conweb is being transferred to Seoul Headquarters and, against my wishes, he's trying to take me with him."

The Sergeant held the cool soda bottle to his forehead. "That's what you get for being indispensable. I know what that's like. Every officer has his little non-com (non-commissioned officer) doing his job for him, and he drags the non-com around wherever he goes because the stupid non-com does his job better than he does."

Max frowned at the Sergeant. "But, how do I avoid the transfer?"

The Sergeant took another sip. "You can't, as far as I know. He can request whoever he wants, as long as it's 'in the best interest of the service.'"

Max's frown deepened. "Do you know who's replacing Conweb?"

The Sergeant smiled at Max. "Your friend, that Lieutenant who sponsored your talent show."

199

Max's frown changed to an expression of hope. "Can he request I stay in my present post, 'in the best interest of the service?'"

The Sergeant tilted his head sideways. "I don't know."

Max asked, "Who would know?"

The Sergeant shrugged his shoulders. "I don't know. I guess, somebody in the Provost Marshall's office."

Max asked, "Do you know anyone in the Provost Marshall's office?"

The Sergeants' brows knit. "Why do you ask? What do you mean by that?"

Max looked confused. "I asked because you said....What I mean is, do you know anyone in the Provost Marshall's Office who would advise me confidentially how to avoid this transfer?"

"Oh!" The Sergeant shook his empty soda bottle and frowned at it. "Yeah, I know someone. But you can't tell anyone I hooked you up."

****

Sook Cha helped Old Mamasan expand the kitchen garden until it started to produce a surplus, whereupon Young Mamasan became a sales agent for the surplus. Seeing her managerial skills, the farmer solicited her help as his accountant and sales agent, and the two began a business alliance that looked forward to the farmer re-acquiring the last of his lost rice paddies. The money from the house sale had bought the farmer needed supplies and half the former paddies, but the last few completing the floor of this small valley remained economically out of reach.

200

After the farmer and his son left dinner one evening and returned to their little house at the rear of the hill, Young Mamasan said to Max and Sook Cha, "Farmersan speakee catchee old rice paddy, makee new. Farm farm much rice, mebbe mo wegetable. Need dollar for paddy. Need his brodder come help farm farm. Him speakee marry me, I buy paddy."

Max and Sook Chas' eyes widened and they smiled at each other.

Young Mamasan frowned at them and continued with a hint of anger in her voice. "I speakee no marry. I speakee makee paper, me partner."

Max was about to agree when she continued talking over him. "You let me buy half Sook Chas' house. Mebbe you like buy part of farm, we all become partner, farmersan, farmersan brudder, Sook Cha, Max, me. We pay Old Mamasan salary, mebbe boysan when they mo' big."

Sook Cha looked at Max quizzicly. Max mentally juggled how much money was left from the picture story sale before he spoke up. "Dai jobi, but only you, farmersan, his brother, and Sook Cha. I'll pay for Sook Cha, she'll be your partner."

Sook Cha beamed at Max, then looked at Young Mamasan. "Dai jobi, I workee farm, we share four way." She turned to Max questioningly, ":Okay, Max, you shoe dai jobi?"

Max took her hands in his and smiled. "Yes, I'm very sure, tauksan dai jobi."

****

As Max entered the movie tent, the movie *Caddy Shack*, starring Dean Martin and Jerry Lewis, was half over. The tent was the same size as the residential tents

201

designed to house eight men, but, without cots and foot lockers, there were usually thirty to fifty men crowded onto wooden benches and standing around the perimeter wall. Max stood beside the noisy clickety-click of the 16mm projector and squinted to see the black and white image on a white sheet tacked on the far wall of the tent. He was looking for Guido, whose short frame would be hard to find in this fatigue green smelly sea of GIs. As luck would have it, when Dean Martin began to sing *Amore*, Guido's voice sang out like a beacon, "When the moon hits your eye like a big pizza pie, that's Amore!"

Max stooped down behind Guido and whispered, "Guido, when the movie's over, can I have a word with you?"

Guido swivelled around with a wide eyed grin. "Sugar, you can have a lot more than a word, a sentence, a paragraph,. Hell, you could have a whole damn book if you like." Then Guido pushed the guy next to him, saying, "Move your fat ass down, Mary, and make room for my gorgeous friend."

The six foot beefy looking GI retorted, "Screw you, Faggot!"

Guido giggled. "You wish."

Max raised his hands in protest and whispered, "That's okay, Guido, I'll just..."

Guido's stretched his face up to the GI's and his voice raised three notes and ten decibels as he warned, "I'm the one who provides your clean sheets, heater fuel, and everything else it takes to make life livable here. Now move your fat ass over."

The GI and the other five men on the bench reluctantly moved over and Max self consciously sat down, offering the GI an apologetic, "Sorry, thank you." Then he turned to Guido, saying, "Guido, I..."

Guido stopped him with a raised hand. "Shhhh! Sit down, shut up, and watch the most beautiful man you will ever see in life, my future husband, Deano!"

The beefy GI spoke out of the corner of his mouth, "You wish!"

After the movie, Max and Guido walked back to the squadron area. Max asked Guido, "Man, how can you be so blatantly campy? Don't you worry about the law, or one of those cro-magnon homophobes cornering you in a dark alley somewhere?"

Guido gestured with his hands as he spoke like a professor lecturing at a university. "First of all, Max, forget about the law. In our case here, half or more of the law are homos themselves. Commissioned officer homos are super cool at staying in the closet, because they have so much to lose, even though they have a wealth of legal knowledge to protect themselves. Peons like me, who have little to lose, other than our lives, learn to brown nose the legal homos for protection from the law. As for protection from the cro-magnon homophobes, I learned very early on the streets of Chicago that the best defense is an offense. Part of my offense is to have some dirt on everyone possible, hence the saying, 'keep your friends close, but keep your enemies closer.' That bully that dared to suggest that Dean Martin is not my fiancé, he knows that I know enough to put him in Levenworth for the rest of his life."

Max smiled with respect. "Wow, Man, are you related to Machiavelli?"

Guido unlocked the supply tent door. "I don't think they're from Chicago. I never heard of them." He opened the door and gestured for Max to enter. "So, you wanted to have a word with me."

Max hesitated, then said, "Yeah, a word."

203

Guido entered ahead of him. "Oh, come on in, Max. I'm not going to grope you. Poor Sarge told me about that night in the latrine. I'm sorry if I contributed in any way that made either of you uncomfortable."

Max took his cap off and stuck it in his belt. "No sweat. We're past that, and he's proven to be a friend in need."

Guido pulled out a bottle and two glasses, proffering one to Max. "Well that's good. So, what do you need from me?"

Max declined the glass. "I wanted to ask you about all those tin cans I saw. How do they seal those things?"

Guido poured himself two fingers of Scotch, set the bottle down, then began looking among the shelved boxes, finally pulling one down and opening it. "Voila!"

Max's eyes widened and his heart skipped a beat. There in the box was what he had seen in his mother's kitchen during childhood. A hand cranked canning machine, all tin coated and shiney new. He had to swallow before he could speak. "Guido, how, when, and where are they gonna use this stuff? Is it critical to the war effort?"

Guido swallowed a mouthful of Scotch and smiled warmly at the glass he held before his eyes. "Like I told you, they turned thumbs down on local produce because of sanitation. This stuff ain't worth shipping back to where it came from. Next shipment that comes in, I'll have to toss it. It's not like something I could barter to anyone on base."

A smile illuminated Maxs' face. "Guido, you like pretty things, right?"

Guido smiled a Machiavelian smile. "Pretty as in who, what, when, where?"

204

Max unbuttoned one of his shirt buttons, reached under his shirt, and pulled out a folded cloth. "Let me show you some beautiful embroidery a friend of mine does."

****

Korean civilians were employed in a variety of capacities on American and other United Nations bases. To minimize the number of American personnel needed in some support services, most menial jobs were given to civilians such as one house boy for each eight man residential tent to clean, make beds, and maintenance and monitor the oil burning space heater. For health and security reasons, support services such as food service, supply, hospital, motor pool, and waste disposal workers were entirely military personnel. Semi skilled non critical jobs such as the laundry workers, tailor shop employees, barbers, and Kim, the darkroom assistant, were filled on the basis of available Korean civilians who possessed such skills, spoke a reasonable amount of English, and could fulfill the medical and security screening required.

Kim was in his early twenties, lived in Kimpo village with his teenage wife and two babies, and had graduated from being a houseboy where he learned an American street version of English richly laced with slang, colloquialisms, and obscenities. He was exposed to the American GI's predilection for 'snap shooting' and, because he was honest and did not steal personal items like some other houseboys, he was gifted by his tent resident employers with one of the cameras he so admired, plus film and lessons in photography. Ned was one of his employers, had been instrumental in getting Kim his job as darkroom assistant, and had asked Max to tutor Kim in photography. Though semi-illiterate in both Korean and English, Kim was a quick learner and, despite a few serious mistakes in darkroom protocol along the way, became a competent darkroom assistant and a great asset as a verbal interpreter.

Kim had escorted Max through Kimpo Village when Max had photographed the girl bathing in the wing tip tank bathtub, the photo which had gotten Max in trouble with Lieutenant Conweb initially. Kim had introduced Max to the Kimpo Village Orphanage for which Max had negotiated donations when he took the talent show on the road. Kim had negotiated the cooperation of other Korean civilian base employees such as the laundry worker who posed as a farmer with Lieutenant Conweb and the seamstress that modified the nurses uniform for Sook Cha. Kim was also savvy enough to understand the interoffice conflicts between Lieutenant Conweb and his staff, and Kim identified with Ned and Max and was loyal to their interests.

One of Kim's acquisitions from his days as a houseboy had been the gift of a battered old Martin guitar from a tent resident who was returning stateside. Knowing that Max was a pianist, Kim asked if he could teach him how to play the guitar. It so happened that Max had taught himself enough chords in the first position to get by with a few French songs he learned from fellow entertainers on Bourbon Street in the French Quarter, and a few Spanish songs he learned from the sailors at La Marina bar on the Decateur Street waterfront. To these he added a few strumming tricks on the strings and a few percussion tricks of rapping his knuckles on the guitar body in between strokes.

Kim wanted to learn *On Top Of Old Smokey*, a favorite of his benefactor, the former Martin guitar owner. Another request was *China Nights*, a popular

Chinese song at the time whose opening lyrics, "Shina No Yoru," were satirized by some GIs as, "She ain't got no yo-yo." The final choice was the easiest of the songs Kim had heard Max perform on the guitar, *La Cucaracha*, replete with the unabridged English translation, "The little cockroach, the little cockroach, he can't walk good anymore, because he doesn't have, because he cannot get, marijuana for to smoke."

Kim learned the guitar chords fairly well because he had the aptitude to visualize chord symbols on the frets of the guitar neck and he had a sense of rhythm, but, with the Korean language problem with "R's" and the difference between the oriental and western tonal scales, his singing usually elicited unintended laughter, which he bore good naturedly.

Max conducted the lessons in his tent area, knowing that it would lead to problems in the office. He extracted a promise from Kim to trade him off base translator services in equal amount, although Kim would have been delighted to do so for no compensation, any traveling in a vehicle to any place beyond Kimpo Village being an adventure to him. Now that the ladies had become entrepreneurs in the food supply business, Max felt Kim's familiarity with English and the American military might make him an excellent future ally for them. Max invited him to the house on the hill and told him to bring his guitar.

Korean civilians, even those with military employee ID's, were the last allowed to board the military shuttle buses. If the bus was filled with military personnel, the civilians had to wait for and hope there would be space on the next one. When Max took Kim with him on a shuttle bus that was fully loaded, poor Kim had to sit in Max's lap in order to be admitted, which made holding the guitar case while the bus bounced over pot holes a bit of a balancing act.

But Kim was proud to have been invited to visit the home of Max's girlfriend, even though he had to swear to keep the trip a secret from Lieutenant Conweb. He realized he would be in the company of high class people because Max had also cautioned him to restrain his use of the obscene vocabulary he had learned from the GI's. He was particularly impressed when he heard the name of Young Mamasan's deceased elderly husband.

Max had explained his purpose for introducing Kim to the ladies beforehand, and they received him graciously. Young Mamasan recognized Kim's value to their business interests, and she became the pivotal figure during his visit.

After a dinner attended by only Max, Kim, and the ladies, Max picked up the guitar and asked Kim to try and translate a song. Max played the *Guardsman's Song* he wrote the last night he stood guard before going into the hospital, singing it once in English without stopping, then repeating it one line at a time while Kim attempted to translate. Kim obviously had difficulty understanding the nuances of the English and capturing the prose of the words, and Young Mamasan was obviously frustrated with his translation. After the first effort at translation, she stood up and requested Max and Kim to repeat it one line at a time, and she attempted, through words and pantomime, to re-translate Kim's Korean words back into an operetta style art form.

With wiggling fingers to indicate falling snow and shuddering body to communicate cold, with a military stance and march with a brazier poker for a gun, Young Mamasan cleverly and, insofar as Sook Cha was concerned, successfully managed to convey the poetry of Max's song. Everyone applauded her performance, after which Sook Cha flung her arms around Max, Kim snatching the guitar away from him just in time.

Kim performed his first vocal and guitar recital for the ladies who most enjoyed *China Nights* and were amused by the translation of *La Cucaracha*, but politely applauded his entire performance. Then Young Mamasan engaged Kim so Max could go out into the night with Sook Cha and the guitar.

Max sat on a wooden stool with the guitar in his lap and Sook Cha sat on a tatami matt on the ground beside him, leaning against his thigh. The sky was clear and the almost full moon illuminated the still waters of the paddies which reflected the bridge on the pathway fulfilling the perfect circle that gave it the name 'moon bridge.' Sook Cha looked up at Max, his blonde hair back lighted by the orange glow of the candles in the house, his chiseled face painted blue by the moonlight. She ran a finger softly across the strings of the guitar, smiling as the discordant sounds reverberated through the body of the instrument. She asked, "Sing song fo' me, Max, a song you likee."

Max positioned the guitar on his right knee and sang one of his favorites, first in the original French until the title *Autumn Leaves*, then in the American translation titled *September Song*. At first he did not realize how prophetic its lyrics were of their relationship, his voice becoming more hesitant and sad as he realized how true the words were, particularly when he came to the bridge line, "And the days dwindle down, to a precious few, September, November."

In the past, Max had always performed *September Song* so skillfully that it often brought tears to some listener's eyes. This time, however, was the first time it held a personal meaning for him, and the first time it brought tears to his own eyes. Sook Cha did not see the tears in his eyes and would not have understood them because she did not understand the English lyrics, but she certainly sensed the emotion. She said, "That tauksan stecky, Max, but it tauksan sad. Make me happy, Max, sing my song again." And Max, once again, sang the song he had composed for her, *The Guardsman Song*.

****

When Max walked into the Provost Marshall's Counselor's Office, he recognized the guy with the crew cut from Guido's supply tent party, the Officer who had delivered the envelope with the base pass offered by the Sergeant. Max explained he was only seeking counsel and asked if the normal confidentiality of lawyer client relationships existed here in a military environment.

The Officer replied, "For your own protection, I should tell you that, in the military environment, those rules of confidentiality are often ignored when it comes to 'the best interests of the service.' In this case, however, I'm extending to you my personal guarantee of confidentiality as practiced by everyone you met at the party where I met you, and I'm reminding you that confidentiality extends both ways." He smiled pleasantly at Max and added, "Did I make myself clear and are we in agreement?"

Max sat up straight and gave a smart, "Yes, Sir!"

The Officer leaned forward and put his elbows on the desk. "You can take some of the starch out of the 'yes sirs' until and unless someone else is in the room. Now, what do you need counseling about?"

Max took a deep breath. "In a nutshell, my boss got a promotion which transfers him to Air Force

210

Headquarters in Seoul and, against my personal desires and what I consider to be my best interests, he has volunteered me to be transferred to the same post where I will be obliged to continue to work for him."

The Officer smiled. "Wow, that was a long convoluted but concise sentence. Sure you didn't study to be a lawyer?"

Maxs' brow furrowed. "No, Sir."

The Officer leaned back in his chair. "That was a rhetorical question. Anyway, between the Sergeant giving me an overview of the situation and your friend, Ned, running his mouth at the Airmans' Club, I think I have most of the picture. Correct me if I'm wrong and forgive me if I don't use the appropriate legal terms, because I don't ever want to be quoted saying those exact words. Prior to Lieutenant Conweb's becoming your boss, there was a precedent of each Correspondent and photographer in the PIO Office receiving recognition for their work via a byline on their articles and photos. Since his posting at this base, it would appear that Lieutenant Conweb feels proof reading and making minor editorial corrections to the articles you wrote entitles him to place his byline on what originated as your work, and to eliminate photo credits entirely. In turn, these articles and photos have earned him a promotion, but he needs you to continue this level of performance at his new post. You, however, would prefer to remain at your present post. Am I correct?"

Max gave a pained smile. "Yes, Sir. Very tactful, but very accurate."

The Officer leaned forward again. "Okay, that established, let me tell you some things you may or may not be aware of. Your boss sometimes vents at the officer's club, often just out of earshot from your piano bar. He claims your attachment to a Korean girl is

211

destroying your marriage and that all his pressure on you is to save your marriage. What can you tell me about that?"

Max wondered if he was in a lawyer's office or a psychiatrists' office. "I was estranged from my wife before I entered the service. Since my arrival in Korea, my wife has been having an affair with my best friend. Two weeks ago I signed and returned divorce papers to her lawyer. And, yes, I have had a happy relationship with a Korean girl for some months now."

The Officer's eyebrows raised as his smile broadened. "Divorce? Okay! Now, one other area of questioning. I notice you're an Airman Basic. Did Lieutenant Conweb bust you?"

Max bit his lip before replying. "No, Sir. I was busted before Conweb arrived for being in a brawl at the Airman's Club which I was accused of initiating by stating that I thought President Truman was killing American military men by establishing a no win situation in order to deny General MacArthur a victory and thereby eliminate him as a competitor for President."

The Officer chuckled. "Man. You should've gone to law school."

Max pleaded, "But, Sir, the other guy threw the first punch, and then it became a melee."

The Officer waved it away with his hands. "Doesn't matter now. What about this disciplinary action, thirty days base confinement for a first offense of being in an Off Limits area?"

Max sucked in a lung full of air. "My Korean girlfriend was very ill and needed penicillin. The Doctor didn't tell us he was signing her up as a prostitute in order to get the penicillin. Conweb got the information and sent MPs to post her house as Off

Limits, probably suspecting he'd catch me there on Sunday. The MP Captain did not arrest me because it wasn't posted Off Limits when I entered the house, but he put my name on the report, and Conweb disciplined me on the basis of that report. First his discipline was putting me guard every other night, but when I was hospitalized as a result, he settled for thirty days confinement to base."

The Officer looked amazed. "Wow! The man is Draconian! One last question. Just in case it escaped your records, in all the months that you've been winning kudos for him, did Lieutenant Conweb ever give you a promotion or a commendation?"

Max lips tightened. "No, Sir."

The Officer stacked the papers on his desk and put them back in a folder. "I think that's all we need. I looked at your transfer papers. Lieutenant Conweb signed your name on them which, on a battlefield, might be acceptable, but, as I explained to him, was not legally acceptable in the here and now. You can refuse to sign the transfer and, if Lieutenant Conweb can get the Base Commander to honor his request for your reassignment to his new post, we can probably challenge that. But, for one, I don't think Lieutenant Conweb would want all we've discussed to come up in a hearing, and, two, I don't think the Base Commander wants you to leave the piano bar. So, no guarantees, but I think you don't have anything to worry about."

Max frowned. "If I don't sign the transfer, Conweb is going to lean on me even harder."

The Officer nodded assent. "Probably, but he isn't going to be here that long, so you'll have to live with it. In the meantime, two things, one, other than in private conversation with me, you'd be wise to show him the respect of referring to him as 'Lieutenant'

Conweb, and, two, don't sign anything he puts in front of you, not even an autograph at the piano bar, until you have me read it. Okay?"

The two men rose and Max saluted, saying, "Yes, Sir. And thank you, Sir."

The Officer returned the salute, smiled, and extended his hand in a warm handshake, saying, "You're welcome, Max, and good luck."

****

The farmers' brother arrived to help cultivate the newly acquired paddies, and he was obviously a much younger brother and, as everyone noticed, was every bit as handsome as his older brother, the farmer. In conversations with Max, they began to refer to 'Young Farmersan' and 'Old Farmersan.' Although Young Farmersan was no more sophisticated than Old Farmersan, he was as much a gentleman as his older brother, very respectful to the ladies, and, even moreso than Old Farmersan, a little fearful of Young Mamasan.

However, the elephant on the hilltop that no one would express openly was the obvious fact that Young Farmersan was quite smitten with Sook Cha. It was little consolation to Max that Young Farmersan showed him appropriate respect and acknowledged him as Sook Cha's boyfriend, and that Young Farmersan almost tripped over himself trying not to be too close to her or linger in her company too long. What was unavoidable was the longing in Young Farmersan's eyes as he looked at Sook Cha from afar. All of which made Sook Cha feel obliged to act aloof and indifferent to him, almost to the point of rudeness when she would not even acknowledge his presence or make him repeat himself to her as if she had not heard him initially.

214

After the farmers retreated from dinner one evening, Young Mamasan began one of her monologues which she probably initiated to make Max feel more secure about Sook Cha. She told stories of how dictatorial her father was and how, despite his being a good provider and essentially a kind and educated man, she regarded most Korean men as chauvinists and domineering husbands. Young Mamasan referred to Old Mamasan's stories of the treatment of Korean women under the Japanese occupation, and added that, in the seven years since the end of World War II, women's rights were almost as non-existent as they had been under the Japanese. With the commencement of the Korean Civil War between the Communist North and the Democratic South, only the intervention of the United Nations as a governing body brought about some semblance of women's legal and voting rights. Even Sook Cha agreed that the South Korean farmer who tried to trade her like an animal to the North Korean troops or his neighboring male farmers had no respect for a woman's rights, South Korean or otherwise.

Young Mamasan concluded her discussion as an explanation of why she refused to marry the farmer, and instead chose to maintain her personal rights and material assets solely in her own name. She admitted that, under the new young democratic government, it might be hard to assert and hold on to her rights and property as a woman, but she wanted that for herself and Sook Cha. Then she turned to Max and spoke reverently. "I teach my Boysan be good like you wit' Sook Cha. You no loud loud, no mean mean wit' woman. You speakee good for woman. You touchee good for woman. You okay, Maxsan, make ichi bon boyfwen'."

Max bowed his head low and responded softly, "Domo arigato, Mamasan. Domo arigato."

Sook Cha stroked the back of his head, put her arm around him, and leaned her head on his shoulder. "Is twoo, Maxsan. Wery wery twoo."

Max lifted her hand to his lips and kissed it.

Chapter Twelve
CYCLES OF LIFE

Max stood stiffly before Lieutenant Conweb's desk and made a sharp salute, swiftly returning his right hand to his right side. The Lieutenant sat with his hands folded over his desk blotter and looked at Max without emotion. "Airman, when you salute an officer, you hold that salute until the officer returns it."

Max snapped his right hand back to his brow, holding it there as he barked, "Yes, Sir. Sorry, Sir."

While Max held his salute at attention, the Lieutenant casually reached to one side for a folder and removed a paper from it, placing it before Max before he slowly returned the salute. After completing the salute, thereby allowing Max to return his right hand to his side, his boss tossed a pen on top of the paper and casually said, "Now sign this."

Max didn't need to look at the paper. "Sir, I respectfully request permission to have that document reviewed by a counselor at the Provost Marshall's office, Sir."

A muscle at the side of the Lieutenant's receding jaw line twitched and he spoke tensely. "Permission denied. Now sign it!"

Max stared at the 'Military Slogan of the Week' above his bosses head, the Lieutenant's abbreviated version of another Ben Franklin proverb, "No Pain, No Gain." Max responded in a firm tone that was less tense than his boss.' "Sir. No thank you, Sir."

Just then Ned peeked timidly around Max and said, "Excuse me, Sir, but...."

Lieutenant Conweb barked, "Not now, Ned!"

Ned raised his eyebrows and tried again, "But, Sir....."

The Lieutenant moved his eyes off Max to give Ned a withering stare and shout, "Dammit, Ned, I said not now!" Lieutenant Conweb slapped the manilla folder down on his desk and his voice rose slightly in pitch and volume as he glared at Max. "There are no 'thank you's' required here. Although I'd think you'd be thanking me for providing you the opportunity of a lifetime. Sounds like you're disobeying a direct order, Airman. On a battlefield, I could summarily shoot you for that." The Lieutenant paused expectantly, but, when Max did not respond, his boss slapped his hands on top of the folder and blurted, "Well, Airman, what do you have to say for yourself?"

Max stared at Franklin's proverb and spoke in a monotone. "I respectfully decline to sign that paper without counsel. I respectfully decline to volunteer for re-assignment. I respectfully request permission to be dismissed."

Lieutenant Conweb leaned forward and began to fan himself with the manilla folder. He adopted a crocodile smile and affected a friendly tone. "Ohhhhhh, Maxie, Maxie, Maxie. I can't dismiss you when we have so many unresolved issues."

Max stared straight ahead. "I am resolved, Sir."

His boss continued to smile painfully. "After all I've done for you, trying to save your marriage and..."

Max interjected impassionately. "I'm divorced, Sir."

The Lieutenant's eyes widened. "Right, and that wouldn't have happened if you hadn't been dipping your wick in every little yellow whore you could find." His boss' voice rose as he began to argue passionately.

"Even when I gave you guard duty every other night to keep you busy, even when I confined you to the base for thirty days, even when I gave you the opportunity to immortalize your photography in print, you were dragging your ungrateful ass off base to every disease infested bordello you could find!"

Ned intruded again. "Sir, I'm very sorry, but...."

The Lieutenant glared at Ned and angrily hissed, "But what, Ned!"

Ned gestured toward the office door. "Sir, like I tried to tell you, the Base Commander is here to see you."

Lieutenant Conweb bolted to his feet to face the Base Commander standing in the office doorway, saluting him so abruptly he almost struck himself in the eye. Looking at Max out the corner of his eye and speaking through his teeth, he whispered hoarsely, "Max. Salute the Commander."

Max made a sharp quarter turn and smoothly saluted the Commander. The two men held the salute while the Base Commander slowly walked from the office door through the little swinging gate of the Lieutenant's little fenced off desk area, without speaking or taking his eyes off the Lieutenant. The Commander stopped before Lieutenant Conweb and slowly raised his hand to return the salute, whereupon the Lieutenant began to drop his salute, but, realizing the Commander had not lowered his hand, returned his own hand to his forehead to maintain the salute. Out of the corner of his eye, the Lieutenant noticed that Max had not dropped his salute. The Commander held his salute a full ten seconds before dropping it and saying, "At ease, Gentlemen."

Lieutenant Conweb dropped his salute and started to don his Ike jacket from the coatrack near his

219

desk, saying, "Well, Sir. To what do I owe this unexpected honor?"

The Commander stepped over to the little swinging gate and started to play with it, moving it back and forth which made a little squeaking sound. "Actually, I was passing by and thought I should stop in and congratulate you on your USAF (he pronounced it 'you-saff') Headquarters assignment."

Lieutenant Conweb finished buttoning his jacket and brushing his single row of citation ribbons with his cuff. "Thank you, Sir! Very kind of you, Sir."

The Commander again stared at the Lieutenant. "Thought maybe we'd have a drink, but I had a bit of a wait as it seems you were rather busy."

The Lieutenants' eyes blinked several times uncontrollably. "Yes, well, a disciplinary matter, you know. It's a never ending job."

The Commander's eyes moved to Max with the barest hint of a smile. "So it seems. Well, even if I don't have time left for a drink, perhaps you'd like to celebrate your good fortune by giving your staff the rest of the day off. I'm sure they'd like to go to the Airman's Club and drink a toast to you." The Commander looked back at the Lieutenant questioningly.

Lieutenant Conweb's jaw dropped and he had a momentarily surprised expression before he recovered and said, "Oh yes, of course. Ned, Max, finish what you're doing and then tell the guys in the lab to take the rest of the day off, too, before you leave. You're dismissed."

Ned and Max saluted the Lieutenant and Commander sharply as Ned responded enthusiastically, "Yes, Sir! Thank you, Sir!"

As they passed by the Commander, he addressed both of them warmly by name. "Ned. Max." The two men peeked over their shoulders to see the Commander extend a handshake to their boss and heard him say, "Congratulations. Maybe you should just take it easy these last few days. Your replacement can handle the loose ends. Just look forward to fulfilling your new assignment."

Lieutenant Conweb reluctantly let go of the Commander's handshake, saying, "Yes, Sir. I'll try to do that." The little gate squeaked as the Commander went through it, the office door slapped shut as he exited, and the Lieutenant looked around the empty office with a scared expression on his face.

****

With Guido's help, Max commandeered a personnel carrier to transport the boxes of tin cans, 2500 in all, to the hilltop, everyone forming a 'water bucket brigade' to get them from the main road down the narrow pathway to the houses. No one quite understood what the rattling boxes contained until Max ceremoniously opened the final box, removed the hand cranked canning crimper, and began to demonstrate.

For demonstration purposes, Max had created a black and white label for the cans with Old Mamasan's picture in the center, English lettering above announcing *Old Mamasan's Authentic Korean Kimchi*, and Kim's hand lettered Korean below paraphrasing the same words. Max had borrowed a Leroy lettering set from one of the draftsmen in the Reconnaissance Squadron, and created a frame around Old Mamasan's picture by pasting artwork cut from magazine ads, copying the whole thing photographically so that Kim could provide

221

reproductions of the labels in the future. Without bothering to explain the sterilizing process that would be necessary in actual production, Max got the point across to the assembled family by filling a can with kimchi, using the machine to crimp a lid on it, and pasting a label on the initial sample. Max handed the can to Old Mamasan who beamed with pride before it was passed from one family member to another, eliciting expressions of surprise, delight, and amazement. When the can had made the rounds and returned to Old Mamasan, she walked up to Max and held the can between their two faces while everyone applauded.

On the hilltop above the rice paddies, the new alliance of the ladies and the farmers prospered materially and benefitted interpersonally as a business and as an extended family. The farmers profited sufficiently to purchase two oxen instead of renting one part time from a neighbor. The compost bin and chemicals Max had promoted with the picture story helped expand the vegetable garden which produced a larger and safer surplus available for sale and for kimchi production. Max saved the used fibreglass five gallon containers the darkroom chemicals came in and the ladies scoured them thoroughly to make them free of contamination. Old Mamasan used these to make many smaller more portable batches of kimchie which could be rotated more frequently in their curing cycles, allowing them to transport five gallon quantities without having to transfer them to another container. At the base, Max dismantled a two wheel dolly with a curved back used for loading bombs on the underside of jet fighter planes, then reassembled it on the hilltop so Old Mamasan could use it to transport the five gallon kimchie containers.

The ladies English improved via Max's tutoring and Young Mamasan's creative use of his battered little Korean-English Dictionary. Because Max couldn't find an 'English As A Second Language' program in Korean, Young Mamasan retro-engineered the little dictionary in order to teach English to herself and Sook Cha. Max coached them on the 'V's and 'R's that are so difficult for most Asian speakers to master, and he compiled special vocabulary lists they would need to negotiate business with the United Nation military bases which were the most desired volume buyers of local foods.

Every chance Max had to commandeer a vehicle, he made a project out of teaching Sook Cha how to drive and maintenance an automobile. This was complicated by the fact that all the military vehicles available to him were both manual transmissions and four wheel drive vehicles. There were precious few of the little Japanese three wheel and four wheel mini-cars which had survived from World War II, and the most likely vehicle the family would acquire would be from future American military surplus sales, so mastering the manual four wheel drives was essential. He also showed the farmers how the trailer hitch on the vehicles worked and tried to explain how it would apply to future replacement of the oxen for some tasks.

Through Guido, he procured two motorcycle front wheels and enough metal parts to build a utility trailer just wide enough to fit the narrow pathway between the hilltop to the main road, and capable of being towed via a standard trailer hitch on a motor vehicle. He attached a bubble level to his rangefinder camera and used it like an civil engineers transit to draw a map with reasonably precise linear dimensions and elevations of the hill, pathway, and main road, then had his draftsman friend at the base make construction drawings for a roadway between the hill and main road that might someday support a sizeable truck.

Max had the base seamstress attach Young Mamasan's embroidered patterns of Kimpo Village and the jet fighter plane to two plain jackets he bought at the PX. Using them as samples, he then took orders from the PX for more of them as souvenir items providing a considerable profit to Young Mamasan for her embroidery. He provided Young Mamasan a supply of jackets, scarves, and visored caps to embroider for future souvenir item PX orders which Kim could deliver.

Max's introduction of Kim provided more than just a verbal interpreter, Kim also had a knowledge of electrical apparatus and photography, and a wealth of potential business connections with both Korean civilians and military personnel working on the base. Max encouraged the ladies to consider Kim as a potential agent and consultant in their future business relations with United Nations military markets.

Max removed the chevrons, stripes, and military buttons from one of his dress uniforms that would fit Old Farmersan, then had it dyed black so it would serve as a business suit for him in later negotiations with UN personnel. He advised Young Mamasan to consider bringing Old Farmersan to business meetings as an alleged 'Senior Partner,' and, acting as his alleged interpreter, she could control the negotiations entirely on her own, while his presence would minimize any doubts of credibility and awkward social situations a Korean business woman acting alone might face.

At night, Max and the two young women would plan a future which they all knew would come much too soon, a future when Max would no longer be there. They were trying to secure not just a fledgling business, but the safety and well being of three woman and a small child in the postwar world of South Korea which, in the year 1953, was a chaotic environment where women's rights were a strange new concept. They were not selfishly thinking that they would become one of the earliest and most successful new entrepreneurs of a brave new capitalistic South Korea. They were simply trying to build a wall of security between the horrors of the past and a future without Max.

****

The new PIO (Public Information Officer), the Lieutenant who had sponsored the talent show, was no more or less competent than Lieutenant Conweb had been when it came to journalism, but, as a boss, he was a vast improvement in the eyes of the staff. He was a little stage struck and aspired to be a comedian, having believed that his recitation of 'Casey At The Bat' in Korean 'pidgeon English' dialect had been a success, when in fact it had gone over the heads of the military audience and offended some of the Korean civilian staff. Mercifully oblivious to this reality, the good Lieutenant decided to eliminate the 'Military Slogan of the Week' and replace it with his 'Quotation of the Week.' These alternated between actual famous quotes and fictional quotes he made up which were actually malapropisms, limericks, and puns he considered funny

He began with General MacArthurs' famous quote when the General was forced out of the Philippines by the Japanese at the beginning of World War II, "I Shall Return." Kim was obliged to hand letter these and, unfamiliar with MacArthur and thinking it as a joke, tacked a photo of Lieutenant Conweb above it.

225

When the staff first saw it, everyone's jaw dropped and Ned said, "Oh, my Gawd, I hope not."

As for the comedy quotes, the Lieutenant made good use of Yogi Berra's most famous malapropisms such as, "When you come to a fork in the road, take it." Sometimes he would risk one of his own puns such as, "All that glitters is not brass," paraphrasing Shakespear from *The Merchant of Venice* ("All that glisters is not gold"), which the good Lieutenant intended as praise for his staff, acknowledging they were the true journalists and he was just 'brass,' in that officers wear brass insignia and are therefore known as 'brass.'

Despite his convoluted efforts at comedy, his staff greatly appreciated his efforts to reverse the injustices of his predecessor by re-instating each Correspondent's well deserved bylines and each Photographer's well earned photo credits. In his first report he put everyone in for a promotion, Ned getting his third stripe and Max recovering one of the two he had lost. Although his divorce was not yet final, Max had succeeded in having the allotment to his wife stopped and, with his promotion, Max was now receiving his full pay for the first time since he had entered the service.

****

Sook Cha's room in the hilltop house was ten feet by ten feet, roughly three times the size of her room in Yeong Deungpo, and it had no bomb hole in the ceiling and floor. Most of all, it had no visitations from the Jee.

It did have a hardwood floor, a two foot diameter round window opening which Max had glazed with quarter inch thick clear lucite plastic salvaged from an airplane window, and the pictures of the moon bridge from the calendar, the magazine photos of Burt Lancaster and the American girl in the white dress, and numerous photos of Sook Cha and Max and all of the family. These were all now framed and comprised a montage of memories on the wall opposite the window that illuminated it.

At the front of the house there was a small terrace that Max had defined with a curved railing made from a steel tubular ladder which he had softened in sections with white hot coals from the brazier in order to bend it into a curve. It was secured to posts made from young pine trees driven into the ground twice as deep as they were above ground, the whole thing painted flat black to make it look like wrought iron. The floor of the terrace was made of pavers Max had made from mud and a few sacks of Portland cement he had managed to acquire from the base one day when he had the use of a vehicle. The terrace looked out on the North side of the house toward the highest mountain which looked pale lavender behind the green of the terraced foothills and bright green of the paddies below. To the left was the earthen pathway to the main road with the mini moon bridge at its center, to the right a valley filled with paddies which were hidden by fog most mornings.

Max had a three day pass before he would board the plane that would take him stateside, ending his tour of duty in Korea. He spent the first morning in a final shopping frenzy at the Post Exchange and negotiations with Guido. He arrived at the hill late in the afternoon, loaded with as many packages as he could carry.

For the men and boys there were colorful tee shirts and comfortable house robes. For the three ladies there were beautiful silk scarves and carved ivory bracelets. For Old Mamasan there was an elaborate packaged array of spices. For Young Mamasan there was a luxurious writing kit with a cut glass ink well, a variety of bottled inks, a wide selection of writing brushes for writing Korean, a selection of colored and textured stationary, and a beautiful abalone inlaid abacus for her accounting needs.

For Sook Cha there were several packages. The first was a jewelry case containing a strand of genuine pearls with matching earrings. The second was a package contained one hundred stamped envelopes with Maxs' stateside address and a card with Kims address and work phone number so he could put letters from Sook Cha into the U.S. Mail system. The third contained Max's rangefinder camera with a fresh package of twenty rolls of film and, again, Kim's contact card so he could process the film for her.

There were two final gifts that Max did not give her until they were alone in her room. When Max had helped make repairs on the house, although there was no need to create a trap door for Max to hide under, they did make a small trap door in the floor of Sook Cha's room large enough to hide valuables. In a small wood box that had originally held tea, Max had gift wrapped twenty American ten dollar bills, and he told her to hide these under the trap door for emergencies. The other gift was also for emergencies, and, as she opened it, he said, "Sook Cha, I hope you never have to use this. If you wish, you can sell it and use the money. I offer it only because I want you to be safe, and, because I cannot be here to protect you, I'm offering this as the best protection I can think of."

Sook Cha lifted the heavy .45 caliber automatic pistol out of the box with one hand, and the little tin can of one hundred bullets with the other. Her eyebrows raised, her eyes teared, and she looked at Max with a pained smile. She dropped the weapon and bullets back into the box with a thud and threw her arms around him, burying her face in his chest and sobbing. This was the final tangible evidence that he was going, and she would probably never see him again. He had provided for her future as best he could, but she would have to face that future without him.

For the next two days, the family left them alone as much as possible. Sook Cha did not work and even the farmers took their meals in the little house at the rear. Max and Sook Cha took their meals together with the other two ladies, but nothing was said about his coming departure. Funny memories were recalled eliciting laughter, happy memories were recalled eliciting smiles and happy tears. And there was lots of touching, lots of hugging, lots of smiles beneath tear filled eyes.

Their last night, Max and Sook Cha explored each other like there was no tomorrow, because there would be no more tomorrows together. She tried to remember and recreate every carnal pleasure he had taught her and they had shared, even trying to invent news ways to prove that she would give every part of herself to him, without reservation, without restraint. He tried to enmesh her body into his and his body into hers, trying to somehow mold their two bodies into one being that could never never be separated; not by oceans, not by continents, not by time or space.

The first rays of sunrise turned the round window a golden color and illuminated all the pictures on the wall above them. Sook Cha slept with her head on his chest, one leg nestled between his two legs, one hand intertwined with his fingers. He had spent the past week agonizing over the circumstances that prevented him from taking Sook Cha with him. Legally his

229

divorce was not final. Financially he did not have the means to bribe his way through the process of getting her into the states under false pretenses. And when he tried to imagine what it would be like if he could actually get her to the states, the image of the black maid in the French Quarter nightclub kept appearing and saying to him, "You're in the segregated South, Dum Dum."

There was a gentle knock at Sook Cha's door. Max extricated himself from her grasp, slid the door partially open, and saw Old Mamasan's face smiling, but with tears in her eyes. In a soft voice she said, "GI all run run home, catchee shuttle bus. Ne?" Max smiled back at her, nodded assent, and gently shut the door.

Outside the sun was losing a battle with a cold cloudy overcast, and, by the time Max appeared, a light snow was beginning to fall. The two farmers and two little boys stood in a line. Max shook both farmer's hands, Young Farmersan avoiding his eyes as he did so. Max lifted each boy in a final playful shake, tousling their hair as he set each one down. He hugged Old Mamasan and, as he stepped away, she playfully raised a brazier poker.

As he stepped before Young Mamasan, Old Farmersan lowered his eyes to the ground like his brother beside him. Max and Young Mamasan put their arms around each other and stared into each others tear filled eyes a long time before their lips met and their arms closed around each other tightly.

As Max turned toward Sook Cha standing on the terrace, he froze in his tracks. She stood erect in her white dress, white hose, white high heeled shoes, white pearls at her neck and ears, ivory comb in her hair, and silk scarf around her neck blowing in the breeze. Behind her the morning fog hoovered over the paddies

230

and painted horizontal stripes across the green of the foothills and the lavender of the mountain.

Max was acutely aware of the crunch of the thin carpet of snow beneath his feet, the whipping of her scarf in the wind, and, as he stood inches before her, the sound of her measured breathing, as if each of these remaining seconds were so precious they must be remembered forever. He held her face in his hands and kissed the tears from her eyes, but they instantly reappeared. She put her arms around his back and laid her cheek on his chest, his arms enfolding her, pulling her to him in one last embrace, his tears dropping into the blue black of her long straight hair melting the few snowflakes that landed there. They moved slightly apart and he tilted his face down for one last tender kiss as their hands released each other until their bodies were only connected by their lips. Their lips seemed stuck together until, finally, this last connection was broken.

They both felt like they were in a vacuum of silence. From both their perspectives, Max seemed to be moving in slow motion as he headed down the earthen snow spattered pathway toward the main road. From the top of the mini moon bridge, he could still see her standing on the terrace, the wind whipping her white dress about her firmly sculptured body, the lightly falling snow matting her hair into the tears that streaked down her immobile face. Each step he took made her a smaller figure in the distance, yet each step he took was burdened with a thousand memories, a thousand regrets.

Max knew he was experiencing the end of what might be the most beautiful experience and the greatest adventure of his life. He knew that life was not like fairy tales or movies, there was no 'happily ever after.' Happiness lives side by side with tragedy, and they both live only in the here and now, and he was departing the here, and he had outlived the now.

His only salvation would be to appreciate the lessons of the horrors of the past year, and to savor the joys that had made those lessons endurable. And, if he were very very fortunate, perhaps the future might provide other 'here and nows' as sublime and as scary as those he had shared with The Josan and the Jee.

THE END

ABOUT THE AUTHOR

 William Karl Thomas was born 1/25/33 in Bay St. Louis, Mississippi, a small Gulf Coast town in which Tennessee Williams lived and wrote about in his works. In 1951 Thomas married his former high school teacher and was divorced after a four year childless marriage. His checkered background includes being a cocktail pianist in New Orleans French Quarter, serving a year of combat in the Air Force during the Korean War, being a photographer, a journalist, a feature/documentary cinematographer, a screen writer, an industrial film producer, a public relations executive, and a book author. He has worked for and with such notables as Frank Sinatra, the Rat Pack, Lenny Bruce, and others..

The Manchester Guardian has stated, "He superbly evokes the seedy atmosphere of the cheap Hollywood clubs and coffeehouses," and "His work sometimes reads like a Bogart script." Kirkus refers to, "His historically astute depiction of the country and era" and "(He) aptly conveys the heights and depths of human capability," and refers to *The Josan and the Jee* as *"An emotionally challenging but rewarding war novel."*
Readers reviews say " One of the best books I have ever read; maybe the best," and "This story will make you sad and happy at the same time. It is difficult to put the book down."

MORE BOOKS ON NEXT PAGE

OTHER BOOKS BY
WILLIAM KARL THOMAS

All books are available in print and digital editions from Amazon.com. Find details and excerpts of all books, or order autographed copies at Media Maestro - Book Division, P.O. Box 50672, Tucson, AZ 85703, or online at www.mediamaestro.net/books.htm

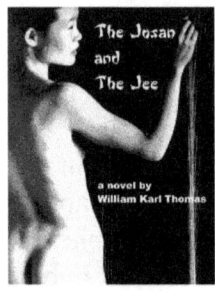

THE JOSAN AND THE JEE
The book you have just read is available in an E-edition for your Kindle, Nook, I-pad, or other E-reader, or read it on your computer by downloading Amazon's free E-reader application. Tell your friends they can buy the E-edition online for less that it would cost to mail your print copy across the nation.
ISBN #978-1-62768-001-1 Softcover $9.95
ISBN #978-0-9799477-5-9 Digital E-edition $4.99

CLEO
A novel about a beautiful and talented black female journalist who is an intimate friend of black entertainment and political celebrities during the turbulent civil rights era in the 1950's and 1960's. Her professional and private life takes a quantum leap when she crosses paths with a cynical but equally talented white male publicist.
ISBN #978-1-62768-002-8 Softcover $9.99
ISBN #978-0-9799477-6-6 Digital E-edition $4.99

THE PIANO LOVER a trilogy

In New Orleans French Quarter during the 1950's, a young male cocktail pianist's life is complicated by four beautiful women: two young women from opposite poles of society who love him in diverse ways, and two middle aged women who seek to control him for their own secret reasons.

ISBN #978-1-62768-005-9 Softcover $14.95
ISBN: 978-1-62768-006-6 digital E-edition $4.99

PIANO LOVER THE MUSICAL

The second novel of *The Piano Lover* trilogy includes the script and score of an entire original musical stage production. Follow the careers of the talented alumni from New Orleans French Quarter who helped create the 1950's and 1960's counter culture.

ISBN #978-1-62768-011-0 Softcover $14.95
ISBN: 978-1-62768-012-7 digital E-edition $4.99

PIANO LOVER THE MOVIE

In the third novel of the trilogy, the musical is made into a movie. The entourage experience professional and romantic adventures in Hollywood, San Francisco, and exotic foreign capitals with their famous and celebrated show biz peers.

ISBN #978-1-62768-013-4 Softcover $14.95
ISBN: 978-1-62768-014-1 digital E-edition $4.99

MORE BOOKS ON NEXT PAGE

A PLACE FOR US

The biography of Wendy Wolf who entered an iron lung at the age of four and emerged a polio survivor whose life illustrates the challenges of opportunity and acceptance people with disabilities face and the triumphs and successes this extraordinary woman achieved.

ISBN: 978-0-9799477-2-8 Hardcover $29.95
ISBN: 978-1-62768-004-2 Softcover $9.95
ISBN: 978-0-9799477-8-0 digital E-edition $2.99

THE GENTEEL POOR

A memoir telling the story of four generations of the author's colorful and talented family spanning the Civil War, World War I, the Great Depression, and World War II. This coming of age memoir deals with the social and ethnic evolution of the New Orleans/Gulf Coast area a century before it was devastated by Hurricane Katrina.

ISBN: 978-1-59663-565-4 Hardcover: $29.95
ISBN: 978-1-62768-000-4 Softcover $9.95
ISBN: 978-0-9799477-9-7 digital E-edition $2.99

LENNY BRUCE: THE MAKING OF A PROPHET

William Karl Thomas' intimate and poignant memoir of his ten year collaboration with the most controversial comedian of the 20th century, a martyr to First Amendment rights. The book begins before Bruce's rise to international fame and continues through the night Bruce died.

ISBN #978-0-9799477-0-4 Hardcover: $24.95
ISBN #978-1-62768-003-5 Softcover: $9.95
ISBN #978-0-9799477-4-2 Digital edition: $2.99

THE CANDY BUTCHER

The amazing biography of screenwriter, film producer, playwrite, actor, nightclub comedian Frank Ray Perilli, creator of such notable films as *The Doberman Gang, Harlow* and such cult films as *Dracula's Dog, Little Cigars, Fairytales, Cinderella, The End of the World, Alligator,* and more than two dozen unique offbeat films and plays.

ISBN #978-1-62768-019-6 Softcover $9.95
ISBN: 978-1-62768-020-2 digital E-edition $2.99

MORE BOOKS ON NEXT PAGE

HOLLYWOOD TALES FROM THE OUTER FRINGE

Thomas' career brought him in contact with 'A' list celebrities and the armies of 'little people' who served them. This anthology of 12 stories reveals the intimate relationship between the two set against a historically accurate 1950's-1960's background. Love Hollywood's down and dirty side, then you've gotta love the torrid twisted "Hollywood Tales From The Outer Fringe."

ISBN #978-0-9799477-3-5 Softcover: $9.95
ISBN #978-0-9799477-7-3 Digital edition: $2.99

T

IMMORTAL: a science fiction trilogy

A millennium into the future, three alien archeologists attempt to determine how humanity self destructed themselves and their planet. Their discovery of a dormant android guarding a human gene bank on a Saturnian moon leads to a conflict among them regarding humanity's potential future. Share the alien archeologist's discovery of human evolution and the turning points that shaped earth's civilizations in the first book of this trilogy.

ISBN: 978-1-62768-007-3 Softcover $9.95
ISBN: 978-1-62768-008-0 digital E-edition $2.99

IMMORTAL: RESURRECTION

In the second novel of the trilogy, the alien female allies with the android's desperate attempt to resurrect humanity while alien forces mount an expedition to rid the universe of human dysfunctional behavior.

ISBN: 978-1-62768-015-8 Softcover $9.95
ISBN: 978-1-62768-016-5 digital E-edition $2.99

IMMORTAL: ARMAGEDDON

In the third novel of the trilogy, a small band of newly created humans defend the survival of the human race against an alien expedition determined to rid the universe of future human folly.

ISBN: 978-1-62768-017-2 Softcover $9.95
ISBN: 978-1-62768-018-9 digital E-edition $2.99

.

239